DOCTOR·WHO

The Monsters Inside

Collect all the exciting new Doctor Who *adventures:*

THE CLOCKWISE MAN
By Justin Richards

WINNER TAKES ALL
By Jacqueline Rayner

The
Monsters Inside

BY STEPHEN COLE

BOOKS

Published by BBC Books, BBC Worldwide Ltd,
Woodlands, 80 Wood Lane, London W12 0TT

First published 2005

10 9 8 7

Commissioning Editors: Shirley Patton/Stuart Cooper
Creative Director and Editor: Justin Richards

Doctor Who is a BBC Wales production for BBC ONE
Executive Producers: Russell T Davies, Julie Gardner and Mal Young
Producer: Phil Collinson

Cover design by Henry Steadman © BBC 2005
Typeset in Albertina by Rocket Editorial, Aylesbury, Bucks
Printed and bound in Great Britain by
Cox & Wyman Ltd, Reading, Berkshire

For more information about this and other BBC books,
please visit our website at www.bbcshop.com

For Jason Loborik,
who just smiled when I couldn't tell him a thing

Wherever it was, it wasn't Earth.

Rose Tyler threw open the TARDIS doors and stood looking out, a massive grin on her face. The sky was a shimmering green. Three suns shone through the haze, their heat prickling her skin. The muddy ground was the colour of olives and sloped up sharply, while beyond it a range of pale mountains, perfect pyramids, stood like pitched tents on the far horizon.

It wasn't Earth. She was, officially, Somewhere Else.

'Another world…' Rose closed her eyes, opened her arms and leaned out a little. She felt giddy for a moment as a gentle breeze blew up and ruffled her long blonde hair about her shoulders.

'You did it, then,' she called to the man who'd brought her here.

'Huh?' He sounded preoccupied. 'Oh, yeah, right. The alien planet thing.'

'And about time. We've done space stations… space-ships…'

'We've done *your* planet so often we should get T-shirts made up.'

Rose heard him crossing to join her and smiled to herself. 'What, you mean, like, *I saved the Earth and all I got was –*'

'Aggro?'

He gave Rose a gentle shove in the small of her back and she stumbled outside. The alien soil squidged beneath her white trainers. 'Oi! Doctor, I was building up to that!'

The Doctor grinned at her. He was a tall, imposing man with heavy features and dark, close-cropped hair. His leather jacket, jeans and T-shirt lent him a casual, unassuming air. If you passed him on the street you wouldn't look twice. But up close, there was an intensity about him that crackled through every movement, each lingering look.

'What were you gonna do?' he said. 'Plant a flag? Make a speech?' He stepped out after her, looking all about. 'Nah. Take a giant leap for humankind, and nine times out of ten you squash whatever's beneath you. The best things are always just stumbled upon.'

'The way you stumbled on me, you mean?' she asked cheekily. That had been back on Earth, in the middle of an alien invasion. They'd beaten it together; he'd shown her she could make a difference to things. Now she travelled with him, and felt a sense of belonging she'd never dreamed possible.

'Look,' he said softly, pointing to something just the other side of the TARDIS. A single flower.

Rose went over to see. It was a scraggly specimen, but smelled sweet, and its red petals were the only splats of colour in the muddy desert.

'There you go,' the Doctor murmured. 'Your first contact with alien life on its own turf.'

'Literally.' Rose picked up a fallen petal. It felt velvety between her fingertips, made them tingle.

'This could be the rarest flower in the universe, the last of its kind.' The Doctor's eyes fixed on hers suddenly, clear and unnervingly blue. 'Or it could be one of billions. Common as daisies. Just the first to poke its head through the soil to greet the three-sunned springtime.'

She smiled. 'Doesn't matter, does it? It's here, and so are we!'

He grinned back.

'But *where* are we?'

He shrugged. 'Dunno. Edge of the galaxy somewhere.'

She got up. 'TARDIS not telling?' TARDIS stood for 'Time And Relative Dimension In Space'. This was supposed to explain how come you could disguise a massive control room inside a poky police box and travel anywhere and any time in the universe, but it left Rose little the wiser.

'Might be on the blink. We landed quicker than normal, like something in the area drew us down…' The Doctor looked bothered for a moment. Then he started glancing all about again. 'What do you think?'

'You're the 900-year-old alien, you tell me!'

'I mean, what do you think of all *this*? Strange air in your lungs. New suns in the sky.'

'That's a point – three suns up there, we'll burn really quickly.' Rose was wearing jeans, a red T-shirt and a white jacket, but her face was still exposed. 'Maybe we should get some cream.'

The Doctor considered. 'Let's have a poke about before we crack open the Ambre Solaire.' He set off up the muddy rise. 'See if it's worth sticking around.'

'Speaking of sticking,' she said, 'how come the ground's so soggy when it's so hot?'

He shot her a sideways glance. 'This isn't Earth. Earth rules don't apply.'

'That's true. I feel lighter,' Rose said, taking a balletic leap after him.

'Less gravity,' he agreed.

'So I weigh about half a stone less, and I'll tan three times as fast.' She smiled as she fell into step beside him, bouncing along. 'We have to stay here for ever, you know that, right?'

'Tell you what. If we like the view from this hilltop, I'll dig out the deck chairs.' He offered her his hand. 'Deal?'

'Deal,' she said, taking it.

They were still hand in hand when they reached the lip of the rise. Rose found they were far higher up than she had realised. And whatever view she had been expecting, it couldn't have been more gobsmacking than this.

'No more flowers, then.' She felt she was overlooking the set of some incredible Hollywood epic. 'I thought those things in the distance were mountains *shaped* like pyramids –'

'But they're the real thing,' said the Doctor.

'And are those real Egyptians?'

In the valley far below, tiny figures were building a pyramid right now. The ground area had to be twice the size of Trafalgar Square, though Nelson's column would barely peep over the second of the five steep steps cut cleanly into the pyramid's sides. These baked-mud plateaux were a seething, sweating mass of activity as workers toiled to disguise the steps and create a true pyramid. Overseers watched, massive arms folded across their well-oiled chests, as scores of sweating men in loincloths heaved huge bricks up ramps of rubble to add to the massive construction. A hundred more were struggling with ropes and pulleys to lower the finishing blocks into position.

'Built the same as your pyramids on Earth,' the Doctor

informed her. 'Buttress walls built up around a central core. Fourth dynasty, maybe.'

'And not what you'd expect to find the other side of the galaxy.' Rose watched as a man stumbled and fell while struggling to push a sledge full of rubble down one of the many ramps. An overseer strode forwards at once with a vicious-looking whip, started laying into him. The man screamed as the leather lashed him.

'There's no need for that,' Rose said fiercely. 'What's going on? I mean, space-travelling ancient-Egyptian chain gangs?'

'Doubt it.'

'They look human.'

The Doctor stared on as a further whipcrack scored through the air. 'Yeah. They act human, too.'

The man, his back burned now with four thick red stripes, was dragged to his feet by two more workers and shoved back towards the sledge. Weakly, he struggled with it once more.

'This is horrible,' said Rose. 'Can't we do something?'

'No.'

She looked at him sharply. 'Oh, yeah? More of your posh alien morality?'

'Oh, no, I'm well up for it.' He was looking back the way they'd come. 'But I don't reckon *they're* keen.'

Rose turned back from the lip of the precipice. Four of the overseers had crept up behind them, swarthy, bare-chested, massive and mean-looking. Each held a heavy whip in one hand.

And a futuristic space gun in the other.

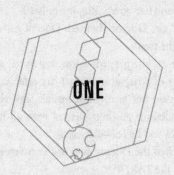

ONE

'OK, so what's the charge?' asked the Doctor, grinning as he raised his hands above his head. 'Trespassing on sacred land? Nicking secrets so we can build bigger pyramids down the road?'

Rose raised her hands too. 'Trust me, whatever you take us for, you're wrong.'

'Put down the guns, and we'll explain why,' said the Doctor.

The four men ignored them, took a threatening step closer. Then one of the whips cracked out. Rose gasped as the leather bit into her ankle.

'Too far, mate,' the Doctor snapped. He kicked the whip handle from the overseer's hand, freeing Rose. Then he tried to wrestle the man's gun away.

Rose took her cue. As the overseers brought their guns to bear on the Doctor, she shoulder-charged one and knocked him flying. Another guard lunged for her but she dodged aside with a speed that surprised even her – lower gravity, she realised. She wrestled the gun from his grip but he swiped it aside, shoved her backwards towards the lip of the precipice.

Rose tried to duck past him but his thick, slippery fingers

clamped around her wrists, digging in hard.

'You OK?' the Doctor shouted. One of his opponents lay sprawled in the mud.

'Never better,' she gasped, squirming in the big man's grip. Then, instead of struggling against her attacker, she plonked herself down on her bum, bent up her legs, shoved her feet against his oiled-up gut and pushed with all her force. That broke his hold and he fell backwards.

'Leg it!' yelled the Doctor, two of the overseers lying at his feet. 'Back to the TARDIS!'

But now the one who'd whipped her was blocking Rose's way. He lunged for her and she backed off. It would be OK, the Doctor was racing towards them and –

The ground started to crumble underfoot. Rose looked back wildly and with a sick feeling found she'd reached the very edge of the precipice. She wavered on the brink, losing her balance. It was like everything was happening in slow motion.

Then a bellow from the guard and the sharp crack of a whip cut through the moment. Her arm burned with a sudden, galvanising pain.

The Doctor was holding the other end of the whip, his face frantic.

Rose's fingers curled round rough leather as the lip of the ledge gave way beneath her and she fell.

The scream had barely built in her throat before she was pulled up short, dangling from the whipcord. She caught crazy, spiralling glimpses of sheer rock, green sky, of tiny figures on the giant stone anthill far below.

'Hold on!' the Doctor gasped, thrusting into view over the crumbling precipice.

'You too,' she told him, her feet flailing for purchase in the side of the mud cliff, trying to pull herself up the length of leather. Low gravity or not, she felt heavy as lead. She focused on the Doctor's face; he was helping her, he was going to drag her to safety.

Then one of the overseers loomed into view behind him, gun raised.

'Look out!' Rose shouted.

The Doctor didn't turn, kept hauling her up, hands moving mechanically, faster and faster. At last her elbows mushed into the soft mud at the precipice's edge, took her weight. His hand clutched her forearm and he gave her an enormous grin.

Then the contact was snatched away. The Doctor was dragged to his feet by two of the overseers and a gun was pressed to the back of his head. Rose was helpless as slablike hands reached for hers, pulled her up, jammed gun barrels into her neck.

'Get off me!' She struggled angrily. 'If you'd just try talking instead of –'

Rose broke off as, with a weird whirring of alien engines, two small vessels rose up over the edge of the rise. They were shaped a bit like helicopters, but in place of rotor blades there blazed a vortex of blue light. One was landing close to the TARDIS. Rose thought fleetingly of the single straggly flower caught beneath it, its life and colour crushed into the earth. The other craft landed beside her, and the shadow it cast was black and cold.

With a sick feeling, Rose found herself being frogmarched towards it.

'Doctor!' she yelled. The gun jabbed in her throat as she stared back frantically over her shoulder. 'Doctor, I can't stop them!'

He was straining to get to her, eyes wide and unbelieving. But the other craft was touching down now, and the overseers were dragging him off in its direction. 'Don't struggle, don't let them hurt you!' he shouted. 'I'll find you. I promise, I'll find you.'

A door buzzed open in the side of the silver ship. Rose dug her heels into the spongy mud but they simply lifted her up, bundled her inside the cold, metal hole that had sprung open.

'Wherever they take you,' she heard the Doctor yelling, 'I'll get you back.'

She kicked and swung at her captors, wild now, not caring about their guns in the cold darkness. Then she gasped as her body stiffened. She couldn't move. The door in the side of the ship was closing. 'Doctor!'

'No –'

The door buzzed shut and she could hear nothing at all in the blackness.

The ship lurched. The air seemed to thicken. There was a pressure in her ears as if she was underwater. She was being taken someplace to face God knew what.

Alone.

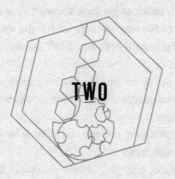

TWO

The Doctor stared as the silver ship with Rose on board whizzed away through the hazy sky. He almost broke the overseers' grips in his haste to get inside the other vessel.

The darkness was oppressive inside the machine. He guessed it was meant to be intimidating. His ears popped as the craft climbed steeply, smoothly outstripping the planet's pull.

It didn't matter what they did to him. He *would* get her back.

Maybe two hours passed before the ship doors snapped back open. The Doctor scrambled out and found himself in a square room, grey and dull. He studied it first for any sign that Rose had been there, then for any clue to his captors. He struck out on both counts. One sealed door, no windows.

Nothing else.

The lights in the room dipped for a few moments. The Doctor's skin tingled as some invisible force played over it. He knew he was being scanned.

'I'm not armed,' he announced gruffly. 'What have you done with Rose?'

No answer.

The Doctor took out his sonic screwdriver and held it to the door. A blur of blue energy appeared at the tip. But the door stayed shut. He frowned. Doors didn't usually stand a chance against this…

Finally, it slid open. But the Doctor's smile soon faded. A crowd of armed guards in grey uniforms were clustered in the corridor outside.

Their leader raised his gun, an ugly look on his florid, doughy face. 'Get back!'

'Wish I could, pal,' the Doctor snapped. 'But I'm going nowhere without Rose Tyler.' He ignored the gun, took a step closer to the guard. 'You must have seen her. Long blonde hair, about so high. Where is she?'

'See this, boys?' the leader said, ignoring him. 'Got ourselves another goldmine. Alien, the scan says.'

'I'm just the Doctor, all right? Now, where am I, the local nick?'

'Talks alien, all right,' one of the guards commented.

The Doctor sighed. 'All right then, am I in custody?'

There were sniggers at this.

'Am I in custody, he asks!' the leader sneered. 'Just in case you *hadn't* noticed, this is Justicia, "pal". Whatever you came here for, you're human property now.'

'You *what*?'

'Found guilty of trespassing on Justice Alpha, a designated prison planet. You and your bit of human skirt.'

The Doctor barged forwards. 'What have you done with –'

But the guards burst into laughter as the Doctor rebounded against an invisible shield and was sent staggering back inside the cell.

'She's nothing,' crowed the leader. 'Already gone, dealt with.

No complications.' He grinned. 'But *you*, goldmine… You're alien. And aliens get the special treatment.'

The Doctor suddenly became aware of a barely audible hiss in his ears. He spun around to locate the source, but the movement made him dizzy. His vision was blurring. He shouted out in anger but it was too late, the gas was doing its work. He sank to his knees. 'Where's Rose?' he croaked. 'What… What did you do…?'

'Right then, boys.' The leader's voice echoed through the darkness in the Doctor's cell. 'Let's get his brain tagged and ship him out. Then it's feet-up time again…'

There had to be over 100 seats in the dull grey cabin, but Rose was the only occupant. She sat listlessly in a corner, looking behind her at the silent lines of padded seats every few moments to check she was still alone.

The silver ship had spat her out into an empty room with dodgy lighting. She'd heard what sounded like whispers in her mind, fingers thumbing through all the thoughts in her head. Then she'd passed out.

When she woke up here, for a moment she almost expected to find the Doctor waiting for her. That everything had just been a mix-up, a misunderstanding.

But no.

Rose rested her head against the tinted glass of the small window beside her, felt its coldness on her cheek. Outside she saw the star-speckled blackness of space. Three suns huddled together in a cloud of incandescence, their white light picking out the stark, mysterious slivers of distant worlds. One of them must be the planet of the little red flower. Her first new world.

The spaceship set off, silently, without warning. Rose wiped the tears welling in her eyes with her sleeve, which was still caked in mud. She noticed a big, lumpy handprint there.

It was the Doctor's.

For a moment she felt the strength of his hand on her wrist again, pulling her back.

Rose placed her own hand against the mark. 'I'll get to you.' She screwed up her eyes, whispered fiercely to herself. 'Just you wait.'

When the Doctor woke he was lying on a metal couch and a woman was watching him.

She was short and plain with a thatch of mousy hair. While her matronly frame was dressed in shapeless grey coveralls, she'd perched a pair of bright pink glasses on her pointed nose, framing her beady blue eyes, as if to say, *Look! I'm very interesting really!*

The Doctor tried to move. He couldn't. 'Where's Rose?' His voice came out as a croak, and he licked his claggy lips. 'The girl I was travelling with?'

'Please don't struggle, Doctor. You're in a restraint field.' The woman referred to the small futuristic clipboard she held. 'I've read the full account of your discovery, capture and dispatch. You've been classified as *Miscellaneous Alien Doctor*. An irregular, disruptive non-human entity.'

'Seems fair comment,' the Doctor remarked. 'But we're wasting time –'

'Doctor, I can promise you there's no shortage of time here.' She looked at him and seemed almost sorry. 'I'm Senator Lazlee Flowers. Welcome to the SCAT-house.'

He blinked. 'What?'

'That's SCAT for Species-led Creative and Advanced

Technologies. An underground complex on the planet Justice Prime.' Flowers gave a deep, bosom-heaving sigh. 'I must say, your resemblance to humans is quite striking. Some of the, uh, entities we have here –'

'I asked you about my friend.'

'Oh, the girl. She's human. Different department, I'm afraid.'

'If you've hurt her –'

'We're not sadists, and we're not savages. We want to re-habilitate her, not to harm her.' Flowers's voice had hardened a touch. 'I don't know how or why you infiltrated Justicia, but you must have known you'd be punished.'

'Didn't see any Keep Out signs.'

'Doctor, the auto-beacons warn off *all* vessels straying with-in two light years of the Justicia system, and the deflection barrier operates at a distance of ten billion miles! Just how big do you need the Keep Out signs to be?'

'Light years? Deflection barrier?' The Doctor frowned. 'Then… this entire solar system is one big prison?'

'I believe people usually try to break *out* of it,' said Flowers wryly. 'But "prison" hardly does Justicia… er, justice.' She tit-tered briefly at her little joke. 'I prefer to think of it more as a testing centre.'

'Testing what?' The Doctor swallowed hard. 'What's hap-pening to Rose?'

Flowers sighed. 'Doctor, putting aside for a moment the question of how you came to be on Justice Alpha, are you hon-estly trying to tell me that you and the girl crossed the void between star systems in a small blue projectile with no visible means of propulsion –'

'Yes.'

'– breached three lines of defences without even noticing –'

'Yes.'

'– and that you really don't have the faintest idea of where you are or what you're dealing with?'

He looked her in the eye. 'What *are* we dealing with?'

Flowers cleared her throat. 'Any unauthorised entity trespassing on Justicia automatically earns a twenty-five-year prison sentence.'

'What about a trial?'

'You were scanned and assessed.'

'Not good enough! Don't you even care what I was doing –'

Flowers raised her voice above his: 'Not my department, Doctor. Inquiry and Appeals will process that information in due course.'

'They'll process it now!' thundered the Doctor, straining against his invisible shackles. 'I must have *some* rights?'

'Er, afraid not.' She came over to him and smiled down wistfully. 'Our treatment of you is perfectly legal, under the terms of the Reciprocal Alien Imprisonment Treaty.'

'Never heard of it.'

She shrugged. 'If your home planet isn't registered then you'll be extradited – once your ambassador has registered a protest, and subject to legal damages being paid.'

The Doctor stared at her. 'And if I *don't* have an ambassador? If I'm on my own?'

'Then here you stay for the full term of your sentence.' She clapped her hands with forced school-ma'am jolliness. 'Still, I'm sure you'll make the best of it.'

'You've got two hopes – Bob Hope and no hope!'

'We try to make things as easy as possible,' she breezed on. 'For instance, a low-level implant has been placed in your brain.'

'So now I'm tagged like a pigeon. Thanks.'

'Not everyone here speaks human, you see. The implant aids inter-species translations, and helps you interface with the automatic systems here.'

'I don't get it, Flowers.' He glared up at her. 'You humans are out here in deep space, thousands of parsecs from home. *You're* the aliens, mixing it up with other races on their home turf. Oh, but hang on – anyone *not* like you gets dumped in a ghetto out here?'

Flowers shrugged. 'EarthGov voted to group together non-human offenders. Alien prisoners have different needs to humans, so it made sense to put them in a customised jail-house.'

'And that's why Justicia was built?'

'Just the SCAT-house at first.'

'Wait. Species-led, Creative and Advanced Technologies… This isn't just a prison, is it? It's a workhouse! A scientific labour camp!'

'It's a business,' she corrected him. 'You may be prisoners, but there's still much you can offer humanity.'

'Like flashier guns for its armies? Bigger bombs? Faster war-ships?'

Flowers got defensive. 'Not all our work is for the military. Besides, if you get good results, you get time off your sentence – as well as a .00137 royalty on intergalactic sales. That's a gross figure –'

'You're telling me.'

'– but still extremely generous.' So saying, she switched off the restraint field.

The Doctor sat up on the couch and appraised her coolly. 'Bit risky, isn't it? Letting me loose? I'm not exactly full of sunshine and love right now.'

'I don't think you'll attack me, Doctor,' Flowers said confidently. 'I'm happy to answer your questions, help you acclimatise. Besides, I know you're an intelligent individual.'

'Clever people can still do terrible things.' He rubbed his arms and legs. 'Like converting an entire solar system into a prison camp. Got bored with the aliens, did you? Thought you'd let in some humans too?'

'The Empire was expanding so fast, colonising planet after planet. The star cops were spread too thinly to police them all effectively. Crime rates began to soar. Prisons became over-crowded, unworkable.' Flowers poured him a glass of water. 'So Justicia approached EarthGov and offered to handle the overspill. Almost had their hands bitten off.'

The Doctor took the glass and drained it. 'What was in it for Justicia? Cash?'

'Expansion. The extra money helped Justicia develop and market inventions from the SCAT-house more efficiently. We've always been the heart of the business.' She poured him another glass. 'Then, as more and more planets decided to offload their prisoners here, and as more and more of this solar system was given over to housing them… Justicia's Executive realised what an opportunity they had. A chance to expand their research from the purely scientific.'

'A testing centre, you said.'

Flowers nodded, her face grave.

'But besides my patience…' He drained the water in a single gulp. 'Testing what?'

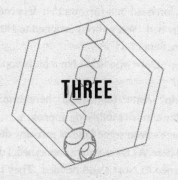

THREE

Rose slept fitfully on the long shuttle journey. She must have lost her watch in the fight, so she had no way of knowing how much time had passed – but the world they'd left now looked more like a marble than a pool ball through the little window beside her.

She rocked in her seat as the ship came to a gentle halt. Instantly she stood up, pressed her back to the wall, wondering what would come next.

A door slid open at the front of the cabin and a man and a woman came inside. Both were black, and wore grey uniforms, peaked caps and sour expressions. They looked as if they'd stepped out of some American cop reality show, and sure enough their voices held a trace of transatlantic too.

'Your name is Rose Tyler?' said the woman. She was slim and wiry, her scraped-back hair emphasising the severity of her features.

Rose nodded, folded her arms. 'That's right.'

'I'm Warder Blanc, this is Warder Norris.'

Norris was big and broad, with a *don't mess* attitude written all over his surly face. His cap seemed too small for him; it plunged his forehead into furrows that deepened to crevasses when he frowned. 'You've been assigned to Detention Centre Six on Justice Beta.'

'Detention? Don't you think I'm a bit beyond writing lines after school?'

They didn't react. Just stood there impassively. Rose decided to try a more mollifying approach.

'Look, there's been some kind of mix-up,' she said. 'I'm not from round here. As far as you're concerned, I don't exist.'

Blanc turned to Norris and nodded. 'They said she wasn't carrying identification.'

'Look, I could show you a credit card or something, but I left my bag in this big blue box thing. If you want to take me back there, I'll –'

Norris snorted, looked at her as if she was dirt. 'We're wasting time.' He nodded to the door, indicating that she should go through it.

Rose didn't move. She didn't want to leave the ship. Didn't want another barrier between her and getting back to the Doctor.

Blanc took a step closer. Her face softened. 'Look, Rose, I know you must be feeling so many things right now. Scared… sorry… Maybe a little out of your depth. You're innocent, you shouldn't be here.'

Norris nodded, unconvinced. 'That's the usual story.'

'In my case it happens to be true.'

Blanc shrugged. 'Whether it's true or not, Rose, you can't prove that to me and Norris right now. And even if you could it would make no difference. We're just warders, there's nothing we can do.' Her eyes were unexpectedly soulful. 'Tomorrow you can put in your plea to the Governor. But right now, you've got no choice but to go through that door. So let's just take it one step at a time, right?'

Rose nodded.

'OK, good,' said Blanc, a little smile settling into place.

Norris gestured she should go through the door now.

Taking a deep breath, Rose did so.

'We brought along some of the girls to help you settle in,' Blanc called after her. 'They're waiting outside. They'll show you the ropes, watch out for you.'

'Thanks,' said Rose huskily.

The door led on to a see-through plastic tunnel. Like the one ET was carried through when he was dying. The two warders didn't move to follow her, and she didn't wait for them. She strode out, gathering momentum with each step. This wasn't a time to show weakness. If this was some kind of borstal, wherever the hell it was, she guessed that showing fear was about the worst thing she could do.

The tunnel led on to a white boxy room. Four girls stood in grey smocks and surly expectation.

'Hi. I'm Rose.' She pushed a hand through her ratted hair self-consciously.

The girls didn't respond except to bunch their fists, their eyes cold and challenging.

Instinctively, Rose knew that if these girls were here to show her any kind of rope, it would be a noose.

She glanced back behind her. No sign of the warders. Nice. She couldn't believe she'd actually fallen for that soft-soap act.

'Back off,' she warned as the girls approached. 'If you knew the kind of day I'd had, you would not mess.'

The girls kept coming, but Rose noticed that three of them

had looked to one to make the decision for them. Their leader was burly but pretty in a trashy sort of way, with short, spiky red hair.

Rose targeted her. 'Here to put the new girl in her place, right?'

The girl smiled. She had no front teeth. 'My name's Kazta. And your *place* equals under my boot.' Suddenly she lunged forwards, her hands clawing big clumps of Rose's hair.

'Scalp her, girls!' Kazta shouted.

Rose gasped in pain, stamped down hard on Kazta's foot. Kazta grimaced but only pulled harder on Rose's hair as her pet thugs lumbered forwards, wielding what looked like metal spoons sharpened to deadly points.

Rose stopped trying to pull away from Kazta and instead scooped her up in a big hug. Kazta squirmed to get free, but Rose held on to her tight, swinging her around like a shield so the others couldn't strike.

Then she pressed her mouth up to Kazta's ear and yelled as loud as she could.

Kazta recoiled, fell backwards into one of her cronies. But Rose was already sprinting for the door at the far side of the room.

It wouldn't open.

'Justicia develops new and pioneering strategies for law enforcement, punishment techniques and mental correction,' Flowers explained. 'All criminals deported here serve a productive purpose. They help Justicia find effective ways of controlling social disorder.'

The Doctor jumped off the couch. 'So you're testing your inmates. Running experiments on them. Like building those pyramids. What was *that* all about?'

Flowers hesitated. 'I believe they're investigating whether spells of hard labour in tough conditions can shock petty offenders into giving up crime.'

'Hard labour?' He snorted. 'Looked more like torture to me.'

'So you were spying?'

'Couldn't miss it!'

Flowers could feel her cheeks flushing. 'Justicia's findings help make policies that benefit countless human societies across the Empire.'

'Policies you flog to them at a tidy profit.'

'They help create happy, healthy colonies with low crime rates and a minimal prison population.'

'Minimal cos they're shipping their crims off here, dirt-cheap!' The Doctor's disgust was plain on his face. 'After all, Justicia needs all the guinea pigs it can get, right?'

'I've no idea,' said Flowers stiffly. 'I've already told you, the SCAT-house is concerned only with scientific research. I'm neither consulted nor informed.'

'Oh, well, that's you off the hook then.' The Doctor stepped stiffly forwards. 'Don't you ever stop to wonder what's happening on the rest of these Justice worlds? What's happening to Rose?'

'Justicia is not run by monsters, Doctor,' said Flowers. 'If anything, the monsters are kept inside. Murderers, rapists, pushers…'

The Doctor looked right into her eyes. 'If anything happens to my friend, Flowers…' He shook his head a fraction. 'Then I'll show you a monster.'

Rose turned, back pressed flat up against the door, glared in defiance at the girls as they advanced murderously.

Then the door whooshed open behind her and she fell backwards into whoever was waiting on the other side. It was a boy. He gasped as he caught her, then set her back on her feet.

'All right, pack it in, Kazta,' he said. 'If New Girl shows up in hospital instead of the blockhouse for check-in, it's *me* who'll get it in the neck.'

'We can arrange that right now, Block-walker,' said Kazta, cupping her ear and wincing. The girl behind her was still holding her sharpened piece of steel.

'Oh, shut it, can't you? I'm supposed to be the one with the testosterone.' Supposed was right, thought Rose – macho was not the word for him. He was about her age, gangly, with a beaky nose. His ash-blond hair flopped down to his eyebrows, as if someone had put a basin on his head and cut around it. 'Just call it a night and get back to your cells.'

'Blanc said it was OK, Dennel,' one of the girls whined. 'She wanted the new girl roughed up.'

'I don't care, Maggi,' he said. 'Blanc or no Blanc, just clear out now and I'll keep quiet. No demerits.'

Kazta sneered at him. 'Can be a dangerous job, block-walking,' she said. 'On patrol, on your own...'

Dennel wasn't impressed. 'You're getting fat, Kazta. Jog back to your cell, yeah? Be good for you.'

Rose breathed out shakily as the girls walked past him and out. But the second they'd gone, Blanc and Norris appeared in the mouth of the plastic tunnel.

'Fake it,' Dennel hissed.

Immediately, Rose leaned on him heavily, lowered her head so her mussed-up hair hid her face.

'Found our new arrival here, Warder Blanc,' Dennel reported stiffly. 'She's been beat up pretty bad.'

'You're designated block-walker, Dennel,' said Blanc. 'It's your job to stop stuff like this happening. You're getting ten demerits for this. Ten more and you can kiss your little suck-up job goodbye and go back to sharing a cell all night.'

Norris smiled. 'And when a block-walker gets bumped back down to regular stir, he finds he don't got too many friends.'

'I'm sorry, warders. Thank you.'

'Just remember, I can get you bunked up with anyone I choose,' said Blanc. 'And I can turn extremely deaf and blind when I need to.'

'Must be a good thing if you have to work with Norris,' Rose murmured.

'What's that?' said Norris sharply.

Rose produced a piteous groan from the back of her throat.

'Just remember, girl,' said Blanc, 'this kind of thing can happen to you at any time. You want to be very nice to me, Rose.'

Rose nodded, her face still hidden by her curtain of hair.

'Get her out of my sight.'

Dennel helped steer Rose through the door and hurried her along a bland corridor painted in putrid pastel shades. Their shoes kicked up a shabby echo on the tiled floor.

'All right,' he whispered, 'they're not following.'

Rose straightened her back and shook her hair out of her face. 'Thanks for turning up when you did.'

He grinned at her, showing crooked teeth. 'I had to – I'm a block-walker, supposed to keep an eye on stuff. Saw Kazta's cell door was ajar, and I know Blanc likes springing these little welcome parties when we get someone new. Knocks any fight out of them from the start.'

'Charming,' said Rose.

They came up against a heavy metal door. Dennel waved a

wristband at it and it ground slowly open – to reveal an identical corridor beyond.

You're in prison, she told herself, with an uneasy feeling of fear and shame. *Mum always said it would be Mickey who'd end up inside, not me.* It didn't seem real, somehow. And the dowdy surroundings certainly didn't seem to fit with the high-tech spaceships and laser guns she'd seen.

'This'll sound weird, Dennel… but what year is this?'

He grinned again. 'How long were you on that transit shuttle exactly? Time crawls on Justicia, but…'

'Please?'

'I know it looks, like, medieval in here, but it's all part of the experiment.'

'Experiment?'

'We may be banged up like it's 1985… but it's 2501.'

Five hundred years out of time, she thought miserably.

'They're seeing if the old-fashioned ways are worth going back to. You know, just locking people up, no implants or limiters…' He smiled. 'You're looking at me like I'm crazy. What you got, amnesia? I mean, I hear some funny stuff walking the blocks, but *you* –'

'Wait a sec.' She looked at him uncertainly. 'Is a block-walker, like, "prison warder lite"? Does that make you some kind of a collaborator, in with the authorities?'

She said it hopefully, thinking he might have some influence where it mattered – but clearly he thought she was accusing him.

'You saw the way Blanc laid into me,' he protested. 'I'm no screw. Block-walker's a new post, part of the Governor's centenary shake-up. I'm meant to wander round, making sure everything's quiet, no one's doing stuff they shouldn't. But

I find I'm sort of like a Samaritan, to the younger kids especially. If they can't sleep, if they got problems, they can talk to me through their doors.'

Rose smiled back. 'Well, you really played Samaritan for me. Sorry you got into trouble for it.'

He shrugged. 'Next time Blanc busts my butt, *you* can help *me*, right? Now we'd better get you a uniform.' He pulled at his grey coveralls without enthusiasm. 'It'll help you blend in.'

Rose looked down at the handprint on her sleeve with a twinge of anxiety. 'I'm not planning on sticking round long enough to blend in, Dennel,' she said. 'I'm only here by mistake, and I've got to get back to someone. I need to see the Governor, as soon as possible, and sort this mess out. Can you help me?'

'Governor always gives new arrivals an interview,' said Dennel cautiously. 'Ahead of Inquiry and Appeals getting round to you. That's when he tells you how long you've got to serve.'

'He decides? He wasn't even there!'

'Most penalties are fixed around here. Automatic.' He looked unhappy. 'I guess I should tell you, Rose. Everyone who comes here, they all of them say they ain't sticking round. You know, they got friends, they got appeals coming through… I was just the same. Juvenile, special circumstances, sob story… Thought I'd walk it.'

'And how long have you been here?'

'Since I was thirteen,' he said. 'Seven years.'

She stared at him. 'They locked you up all that time? Why?'

'Minor charge.' It was all he would say.

'Well, how long till you get out?'

'I'm doing good now, see? I'm a block-walker. Responsible.'

He chewed his lip. 'So, maybe another ten years.'

Rose couldn't believe it. 'Ten years,' she murmured.

'It's Justicia, Rose,' he said, as if this explained everything. 'Reckon you've got a lot to learn.' They came to another heavy door, and he did the business with the wristband again. 'But don't worry. I know the way it works round here, don't I?' He looked at her shyly. 'I can help you out.'

Rose winced as the door slammed shut behind them. If Dennel had got seventeen years for a minor charge...

'I hope to God someone can,' she said.

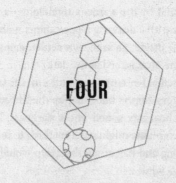

FOUR

Rose wondered if the night would ever end. Dennel stayed with her as long as he dared. Then he left her in a holding room to be 'processed'. She'd waited for hours, too scared to sleep in case Kazta or her cronies crept in to scalp her or worse. For comfort she'd thought about Mum, and the Doctor. About the adventures they'd shared. They'd come through worse than this and still walked away smiling.

And he'd promised he'd get to her. Promised.

Finally a bored, officious woman had come in. Rose found herself stripped, searched, showered and called every name under the sun. Then her clothes and belongings were taken away – earrings, lippy, everything – and she was given the promised saggy grey uniform to wear. It was made of some disgusting fake fabric and felt icky against her skin. She'd stared at herself in a grimy mirror, wet-haired and blotchy-eyed. She looked like death.

A warder – not Blanc or Norris, thank God – had taken her to a cell. Someone else was already there, a girl, half buried under musty blankets, muttering about being disturbed. Warily, Rose had stood there in the middle of the little room, looking around by the warder's torchlight – a narrow bed, a cracked sink with a dripping tap, a cabinet with no doors and precious little inside. Then the warder left and she had to find her way to this strange bed in the dark.

Still dressed in her nasty new uniform, she lay there on the lumpy mattress, fingers bunching up the threadbare blankets, straining to hear any sound in the darkness, afraid that her unknown roommate might try something to harm her.

Half hoping and half afraid that sleep would finally end all this hurt for a while.

The Doctor walked out with Flowers into what seemed to be a massive underground tunnel. It was wide as a motorway and tall as a church. Large steel pillars lined the walls, pinning up the long black shadow of the roof high above them.

Flowers saw him staring around. 'We have a few biggies staying here. When they're queuing up for the canteen we need plenty of room.'

'You make it sound like a jolly little space camp.' He went on looking all around him, hoping to spot some clue to a means of getting out of here.

'If you *can* think of it that way, time will go a lot faster, believe me.'

'You're not a typical warder, I'll give you that.'

'I just don't think things should be needlessly painful,' said Flowers. 'Life's too…' She paused, pushed her pink glasses back up her nose and smiled as if to force a brighter mood into the space between them. 'Look, we're very well equipped here.'

'Good. I need a shovel, a bucket and a vaulting horse, so I can hide mud and rock and stuff.' He grinned, leaned in confidentially. 'You know, for my tunnel.'

'I've told you, Doctor, no one escapes.'

'What's to stop me legging it right now?'

'We're a long way from Justicia's suns, Doctor. The planet's surface is uninhabitable, and the SCAT-house is buried deep underground. It's hard enough for the staff to get in and out, believe me.' Flowers sighed softly. 'Incredibly hard.'

'You could be lying. We could be inside one of those pyramids I saw being built. My ship could be just outside, a hop, skip and a jump away.'

'Your ship, yes…' Flowers consulted her clipboard again. 'Can't be entered. Can't be moved.'

'Local gravity disturbance. Dragged us down. I put the handbrake on so we wouldn't go anywhere else in a hurry.' He smiled. 'You want to see inside? Fine. Take me there.'

'If you *are* inside a pyramid, it could be just outside,' said Flowers casually. 'Why not find out?'

'What, try to escape?' The Doctor rubbed his hands together and started back up the corridor. 'OK, well, *this* door looks interesting…'

Even as he made for it, from out of the shadows of the high tunnel roof there swooped a flock of grey globules. Each was about the size of a football. They stuck all over him like enormous sticky buds. He found he couldn't move.

'Most areas are out of bounds,' Flowers called to him. 'The globs keep a careful watch. If you've taken a wrong turning, you'll soon know about it.'

The Doctor glared at the globs, which up close looked like enormous wads of chewing gum, flexing in and out of shape as if invisible mouths were chewing on them still. Slowly, one by one, the globs floated away like bizarre balloons, vanishing into the blackness.

'They're quick,' said the Doctor. 'Fast as thought. Are they using my implant?'

She nodded, setting off down the corridor again. 'The same thing will happen if you display antisocial behaviour to anyone in the SCAT-house.'

'What if someone has a pop at me? Same story?'

'Exactly. Means we're not overrun with warders, I don't have to play the heavy the whole time and we can all just get on and use our time wisely. Speaking of which...'

He puffed out his cheeks. 'Go on then. What're you doing here? What are you going to make my life's work?'

'There's a choice,' she said brightly. 'For one thing, we're close to a breakthrough on a device that can suppress and confine solar flares.'

'What for?'

'So worlds close to stars can be terraformed. So space traffic can pass far closer to suns.'

He pulled a face. 'Not really me. I don't tan well.'

'OK,' sighed Flowers. 'What about hydroponics – growing and developing plants without soil?'

He waggled his fingers at her. 'Do these look green to you?'

'Never mind. Consul Issabel's shut down those experiments for the time being, anyway.'

'Who's she? The big cheese?'

'She controls the SCAT-house, yes. Now, what about gravity acceleration? Know much about that?'

'Not masses,' he said. They turned a corner into an area marked DORM BLOCK. 'What's the point in speeding up gravity, anyway?'

'With super-accelerated gravity, we hope to be able to bend time and space, distort distance so that journeys into deep space become possible.' This was clearly her thing; she had become suddenly animated. 'My team have experienced many setbacks, but I'm sure we're close to a breakthrough. Then humans can finally make the next leap beyond, crossing to *other* galaxies.'

He shook his head, grimaced. 'I dunno. I usually save planets, rescue millions of people, that sort of thing. I'd be wasted in a workshop.'

'If you opt out, then you'll sit in the communal drop-out chamber and sulk till you rot – with no privileges.' She sighed. 'Still, it's only your first day. You've got over 9,000 to go. I'm sure I'll tempt you with something in time.'

Flowers stopped outside a metal door built into the wall, and slotted a white card into an entry coder. The Doctor recoiled as the door slid open and released a waft of horrid air. It was like a giant with rotten teeth exhaling in his face.

He recognised the smell and looked sharply at Flowers. 'What's this?'

'Temporary accommodation.'

'What's going on?' came a guttural alien voice from through the doorway. 'I just started my rest shift! How about a little peace?'

The Doctor blinked as a towering creature almost three metres tall lumbered into view. It was naked, with sagging, waxy skin the colour of stuff that gets stuck in plugholes. The creature's long arms ended in giant three-fingered claws that almost scraped the floor. Its face was that of a bloated baby, smooth and curious with big round eyes the colour of jet and a slavering hole for a mouth.

The Doctor had met creatures like this before. He had fought them to the death.

They called themselves Slitheen.

Flowers smiled up at the towering creature. 'Hello, Dram Fel Fotch. Sorry for the lack of notice, but this is your new cellmate.'

'Cellmate?' The Doctor smiled tightly at the massive creature looming over him, then turned back to Flowers. 'I'm not normally fussy where I doss, but…'

'Cells are made to order here,' she told him. 'When we have a full house, we have to tunnel out further into the rock.'

'This is an imposition,' said the creature wearily.

'You're telling me.' The Doctor stared up at it. 'You're from the planet Raxacoricofallapatorius, right?'

Dram Fel Fotch shook his head. 'My ancestors were born there. But I have never seen my homeworld.'

'Nor have I.' The Doctor shrugged. 'Just heard of it. I've met some of your people before. Long time ago, as the crow flies. Family by the name of Slitheen.'

'Slitheen?' The creature's head bobbed forwards and it sniffed the Doctor as if he was a suspect puddle in a room just vacated by a dog. '*Slitheen?*'

'*We* are Slitheen,' came a deeper, rumbling voice behind the Doctor. Another of the creatures was looming over him, the twisted fingers of its great claws clacking together over the Doctor's shoulders. 'I am Ecktosca Fel Fotch Heppen-Bar Slitheen. Dram Fel Fotch is my brother.'

'Is that right?' The Doctor took and shook one of the claws. 'Well, good to meet you.'

'Looks like you guys practically know each other already,' Flowers declared.

'Oh, I don't know. Are you lot ruthless, lying killers like your ancestors?'

Ecktosca and Dram narrowed their eyes at him.

'You're perfectly safe, Doctor,' said Flowers awkwardly. 'The globs restrain any and all antisocial behaviour, remember? Now, I'll arrange for a bed to be placed in here. Shouldn't be for long. Make him feel at home, boys.'

Flowers walked away, and the Doctor was left alone in the huge, misshapen shadows of the Slitheen. Their soggy, sticky faces pushed up close to his.

'So,' said the Doctor brightly. 'Who wants top bunk?'

FIVE

Rose was finally, fitfully, drifting off when the lights snapped on. Someone banged on the door, which clanged and creaked as it was unlocked and jumped ajar, yelled at them to wake up and slop out. Rubbing her bleary, gritty eyes, Rose saw a metal pail under the sink.

'You *so* have to be kidding me,' she muttered.

The girl in the bed against the far wall stirred reluctantly. Rose could see only a black starfish tangle of hair on the pillow at first, but gradually the rest of her pushed out from under the blankets. The girl was Asian, small and delicate with wide, startled eyes. An intricate hennaed design ran along her left cheek, and as she sat up her hair spilled down over her grey vest top almost to her waist.

'Hi,' she grunted, her voice almost comically low for such a slight girl. 'Rizwana Mani. Riz, if you like.'

'I'm Rose. Rose Tyler.'

'Cool. Riz and Rose.' She grinned. 'Been lonely round here since I lost my last cellmate, Sally.'

'What happened?'

'I killed her.'

Rose stared at her. Riz stared back, raised her eyebrows.

'You're joking me,' Rose said nervously.

'You reckon?' But Riz couldn't keep her face straight and burst into snorts of laughter.

Rose shut her eyes, sighed with relief. 'You cow!'

'I got you, didn't I?!'

'You never.' But Rose couldn't help smiling too. 'So what *really* happened to your mate?'

'She killed herself.' Riz picked up the bucket beneath the sink. It made a nasty sloshing noise. 'One night in solitary. I never even saw the body.'

Rose waited for her to say she was joking. But there was no laughter this time. She just stared out into space.

'Sorry, I… You OK, Riz?'

'Fine.' Riz forced a smile. 'Come on. We'll empty this and go get some breakfast.'

The canteen was huge, thronging with people. After the nocturnal quiet and emptiness, it came as a shock to Rose just how many people were jammed in here. She scanned for signs of Kazta, then realised she was looking not only at girls but at blokes too. For some reason she'd assumed that Dennel, as a block-walker, was a special case who'd skipped segregation.

'Is this the whole prison?' she asked Riz, standing in a long, long queue for a plate of slops that looked like sick and didn't smell a whole lot better.

'Just the main block.'

'Boys and girls together all day?'

'New directive. They're gonna make all the prisons mixed sex. There's even talk we'll get to work together.' Riz gave her a mock shove. 'What's up, you complaining?'

'God, no,' said Rose quickly. 'Just surprised.'

'So. You got someone?'

Rose thought about the Doctor, and for a moment she could have cried. 'There's someone I need to get back to,' she said.

'Lucky,' said Riz, a dreamy look in her eyes. 'I've been here six years. Never had no one. And even if I did, can't do much about it here. Not till they let us work together, anyway.'

'What did you do?'

'My mum was a benefit cheat. She was claiming for me and two brothers and sisters that didn't exist. They put her away… and put me in here till she gets out.'

'That stinks! You didn't do anything wrong!' Rose shook her head. 'Then again, what did *I* do?'

'What *did* you do?' asked Riz.

So Rose told her story as they shuffled along in the queue. The fight with the overseers. The long journey here through space. Blanc and Norris stitching her up. Kazta.

'Kazta is such a bitch,' said Riz. 'But she's not alone. This place is full of psychos.' She gave a weird nervous laugh that suggested it took one to know one. '"S all right, though, I'll tell you which girls to stay away from… and which boys are hot!'

Rose smiled. 'What about Dennel? He's not a looker, but… well, he's nice. Sort of kind.'

'Oh, Dennel's hot all right.' Riz laughed her funny laugh. 'You're playing with fire there, Rose.'

'All right, all right!' she said, smiling. 'He's the first guy I've met, give me a chance!' She looked round again. 'God, it's so weird, though, isn't it? Girls and boys together in a prison.'

Riz shrugged. 'They like trying out different things. It's all just a big experiment, see.'

'Yeah, Dennel said something about that.'

'I'm just glad I'm not on Justice Alpha. All historical recon-structions and heavy labour.' She screwed up her nose. 'Bring the past to life while they work you to death. Shove you down old-fashioned mines, make you row in old galleys – even make you build pyramids!'

'Don't I know it,' murmured Rose, picking up a plate of congealed pasta. 'But why bother with the history stuff?'

'Adds a new twist, dunnit?' Riz grabbed a plate of slops. 'Any planet can put their crims in a labour camp. But, like Robsen says, spice it up with a bit of history and you can sell it to a colony world as a "punishment solution". It brings the tourists in, and it's educational so you get the school trips too.'

'That's sick. Who's Robsen, anyway?'

'One of the screws. Soft touch.' They sat at an empty table, Riz's eyes quietly sparkling. 'He's not bad for one of them. Used to work on Alpha, but he left. Didn't like it.'

Rose shuddered at the memory of the overseers with their bloody whips. 'Don't blame him. What else has Justicia got going?'

So Riz told her. Rose found the grisly details still harder to swallow than the food.

After breakfast you had to tidy your cell for roll call. Didn't take Rose long; she had nothing to tidy. A warder gave her a kind of credit card thing and told her where she could buy stuff like make-up and chocolate. She would have to earn the money, of course.

Rose had been assigned to the kitchens. She wished she'd been sent to the launderette like Riz. She would be alone again and she felt a nag of worry in her stomach at the thought.

But at lunchtime she was due to see the Governor, to talk through her crimes and her punishment. She knew she must play things *very* carefully. No way was she going to stay lost in the system for the next however many years like Dennel and Riz and probably most of the others. She *had* to get out of here and get back to the Doctor. Riz had filled her head with so many horror stories of where he might be. The Middle Eastern jail colony on Justice Gamma... the acid plantations on Epsilon... But there was meant to be a place in Justicia for alien brainboxes. He had to be there. Had to.

Surely she could work things out with the Governor, explain what an awful mistake had been made? It wasn't even as if they'd landed on the pyramid planet through choice. They'd been dragged down. The Doctor had said so...

Her nerves built all morning. Her stomach griped and growled, she could hear its running commentary even over the roar of ovens and fryers, the clanking and clanging of crocks and pans. The kitchens were hot as hell and smelled worse. Within minutes, Rose's hair was hanging wetly down over her face. Sweat trickled into her eyes, down her back, made her squirm and itch.

She was peeling spuds. About a billion of them in a muddy mountain. The peeler was blunt and next to useless, presumably in case she went mad with despair and used it on her workmates. No blokes in here. All the girls wore vests like the one Riz had slept in, blackened with huge rings of sweat.

Rose recognised someone washing up at the giant sink across the steaming room. It was one of the girls who had gone for her last night, Maggi. She was on her own now. She smiled at Rose, a little self-consciously.

Then Rose jumped as the mound of peeled potatoes beside her seemed to explode. Spuds were suddenly rolling everywhere.

A tall, thin girl with almond eyes gave her a spiteful smile. 'You should put them in the pan. Not on the table.'

Rose glared at her, went to pick them up. But the girls nearby were sniggering and stamping on the potatoes, crushing them, kicking them around.

'Oh, grow up, can't you?' Rose complained.

'Grow up, can't you?' said someone nearby. 'Grow up, can't you?'

The childish chant went up, ragged at first but soon gaining in volume and enthusiasm. Everyone stopped what they were doing to look at her and soon they were all joining in, even smiling Maggi.

'Pack it in!' Rose shouted. And she was busy yelling it again just as the chanting stopped.

Warder Blanc had entered the kitchens, Norris by her side. She stared balefully at Rose and then down at the pulped potato mess over the floor.

Wonderful. It couldn't be Riz's mate, Robsen the soft touch, could it? No, not for her.

'Did you make this mess, Tyler?' asked Blanc quietly.

Rose looked around at the flushed, surly faces ranged around her. She knew she was going to get done for this through no fault of her own. But she wasn't a grass.

'Yeah,' she said. 'Sorry. I must have slipped and knocked them.'

'You slipped all right,' she said. 'Come with us.'

'Where to?'

'Don't question me,' Blanc barked. 'Move.'

Rose ignored the smirks and the gestures and the mouthed threats as she trailed out of the kitchens after them. At least she was getting out of this particular corner of hell.

'Looks like Kazta went easy on you last night,' Blanc observed. 'You'd better hope that the Governor's feeling as lenient.'

'The Governor?' Rose frowned. 'But I'm due to see him in a few hours anyway.'

'That was before you screwed up,' said Norris. 'Shame. Never makes a good first impression – you know, being sent to see the big man on a charge before he's even welcomed you.'

Rose shut her eyes. 'That's not fair.'

'Last night you start a fight, this morning you damn near start a riot in the kitchen block over a few potatoes –'

'Riot? Oh, come off it –'

Blanc turned on her, gripped her by both shoulders. 'You're a disruptive element, Tyler,' she hissed. 'And I'm going to make sure the Governor knows that, ahead of any appeal you might be hoping to make.'

Rose looked at her unflinchingly. 'How come you ended up such a bitch?'

Blanc raised her hand to strike Rose. But Norris caught her wrist, shook his head. Blanc's eyes flashed, but then she nodded, took a deep breath, calmed down. She seized Rose by the sodden scruff of her neck and marched her forwards down the corridor.

Soon they reached the Governor's block. The decor became softer, there were carpets on the floors and decorative plants about the place. Air conditioning whirred softly in the background. A desk stood empty beside them.

'Where's his assistant?' muttered Blanc.

There was a rustling noise from further down the corridor.

'Sir?' called Blanc. She propelled Rose ahead of her, Norris following just behind. 'Sir, I'm sorry to disturb you…'

But it looked to Rose as if the Governor was disturbed already.

The heavy oak door to his office was ajar. An eerie blue light sparked and flickered inside, like electricity. A ripe smell of decay wafted out through the door.

'Sir?' Blanc frowned.

Rose froze. She recognised the light and the smell from times past with the Doctor. The terrifying memories came rushing back.

Blanc started forwards but Rose grabbed hold of her arm. 'Don't go in there,' she said. 'That's not your Governor.'

'What are you talking about?' Blanc pulled free crossly. 'You've never even *seen* the Governor.'

'It's a Slitheen!' said Rose, backing away. 'Or from the Slitheen planet, anyway.' She felt Norris's slablike hands settling around her arms. 'They're evil. Killers! They dress up in human skins – they have a machine that squashes up their bodies, see, and when they unsquash, that light starts up and…'

'Shut her up,' growled Blanc. 'She's crazy.'

Rose struggled in Norris's grip. 'I'm telling you, your Governor's dead,' she said desperately. 'There's a monster in there now. And if we go inside, we could wind up dead too!'

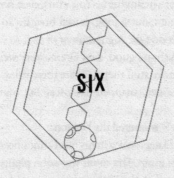

SIX

The Doctor lay on a thin mattress in the corner of the Slitheen cell. As digs went, he'd known better. The room was more like a large cave burrowed out of the bare rock. The walls were plastered with pictures of Raxacoricofallapatorians, some butt-naked like Dram and Ecktosca Fel Fotch, others peeking out cheekily from half-shucked body suits, impersonating all kinds of creatures from Meeps to Kraals. The ceiling might have been thick with pictures too, but it was lost to blackness and shadows. If you squinted you could just make out the glimmer of globs perched somewhere up among the rafters.

Instead of beds, both Dram Fel Fotch and Ecktosca sprawled in elaborate sticky nests. The floor was tacky, as if fizzy pop had been spilled all over it – the Doctor had almost lost both shoes crossing to his temporary bed. A smell of rotting rubbish filled the room.

'Cosy round here,' said the Doctor. 'You've done so much with the place. Like it.'

'I still say having him here is a cheek,' mumbled Dram Fel Fotch. 'If it wasn't for the globs…'

'I don't snore or anything. You won't even notice I'm here.' The Doctor blew out a long, bored breath. 'So is it all right round here? Food OK? A good library?'

'Solar workshop's good,' said Dram. 'Very well equipped.'

'Can you make stuff there? Or are there rules?'

'There are rules,' snapped Ecktosca. 'But one learns to get used to it.'

'Does "one"?' muttered the Doctor.

A moment later a voice in his head announced, 'Lights out!' and made him jump. The room was soon plunged into blackness. He listened to the Slitheen grunting and stretching and settling down for sleep. Then the sound of wet snuffling.

'He smells like a cool little customer, this one, doesn't he, Dram?' said Ecktosca.

'Exotic,' Dram agreed.

'He looks as ugly as a human but his scent is rare and subtle. Brash and distracted and ever so slightly sad…'

'A tough little morsel, too.'

'You would make a glorious hunt, Doctor,' said Ecktosca. 'I shall dream of hunting you down and tearing you into chunks. No offence.'

'None taken. So long as you don't sleepwalk.' No reply. He glanced up at the glimmering globs. *Don't go anywhere.*

A minute passed. The Doctor soon grew bored listening to the rush and whoop of Slitheen breathing as they settled down for sleep.

'So,' he said loudly, 'are you lot still running the family business? Impersonating aliens, nuking their planets and selling off the radioactive chunks as cheap fuel for every bargain-bucket spaceship in the galaxy?'

The heavy breathing stopped for a few seconds.

'How do you know that?' demanded Ecktosca. 'Are you a historian?'

The Doctor considered. 'Sort of, yeah.'

'The Slitheen haven't been in that line of work for hundreds of years. The old firm went bankrupt.'

'Our ancestors turned to chizzle-waxing for a while to make ends meet,' Dram added. 'But it's such a messy business…'

'Is that how you wound up in Justicia?' asked the Doctor. 'Chizzle-waxing?'

'What d'you take us for?' Dram complained.

'Dram Fel Fotch and I have been researching our roots,' said Ecktosca. 'Did you know that 500 or so years ago, there were Slitheen galloping about in skins many sizes too small for them?'

'Yeah, I did,' said the Doctor. 'And if I didn't, the photos on your wall are a bit of a giveaway. They wore gadgets round their necks, compression fields, so they could adopt the shape of their prey. But it made them a bit gassy. You know, reducing the bulk of something your size into something a bit bigger than me, well – the spare energy's got to go somewhere, hasn't it?' He blew a raspberry. 'Better out than in.'

'You're remarkably well informed.'

'News travels,' said the Doctor. 'The Slitheen almost blew up Earth, you know. In the end they only blew up themselves.' He sighed. 'A waste.'

'The family's fortunes went downhill around then,' Dram noted.

'But as the historians of our clan, we celebrate our failures as well as our achievements,' Ecktosca added. 'We've been finding out all we can about the industrious Jocrassa Fel Fotch Pasameer-Day Slitheen and his compatriots.'

The Doctor shifted on his bunk. 'Sometimes it's best to leave the past well alone.'

'Not for us. You see, we are antique dealers,' Ecktosca explained. 'We have been searching for our ancestors' personal effects. Their compression fields alone would fetch an enormous price among collectors.'

'They were destroyed along with the wearers.' The Doctor paused. 'Weren't they?'

'We heard a whisper that they were recovered from the wreckage of that Earthly explosion 500 years ago,' Dram confided. 'They were stored in a government stockpile, filed away, waiting for the day that humans could actually comprehend the technology involved and make something of it. The trail led here –'

'I do love a trail,' sighed Dram.

'– and we tried to deal with the Executive to get back these valuable heirlooms. But we were betrayed. Consul Issabel directed us to a classified building on Justice Delta. The humans believed that we'd broken in and had us arrested.'

The Doctor pulled a face. 'The boss woman framed you?'

'Wanted our brains,' grumbled Dram. 'We were both given thirty years, here on Prime.'

'Well, your people *are* brilliant inventors,' said the Doctor. 'Good hustlers too. You must have family working on getting you out of here?'

'Oh yes,' said Dram.

'You're laughing then.'

As if on command, the pair of Slitheen started giggling.

Ecktosca cleared his throat, recovering. 'We'll get there in the end, undoubtedly. But it's taking so long. Legal loopholes, evidence going missing… And in the meantime we're stuck working on Flowers's dreary solar power project.'

'We *have* to get out soon,' Dram blurted. 'There's urgent business we need to get sorted.'

'Oh yes?' said the Doctor.

There was a squelch as an alien elbow dug into alien ribs. 'Family business.'

'But not *the* family business, right?'

'It does *not* concern aliens.' Ecktosca Fel Fotch turned over in his nest with a heavy slolloping noise. 'Doctor, you smell positively provocative. I wish we had the room to run about in. I miss the hunt so badly…'

'So have you never thought of escape?'

'Next to impossible,' Ecktosca informed him. 'Even with help from the outside.'

'I'm often stood next to impossible.'

'Do *you* have help from the outside?' asked Dram, his voice striking a mournful note in the darkness.

'The only person who can help me now is stuck like me. Well…' He took in the fetid, stinking darkness all about him and sighed. 'Hopefully not *exactly* like me.'

'You've got to listen to me,' said Rose, still trying to wriggle clear of Norris's grip. 'No way is that your Governor!'

'What are you babbling about?' said Blanc. She knocked on the door. The unearthly blue light had died away. 'Sir?'

'Come.'

The voice sounded human enough. Rose was marched in by Norris, afraid of what she might see.

But it was just a man, broad and overweight and sat behind his desk in a scruffy, ill-fitting suit. Rose looked for the telltale mark of a zip in his forehead – the Slitheen's fleshy costumes opened at the head so that the thing inside could struggle free – but a convenient grey fringe had been combed down over the Governor's forehead and she could see nothing.

The man looked at them expectantly.

'I'm sorry, sir,' Blanc began. 'Only we saw a strange light in here and thought we should investigate…'

'Just my desk lamp,' said the Governor. He flicked it on and it cast a radiant blue light. 'My wife had it sent to me, it's supposed to be relaxing.'

Blanc passed Rose a withering look. But Rose still didn't trust this an inch.

'The stupid thing keeps flickering, I've been trying to fix it.' The Governor fiddled with the flex and the blue light flickered alarmingly. He sighed. 'Not relaxing at all.'

'Yes, well, excuse me, sir,' Blanc began, 'but –'

Abruptly, the Governor burped. Another giveaway, thought Rose. The Slitheen she'd met had all burped and farted like there was no tomorrow when in their human forms; they used something called a 'gas exchange' to help shoehorn their bloated alien bodies into a human form. And since Slitheen were made of living calcium, the gas stank of toothrot, and it certainly whiffed of something unpleasant in here.

'Excuse me,' said the Governor quite casually. 'Something I ate disagreed with me. Now, what's this disturbance?'

Blanc seemed to recover herself. 'You were scheduled to meet this girl at twelve-hundred. I've had to bring her to you sooner for disciplining. She's a disruptive influence, sir.'

The Governor looked Rose up and down. 'Is she, now?'

'In the kitchens, she nearly caused –'

'Thank you, Blanc, I think you'd better let me deal with her,' said the Governor. 'You and Norris may wait outside.'

Blanc and Norris thanked him and withdrew. The door closed quietly behind them.

The Governor looked at Rose steadily. She glanced back at the door, gauging the distance, wondering if she could make it…

'She can be a little irksome, that woman,' he said.

Rose stared. 'Pardon?'

'Warder Blanc. Always stirring things up and looking for scapegoats. But she keeps discipline. And I need discipline here.' He rose from his desk. Rose braced herself for the telltale rip of a massive fart or a burp, but there was nothing. 'I've been sent your file from local processing. Justice Alpha, wasn't it?'

She shrugged.

'Unexplained trespass, yes… I'm afraid that Justicia's Executive recommends you serve a sentence of at least twenty-five years.'

'You're joking me.' She felt sick to her stomach. 'Twenty-five? That's my whole life over, and then some!'

'You had an accomplice.'

'You know about the Doctor?' Slitheen or not, Rose needed to find out all she could. 'Please, can you tell me where he is? I really need to know he's –'

'What were you doing on Justicia, the two of you?' barked the Governor. 'You were able to bypass Justicia's force screen and all her security measures, and yet you allowed yourselves to be captured quite casually on Alpha. Almost as if you *wanted* to be caught.'

'Of course we didn't! We didn't even know we were doing anything wrong!'

'Equally bafflingly, neither of you seem to have any official existence – despite the fact that you, at least, are a human.'

Rose raised an eyebrow. 'Like you, you mean?'

'Yes,' said the Governor, frowning. 'Like me.' He cleared his throat. 'All a little incongruous, wouldn't you say? So perhaps you would like to explain to me where you've come from and what you hope to achieve now you're here.'

'What, you think I *want* to be here?'

'I think you were sent here. What I don't understand is why…'

'Look, we don't even belong in your time –'

'Rumours and gossip. I'll wager that's it, eh? Well? What have you heard about my little prison here, hmm?' He was starting to get flustered, picking up some papers and waving them under her nose. 'I mean, if we had problems, the Executive would hardly be offloading extra prisoners on to us, would they?' His voice was rising. 'But they are, God knows they are. And why? Because we *have* no problems. And even if we *did*, we could cope!'

Rose stared at him. 'I've got no idea what you're on about.'

The Governor calmed himself with visible effort. 'Look, if I knew what you were doing here, Tyler, I might be able to help you. Reduce your sentence, perhaps. Or, we could play things a little harder.'

'That's a threat, right?'

He released a quiet but audible fart in the menacing silence.

Rose nodded to herself. 'Pardon you.'

'I don't excuse myself to prisoners,' said the Governor. 'Dismissed. Blanc and Norris will return you to your cell.' He paused. 'I'll be watching you, Tyler.'

Rose turned and crossed to the door. 'Yeah,' she breathed. 'I bet you will.'

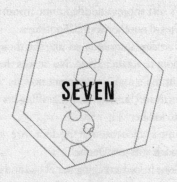

SEVEN

Rose lay on her hard, narrow bunk, as Riz's shallow breaths punctuated the darkness. She was bone-weary from her day working the kitchens, and her night spent on edge in the block common room. She'd made awkward conversation and played bad poker, her cheeks burning under so many curious looks from all around – and from Kazta's spiteful stares.

The clocks here were set to Earth time, and it actually came as a relief that lights-out was 10 p.m. Not that she stood a chance of sleeping, of course. Her thoughts were chasing their ragged tails, trampling through her head, leaving bruises.

One day down, twenty-five more years to go. The idea of it seemed impossible, terrifying. But it was her encounter with the Governor that was really staving off sleep. He *had* to be a Slitheen… didn't he? And if he was, was he planning on nuking this world, turning it into rocket fuel? He couldn't *seriously* imagine she was some kind of undercover agent placed here to stop him…

Of course, he *could* be just an ordinary Governor with a dodgy light and dodgy digestion, paranoid that his prison was up for a secret inspection…

Over Riz's soft snores and the frantic workings of her own mind, Rose heard another sound. Footsteps.

Governor's sending someone to get you, she thought, her heart starting to pound. Kazta? Blanc? No, it was the man himself – the *thing* himself – and any moment now he would strip off his human form and hunt her down, sniffing his way to her cell door, ready to kill her…

'Rose?' came a voice through the door. 'Are you awake?'

Thank God. It was just Dennel.

'I'm here,' she hissed, creeping out of bed and crossing to the door. 'Didn't see you around tonight.'

'I only walk this block. I don't live here.' He paused. 'You OK? Kazta hasn't tried anything, has she?'

'Just the evil eye.'

'She'll get over it, but try your best to avoid her. You'll have work tomorrow morning, and the Governor's lunching in this block tomorrow so you won't get trouble from –'

'The Governor?' Rose frowned. 'What, he's eating with the plebs? Why?'

'Good for morale, I guess. You know, him being seen to eat the same slop as the rest of us. Or maybe he just likes two dinners. Whatever, he eats in all the blocks in turn.'

'You haven't noticed him acting strange at all lately?' asked Rose urgently. 'Maybe smelling a bit different? Can't stop blowing off?'

'Rose, have you flipped or something?' Dennel frowned. 'Though I guess I have heard him let off a few lately… Stressed out, probably. Sounds like Justice Gamma are shipping out a load of their drugged-up prisoners, trying to resettle them into the prisons here on Beta. Must mean a lot of extra paperwork for –'

'Look, never mind that. Dennel, you'll never believe this, but I reckon your Governor's been got at by aliens,' hissed Rose. 'If someone's a bit on the large side, these creatures can squeeze into their skin and no one would know the difference. Not unless they're looking for the telltale signs…'

There was a long, long silence the other side of the door.

'Trust me, Dennel. This is what I do – fight monsters and stuff!'

'When you're not kicking off riots in the kitchens,' said Dennel pointedly. 'Oh yeah, word about you is spreading.'

'Look, just keep an eye on the Governor for me, yeah? Tell me if he's acting funny, or if he skulks off to see other fatties. Or if he tries to get his hands on any nuclear missiles.'

'You're, like, totally insane. And so am I to be listening to this.'

'Please.'

'OK,' he said finally. 'I'll keep an eye and let you know. Gotta go now. Bye.'

Rose shivered, realising how cold it was in the cell in just her night clothes. She crawled back to bed under the covers.

'You're seriously disturbed,' muttered Riz. 'You know that, right?'

'God, yeah,' she murmured. But if she could expose the creature… Make everyone see what was skulking in their midst… That had to be worth a free pardon from the Executive, right? Or at the very least, they might believe her when she said that she and the Doctor had fought these things before. If there were monsters lurking all over Justicia, up to God knew what… well. If they put her back with the Doctor, the two of them could give these people the heads-up, show them what they were up against.

If.

She pulled the musty, scratchy blankets up over herself, and for a few moments dreamed she could be back home in her bed at Mum's, head lost in comfy pillows and gorgeous soft warm duvet piled up about her. But after lingering there a while, she pushed the dream away.

Because she was here, and while things were bad, she knew she could deal with it. She had to.

This was who she was. And tomorrow she might just get to prove it.

The wake-up call sounded to the Doctor's ears like an insane electric chicken laying a square egg, a gibbering hoo-hah that had him up on his feet in seconds. The lights snapped on, and the Slitheen stirred.

'Wakey, wakey,' said the Doctor, slipping on his jacket – the only thing he'd taken off before sleep. 'What happens now? Breakfast?'

The Slitheen squirmed in their nests. Ecktosca Fel Fotch rolled on to his back, his pert little spike of a tail pointing at the Doctor like a rude gesture. 'Slitheen do not break their fast for many weeks at a time.'

'Religious reasons?' wondered the Doctor. 'Or just lazy?'

'Our digestive systems are superior to yours. We process food efficiently and produce little in the way of waste.'

'As your cellmate, I'm glad to hear it.' Suddenly, like a host of lead balloons, grey globs plummeted from the shadows high above and affixed themselves to the Doctor's body. 'What did I do? I wasn't being aggressive!'

The cell door ground open and the globs around him jostled him out of the room.

The Doctor soon found he wasn't the first person up and about in the wide, rocky corridors. An enormous three-legged person ambled past him in the other direction, appraising him with a lazy orange eye. A parade of odd-looking creatures who seemed to be half-dormouse, half-armadillo overtook him, herded by a single glob cruising above them like a lumpy zeppelin. Fellow inmates, off to slave away on their various high-tech projects.

Soon he came to a wide doorway in the corridor. The globs floated off, and he strolled inside a cavernous, circular chamber. A table in the shape of a large, hollow oval filled the room. A variety of chairs, stools and puddles of slime were placed around it, with several spots already taken by fellow prisoners.

The Doctor looked about in fascination. It was more like being in a zoo than a prison. A creature that looked like an orange woolly mammoth with four trunks sat beside a green, skinny reptile-thing with a domed forehead and big webbed feet. Black glistening nodules covered the reptile's body, as if it had bathed in caviar. Someone else pushed past the Doctor, a large blob whose skin was the consistency of sticky toffee pudding. She settled herself under the table in a custard-like splat of fluid, her three stunning blue eyes swaying at the end of frangible marzipan stalks.

'Hey, Doctor,' said Flowers, giving him a little wave. She was sat in a black swivel chair at one end. 'Everyone, this is the Doctor.' A few lethargic hoots and murmurs were made in his direction as Flowers introduced them. The mammoth was Yahoomer. The reptile was Blista. The caramelised creature on the custard cushion had the pretty name of Nesshalop.

'Did you sleep OK, Doctor?' Flowers asked. 'Your room will be prepared in the next couple of days.'

'That casual, fun-camp vibe you're going for doesn't really work when I have to be frogmarched here by a bunch of globs.'

'Only till you know your way around.'

'And to remind me I'm your prisoner.' For all the local colour in the room, the Doctor felt sick at the thought of reporting to the same room day after day, year after year. 'Where's Rose?'

'She's in a detention centre simulation.'

'Is she all right?'

'She's doing her time.' Flowers looked away. 'I told you how it works, Doctor. Help us out, help yourself *get* out.' She gestured around. 'This is the accelerated gravity group. We meet here to go through stuff, share findings, pool our thoughts. Literally.'

Now the Doctor noticed nifty little headsets in front of each place around the table, linked into a gleaming chrome keg-shaped console in the table's centre. He pulled up a seat and stretched the flexible headset. 'Can you pick up XFM on these?'

'The mindmitters interface with your implant to overcome the language barrier. They translate your thoughts and project them on to the screen there.' Flowers pointed to a large glowing rectangle that had appeared in the rocky wall between two steel pillars.

'Yeah?' The Doctor eagerly put on a headset and the chrome console glowed a burnished blue. An image of Flowers dancing the Macarena appeared on the screen, until with a squawk she was buried beneath a massive pile of globs and carried off out of sight.

The other prisoners shook and hooted with mirth, while Flowers gave him a look that suggested she was less than impressed. 'Yes, Doctor, even a simpleton can use them with ease. Shall we get on? Yahoomer, will you present the results of your cyclical gravity experiments on the boosters, please.'

Blista helped slip the mindmitter in place around the mammoth's head. The console glowed fiery red this time and some intricate equations appeared on-screen.

The Doctor skimmed over them. 'Yeah, that's one way of coming at the problem. Normal gravity with go-faster stripes.' He struck a flashy red line through the equations. 'But these boosters will never have enough oomph in them to create a warp-hole in space.'

Flowers blinked and erased his strike-through. 'Doctor, we welcome serious offerings –'

'I'm serious,' he assured her. 'That approach won't work. Wave it goodbye.' He raised a friendly hand at Yahoomer. Then he looked round the curious crowd pointedly, jiggling the hand from side to side and waited…

Flowers jumped as Blista gave a raucous cry. 'Wave!' it said, holding up its webbed reptilian hand as neon green equations danced over the screen. '*Gravitational* wave.'

Flowers bit her lip as the possibilities slowly dawned on her. 'Wave theory, yes… So if the thrusters could generate a gravitational wave –'

'Past light speed of course,' said the Doctor.

'*Past* light speed?' Flowers stared at him. 'That can't be done.'

'What happened to the "C" in SCAT, Flowers? Where's your creativity?'

'Doctor, I really think –'

'What does gravity do? Makes you heavy, right? So to counter heavy, you need light.' He grinned, leaned back in his chair. '*Faster* than light…'

Nesshalop's eyes were bulging on her pale pink stalks. With a high-pitched chittering, she expounded a theory that lit up the screen in icing-pink scribbles. The console in the middle of the oval table glowed a misty gold and began to tremble and hiss.

'Yes, Nesshalop!' grinned the Doctor. 'Just the kind of thinking that's needed!'

'The translation circuits can't handle the equations,' Flowers warned.

'It's all right, I know what she's getting at,' said the Doctor, looking into Nesshalop's brilliant blue eyes. 'But let's add to the algebra – cross the Ts, make the Is dotty, draw a little love heart round the X…'

Flowers stared. She didn't understand everything she was seeing but it was obvious there was some real premise grounding the equations, a proof like nothing she had ever seen before.

The console started to steam. 'Doctor, Nesshalop, stop,' snapped Flowers. 'Take off your mindmitters.'

Globs floated gingerly down from the ceiling, sensing something was wrong. But the truth was, a part of Flowers was willing the two aliens to keep going. They were conjuring some strange mathematical truth into existence. The hairs on Flowers's neck were on end.

The Doctor stood up, knocking his chair flying, and Nesshalop reared up from the ground. The two of them seemed lost in each other's eyes, not blinking, not looking away, while the equations solved themselves and split away. Flowers couldn't keep up or keep track any longer. The console was rattling as if something big was caught inside it, glowing so fiercely that Yahoomer trumpeted with all four trunks and backed away. Blista shrieked, clasped his webbed hands to his head.

Flowers was about to bring down the globs on the Doctor and Nesshalop when a curious thing appeared on the screen.

It was a schematic, showing the orbits of the planets in the Justicia system.

Nesshalop nodded, her eyestalks intertwining, as the diagram burst from the screen into three-dimensional life over the meeting table. And the fiery console was burning a blinding white, gold and yellow, forming surrogate suns for the planets to circle.

Then the console exploded in a spectacular burst of sparks. Flowers threw herself to the floor, landing in an undignified heap.

The globs descended on the Doctor and Nesshalop, but neither seemed to notice for several seconds, eyes only for each other.

Flowers clambered up, choking on smoke. 'What have you done, the pair of you?' Through her smeared specs she saw the console was clearly ruined, and the rock wall where the screen had been was charred and blank.

'Sorry about that, got a bit carried –' The Doctor broke off and gasped. His face contorted with pain, and Nesshalop emitted a pitiful shriek as the same thing happened to her.

The globs had started throbbing with ashen light. In certain cases the bio-organisms were permitted to 'caution' an offender. This apparent vandalism clearly counted.

'Don't hurt Nesshalop!' the Doctor shouted, eyes wide, teeth gritted. 'It wasn't her fault, it was mine… I didn't realise the console's limitations…' He sank to his knees, and stared beseechingly at Flowers.

'Get off them,' Flowers snapped. But the globs persisted, glowing more darkly now, getting sticky and wet like leeches. 'I said get off them! Priority command, voiceprint Lazlee Flowers – release them!'

Grudgingly the globs let go at last and spiralled back up to their space in the shadowy hollows high above.

The Doctor made his way over to where Nesshalop sat sobbing in her quivering puddle of nutrients and breathed gently on her glistening skin: the ritual of expressing regret among Nesshalop's people.

Flowers wanted to join him, but it was taboo. The gesture was socially acceptable only between two equals – and Flowers was not Nesshalop's equal. She was one of her jailers. No matter what she tried to tell herself, these people weren't her friends and colleagues. Their lifestyles and customs were not hers. They were her subjects. She held back, feeling dumb and useless, as they shared their distress with one other.

The Doctor looked up from Nesshalop and gave Flowers an angry look. 'Not sadists or savages, you said.'

'That was out of my hands,' she protested. 'You damaged the infrastructure, the globs are a part of that.'

'Those things wanted to cripple me!'

'I assure you, they're not programmed to be –' She was shouted down by Yahoomer complaining in his vocal alien tongue. Blista too had started hopping crossly on the spot. 'I can't understand them,' said Flowers with a sinking feeling. 'And they can't understand me – the translator's ruined!'

'Never mind.' The Doctor stepped away from Nesshalop, who seemed calmer now. 'You can thank us in any language you like. We've just sorted your gravity problems, after all.'

'What?' Flowers stared at him, not sure if he was teasing

her or getting her hopes up to get back at her somehow. 'I – I understood some of what I saw, but… Doctor, do you mean to say that within ten minutes of your joining this group, you've solved the problems I've been exploring for over five years?'

'Nothing wrong with taking the scenic route,' the Doctor told her, 'lots of pretty views along the way. But I wanted to go straight to the summit, and Nesshalop helped push me along.' He smiled. 'So d'you want to know what we think?'

'Do I *want* to know?' She stared at him, choked off a slightly hysterical laugh. 'Doctor, tell me. *Tell* me. Tell me tell me tell me tell me tell me –'

'I dunno.' The Doctor seemed to consider. 'Maybe Nesshalop should tell you.'

'How! The console's ruined, the translator circuits are burnt out.'

'Oh, of course!' He slapped his hand against his forehead as if this hadn't occurred to him, then stared at her in shock. 'Don't you carry spares?'

'Nesshalop is the only Sucrosian here, Doctor.' Flowers pushed her glasses securely back on to her nose and pursed her lips. 'It will take days to transfer her implant's thought codes into a new translator.'

'Days, eh?' He looked flummoxed by the news. 'So really you can only get this information you're dying to hear from me…'

'As well you know,' she said sourly.

The Doctor raised his eyebrows suggestively. 'Rose is in a borstal, you say? Let's deal.'

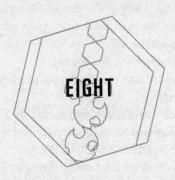

EIGHT

Rose's second morning in the kitchens was almost as grisly as the first. Still hot and hellish, shouts and smoke and nerves. Hands raw and cut and stinging. Warily checking about her, making sure no one was too close, no one was planning to stitch her up again.

The thin girl who'd started everything yesterday was keeping her distance now. Rose wasn't knocking it – she had enough enemies here already – but she idly wondered why.

'You don't want to worry about Nix,' said big Maggi, sidling up to her with a little smile on her gormless face. 'Kazta warned her off.'

'She did?'

'She wants to get you herself, see.'

Rose frowned. 'Oh.'

'Don't go nowhere by yourself. But don't let on I told you.' Maggi looked sad. 'When we give you a thumping, I'll try not to hurt you too bad. 'Kay?'

'Sweet. I'm touched,' said Rose. Maggi smiled again, so the sarcasm was obviously lost on her. 'For God's sake, this is playground stuff. If Kazta wants to play the queen bee round here, that's fine by me so long as she stays out of my way.'

'Sorry, Rose. She has to teach anyone new who's boss. If she doesn't, someone else will.'

'Why are you warning me, anyway?'

'I don't want to hurt you. You've got nice hair.' She smiled shyly. 'It's lovely.'

'Well, when Kazta scalps me, maybe she'll let you have some.' Rose glowered at her. 'Look, you could stand up to her, couldn't you? Together we might be able to...'

But Maggi shook her head and lumbered back to her steaming sink full of dishes.

Rose felt the familiar nervous griping in her stomach.

But maybe there was a way to turn Kazta's spite to her advantage.

At lunchtime, a weary Rose met up with Riz at the canteen. She spied the Governor, sitting at the top table with a handful of warders, Blanc and Norris among them. That was good.

'You sure you don't mind me eating with you?' Rose asked Riz, once they'd queued for their food and she was leading the search for a free table. 'I mean, if I'm a target...'

''S all right,' said Riz, staring distractedly at a group of boys with their backs to her. 'But if Kazta's mob give you a kicking, try not to bleed in my chips, 'kay?' She gave that weirdo laugh of hers.

Rose took Riz towards the top table at the back of the canteen. Either people were understandably shy of sitting too near to the top brass, or the Governor's flatulence was keeping them away in droves. Rose chose a table three down from the Governor and his entourage, and three up from where Kazta sat with her cronies, Maggi included.

Rose gave Kazta a big smile and a cheeky wave. Kazta's face didn't crack. She was seriously checking Rose out. The long intense stare was presumably meant to look intimidating.

'I'm not putting up with this,' Rose said. 'Riz, I could use your help.'

'I ain't fighting.'

'I'm not asking you to.' She grinned. 'Not with your fists, anyway.'

She checked on the Governor. He seemed oblivious to her presence at first, sitting in silence with his plate of slop. Then he looked up, straight at her, like some little Rose-sensor had kicked in.

Slitheen are big on hunting, she remembered.

Rose looked over at Kazta. The look. The smile. The hair, gelled into spikes hard enough to gore you.

She dug her spoon into some lumpy, watery mashed potatoes. When she was thirteen, she'd had a boyfriend in the year above. He was a genius at food fights, the scourge of dinner ladies everywhere. Deadly accurate, he could set whole canteens into chaos with a well-loaded fork and a few subtle flicks of the wrist.

He was a rubbish kisser, but in other arts he had trained her well.

Timing was everything. She waited until the Governor shifted his weight on to one buttock, a small smile suggesting he was discreetly letting one go.

And while he was distracted, Rose took brief but careful aim and flicked her mashed spud in Kazta's direction.

The watery blob of white slime flew through the air over one, two, three tables until it splashed on the shoulder of the girl beside Kazta and sent bits flying everywhere. There was laughter and rebukes and accusations, but all subdued; people were too wary of the Governor and his warders.

Rose knew she had to overcome that.

Kazta's face reddened with fury. Rose blew her a little kiss, hoping to provoke her, but Kazta's mean little eyes kept flicking over to where the big man sat.

So Rose heaped another sludgy mound on to her spoon – not just mash but a few bullet-like baked beans too – and fired again.

This time the missile struck Kazta right in the chest. Rose relished the fury in those piggy eyes, saw the spark start to ignite.

'Food fight?' hissed Riz with an *Are you mad?* look in the direction of the Governor. Then she grinned. 'Guess it beats eating the stuff!'

Riz scooped a huge dollop of potato gloop and flung it over her shoulder at random. It smacked into someone's head with a wet explosion, the soggy fragments snagging in the dreadlocks of a bloke close by, who groaned in revulsion. His tablemates laughed, so he splattered a spoonful in their direction. And at the same time, Kazta – not about to let her victim get away with this, and *stuff* the Governor – loaded her own spoon and hurled a mess of beans and mash in Rose's direction, Maggi and her other minders quickly following suit. But Rose ducked; the mess splattered over the girls on the table behind her. They retaliated by chucking handfuls of their lunch wildly back over their shoulders, hitting others, who yelped and laughed and scooped up missiles of their own...

Within seconds, pandemonium had erupted as a full-scale food fight got under way. Kazta found herself a key target for several splats, as dozens of long-persecuted victims turned on their tormentor – with potato in her eyes, she couldn't see who was attacking, nor where the next assault was coming from.

And just as Rose hoped, the warders leaped up from their seats automatically, yanked their truncheons from their belts and started scattering, bellowing for order. The Governor, red-faced and scandalised, was left alone and unguarded. Rose ducked down under her table and crawled swiftly through a forest of chair legs and stamping size sevens to get to him, heart in her mouth, mashed potato in her hair, yells and shouts and clattering in her ears.

She saw him from under the table, getting up and hurrying for the exit. He would pass by quite close – she couldn't miss this chance. Wriggling frantically from out of her hiding place she grabbed hold of the Governor's leg, pulled on it hard and twisted. He yelled and fell over, smashing into another table, tumbling on to his back. Rose had straddled his chest in seconds, her knees pinning down his arms. She yanked up his thick grey fringe, ready to grab the zip, ready to expose him…

But there was nothing there but his wrinkled forehead.

Rose started going through the hair at his temples like a gorilla picking fleas from its mate, a panicking feeling rising up inside her. She was wrong. No, she *couldn't* be wrong – the blue light, the smell, the flatulence… But there was no zip and so no proof, nothing she could –

Suddenly she was being hauled off him. She caught a glimpse of grey uniform, heard angry voices, her own panicked shouts of '*He's an alien, he's an alien!*' over and over until the truncheon cracked down and the world went silent and black.

With his first day's work over unexpectedly quickly, the Doctor had been sent by Flowers on a proper tour of the

SCAT-house – while she went to see Consul Issabel to outline the Doctor's terms. He'd put a gravitational cat among the pigeons. Now all he could do was sit back and hope it would drag in Flowers and her boss by its force of attraction.

The globs bustled him through a succession of magnificent laboratories and testing areas. In one, he saw the Slitheen bossing around various creatures, doing all the languages and accents as if they were locals. This must be the solar workshop.

'What are you up to?' he called over.

'Big flare's about to rip out from the largest sun,' Ecktosca Fel Fotch replied, sparing him only the briefest of glances. 'We're going for full-on containment.'

'What you using?' Neither he nor Dram, or any of the workers for that matter, bothered to answer, intent on their instruments. 'No, hang on, I'll guess – the mother of all compression fields! Big enough to squeeze a star!'

The Doctor could see a child's excitement shining from the Slitheen's big black eyes. Clearly they were on to something...

Or *up* to something.

'See you later, boys,' called the Doctor, as the globs shepherded him on to the next scheduled stop.

Flowers sat in a hard seat outside Consul Issabel's office, waiting to be seen. But while her backside had gone to sleep, her head was awhirl with the events of the morning, with the snatches of equation she'd seen on the screen and the elusive proof behind them. The idea of generating extreme gravitational waves opened so many new possibilities. It seemed it wasn't so much a question of acceleration as of *volume*... and the Doctor had ideas on how to answer those questions.

Finally, the door to Issabel's office buzzed open. Flowers fair near shot inside and gabbled out her story.

Consul Issabel was a hunched and spindly person in her fifties. Her head looked too big for her sloped shoulders, the pale skin lined and tight over her high cheekbones. And while her eyes burned with a fierce intelligence, she seemed unwilling to look directly at you, staring instead at a shoulder or chest.

'The mindmitter console destroyed, you say?' was her first, rather lukewarm reaction.

'Oh, I expect we can recover the information in the data-core, but until new translation software can be acquired –'

'Breakages must be paid for, Flowers, and a replacement console will not come cheaply.' She half smiled. 'I trust the globs exacted some small retribution?'

'They did,' said Flowers, stony-faced. 'But it hardly seems fair – the Doctor and Nesshalop have broken through the impasse that's been blocking this project for years, in a matter of minutes! We have a way forward now, and I'm convinced it's one that will bring us results.'

Issabel seemed dubious. 'Gravitational waves amplified to break the light barrier?'

'And if we could build spaceships capable of riding those waves…' Flowers felt a flutter in her tummy. 'I remember you mooted a similar theory yourself when we first conceived the project. Imagine being able to propel spacecraft millions of light years in a matter of weeks! *Days* even! True intergalactic travel, and the patents in Justicia's name! And it's perfect timing, too, with the meeting of the Senate tomorrow!' Delegates from all the Justice worlds were coming for the bimonthly presentation from Issabel on the SCAT-house's latest findings. The last two had been cancelled, and it rankled with Flowers that all this year they'd had so little to report. But now…

'I advise you to curb your enthusiasm until you have something a little more concrete in the way of proof,' warned Issabel. 'I abandoned that theory with good reason – it's impossible to generate that level of energy.'

'The Doctor says it *is* possible. He's working on the problem – unconventional but very brilliant.' *He's gorgeous too*, she felt like adding, and started to blush.

'I can see I shall have to meet with this Doctor,' said Issabel thoughtfully.

'Anyway,' said Flowers, charging on, 'the thing is, he claims he needs his friend to help him. An astrophysicist who's currently incarcerated on Justice Beta.'

Issabel's gaze now flicked up to Flowers's eyes and bored into them deeply. 'Oh really?'

Flowers was taken aback by this sudden intimacy and looked down at her shoes. 'He's asked that we give her the chance to let her prove her worth... prove how she could aid him with this project. I know the Doctor is a prisoner and in no position to make demands, but –'

'You feel it would be best to indulge him, to let him explain himself freely rather than attempt to extract the knowledge from his mind against his will?'

'I do,' said Flowers firmly. 'Let's give him the chance to help us willingly, at least in the first instance.'

'You're too soft on the prisoners. This is a labour camp, however you choose to dress it up.'

'I don't care for that term, Consul,' she said, unable to make eye contact now herself.

'Oh, very well,' said Issabel. 'We'll play out some rope to this Doctor and see if he hangs himself.'

'Thank you, Consul. And his astrophysicist friend on Beta?'

Issabel looked at Flowers again. The smile on her face did nothing to soften her drawn features. 'I'll have to give this matter some thought. Have the datacore from the ruined console delivered to me here immediately.'

'But, Consul Issabel, I've already explained that without the translation –'

'Do it!' she snapped. 'I wish to inspect the damage for myself.'

'At once, Consul.' Flowers nodded and rushed from the room. 'You're the boss,' she muttered.

'That's right, Flowers,' said Issabel coolly as the door slid closed. 'I'm the boss.'

A couple of hours later, the Doctor's tour finished as he was returned to his cell. The Slitheen were still out, hard at it in the solar workshops, so the cell was empty.

He lay on his bunk, twiddled his thumbs for a bit. Boring. His eyes started playing over the photos on the wall of the Slitheen ancestors in their alien drag.

It set him thinking about Ecktosca and Dram. Could they really be simple historians with an interest in antiques and their family tree, now filling their days as model prisoners? He supposed that all families had their share of black sheep, and that the Slitheen were no exception. It was perfectly possible he'd met only the evil, ruthless, profit-driven members of the family, and that the rest were lovable, kind and well motivated.

But while all Slitheen undoubtedly looked alike – a strong family resemblance, to be sure – in one of the pictures there was a creature who looked the living spit of Ecktosca Fel Fotch, wriggling with a grin out of a Martian's body armour. Why? Historical re-enactment? Keeping family traditions alive?

With a wicked grin, the Doctor decided it was the perfect time for a quick poke about the nest.

Rose woke up with a splitting headache, alone in a cell under a single burning light bulb. The room was small and bare save for a wooden bench with no mattress and a bucket. Solitary confinement, she supposed, someplace far away from everyone else.

How had she got things so wrong? Rose felt the back of her head to check it hadn't been caved in by the warder's blow. She supposed she had just added another twenty years to her sentence here and made Kazta more mad at her than ever – and all for nothing. She wondered how long she'd been out, and how long before she was *let* out. If their punishments were anything like their jail sentences on Justicia, she could be here for weeks.

'Rose?' She jumped at the sound of Dennel's voice at the door. 'Are you all right?'

'Are you stalking me or something?' she joked. 'What time is it?'

'After ten at night. Just wanted to know if you were OK,' he said. 'You've made yourself into a real celebrity. Rumours are spreading through the blocks about the girl who started a food-fight riot before jumping on the Governor and trying to pull his face off. Is that true?'

'Eyewitness account,' she sighed.

'Because you thought he was an alien. Like you told me.'

'I thought he was…' She groaned, put her head in her hands. 'I *so* thought he was.'

'Well, whatever you thought, you're, like, a total hero to everyone.'

'Total zero, more like,' she countered. 'I've messed up. God knows what the Governor will do to me now.'

'I'll try to find out how long you'll be in here,' said Dennel.

'Should you even be here talking to me?'

'No.'

'What if you get caught? You're crazy!'

'Takes one to know one,' he said. 'Got to go. I can hear someone coming.'

Rose heard his scuffling footsteps retreat quickly from the door, soon to be replaced by a set of precise, military clips and clops on the floor. She backed away from the door, warily, wondering who was approaching and what they had in mind.

The footsteps stopped outside. There was a long, horrible pause.

A grille snapped open in the door.

And a plate of food was pushed through, cold and congealing beneath a thick, rubbery skin.

Rose heaved a monumental sigh of relief, took the food, and slumped back down on the bench.

Then there was a heavy rapping on the door. Rose jumped so high she nearly banged her aching head on the ceiling.

'Tyler?'

It was Norris. Why was a warder knocking before he entered?

'Wha– what is it?' she said shakily.

A key turned in the heavy door. Norris opened it quickly and looked both ways before coming in, as if wary of being seen. As he entered the room his bulk quivered, barely contained by his uniform.

'What do you want?'

He looked at her intently. Little beads of sweat were

dripping down his cheek from beneath his peaked cap.

The peaked cap that hid his forehead from sight.

Rose's mouth ran dry. Suddenly she could picture a zipper running along the length of his head…

'I think we need to talk, Tyler,' said Norris, his mean eyes hard upon her. 'Nice and private. No one else around…'

Rose caught a stink of bad breath as he spoke. She shrank away to the corner of her cell as he advanced towards her.

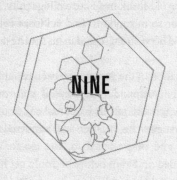

NINE

The Doctor had all but finished searching the Slitheen cell. He'd turned up nothing of interest, and now his hands were sticky with muck. Whatever fluid they used to line their nests, away from their body heat it hardened to a sort of quicklime. It had reddened the skin on his hands, leaving them chapped and sore. Bit of a giveaway, really.

So, he decided, he might just as well get them really dirty.

Beneath the layers of lime, the base of Ecktosca's nest was hard and almost shiny like marble. He rapped his knuckles against this crust and a crack appeared.

Oops. Well, no going back now, then.

He forced his hand right through so that his fingers were exploring a small crevice. The tips scraped against something hard. Frowning, the Doctor hooked hold of it and pulled it out.

It looked a little like a scuba diver's mask, except the front was made of a strange, opaque substance, and the metal frame for it was buckled and clumsily cut. There was no strap, though two holes scored either side suggested there was space for one.

'Home-made compression field,' murmured the Doctor. 'Courtesy of the SCAT-house workshops.'

'And a little old-fashioned Slitheen ingenuity.'

The Doctor spun round to find Ecktosca Fel Fotch in the doorway. He'd been so engrossed in his find he'd not heard the doors open.

'An application of the gear you've been using to control the sun-bursts,' he surmised. 'But why? If you can't find your ancestors' compression fields you'll make your own, is that it?'

Dram burst past his brother and lumbered into the cell, claws raised and outstretched for the Doctor's throat. The globs descended on Dram before he could get halfway across the room, and held him still.

'Don't think about it too hard, you fool,' hissed Ecktosca, moving forwards so that the door slammed shut behind him. 'If the globules detect what we've been up to we're finished. Even if we *have* just given Flowers full mastery over solar flares.'

'You've sorted that out for her, have you? Well done.' The Doctor beamed. 'She's gonna think all her Christmases have come at once. Should put her in a good mood – which is good for me…'

The globs drifted slowly away from Dram's trembling body. His black eyes were still narrowed at the Doctor.

'Poking about in our affairs is *not* good for you, Doctor,' said Ecktosca heavily.

'What do you care? You're going to escape! I bet you've got another one of these gadgets salted away in Dram Fel Fotch's nest… But how are you going to break out without bringing down the globs, eh?' He grinned. 'I get it. Compression field shrinks down your form, alters the molecular state of your mind and body. It'll compress the implant too, confuse the signals enough for you to get away. Right?' He chucked the compression field at Dram, who caught it in one massive hand.

'Thing is – even if you've bypassed the implant, even if you've rustled yourselves up a top disguise on the SCAT-house sewing machine – where is there to go?'

'That's not your business,' hissed Dram.

'And home-made compression fields aren't Flowers's business, either,' said the Doctor brightly. 'But it's weird how these things get out.'

Ecktosca's big black eyes narrowed. 'You wish to stop us?'

'What, and miss having the cell all to myself?'

'Then you wish to escape *with* us.'

'That's a generous offer.' He grinned. 'When are you off?'

'We don't know,' said Dram.

'When help is at hand,' said Ecktosca, just as unhelpfully.

'Fine. I'm not ready to leave yet either. I'm trying to swing a visit from a good friend of mine.' He frowned. 'And even if that comes off, I can't just escape to any old place. I've got property I need to collect.'

'Is that a fact?' said Ecktosca softly. 'Well, then, let's hope you live long enough to do so.'

'What's that supposed to mean?'

The Slitheen lumbered closer, pressed his grotesquely babyish face up close. 'It is not only the globules that watch over us on Justice Prime, Doctor.'

'I think you know why I'm here, Tyler,' said Norris, pausing in front of her.

'You're Slitheen,' Rose croaked, flattening herself against the wall, preparing to bolt.

Norris frowned. 'That name again… What is it with you?'

'I'm not saying another word till you take off your cap!'

He did so. There was nothing there but the mother of all

strap marks right across his head from where the plastic lining
had cut into the skin.

'Satisfied?'

Rose stared. Then she closed her eyes and shuddered with
relief. 'OK, so I'm totally paranoid and I'm feeling completely
stupid right now. What are you doing here?'

'I want to know who sent you,' said Norris.

'Not you too.' Rose sighed. 'Did the Governor send you to
talk to me? He thinks I'm some kind of undercover agent.'

'And you're not?'

'No! Me and my friend came to Justicia by accident and he
got taken somewhere else while I ended up here.'

'The Governor's convinced that someone's coming to check
up on this place.' Norris sighed. 'And he's dead right. It's me.'

Rose gawped. 'You?'

'But how did he get to hear an agent was being sent?' He sat
down on the floor in front of her, and his hard face softened.
'I've been sent by a covert wing of Earth's government to infil-
trate Justicia and report back on the way it's run, the way prisoners are really treated – just what our colonies' money is
funding. Whether what they get is worth all this.'

'How long have you been here?' asked Rose cautiously.

'Nine months.' He shook his head and winced. 'Two weeks'
induction on Justice Delta with the Executive – that's where
they monitor the experiments, co-ordinate the whole system
– and then I was put on patrol here, trailing Blanc around,
junior partner.'

'And you let her get away with treating people...?'

'It's a deep-cover job. I do what I can, but I'm not here to
straighten things. I'm here to find stuff out and report back.' He
rubbed his hands through his close-cropped hair. 'And Jeez,

have I found stuff out. For all the good it does me.'

Rose nodded encouragingly. 'Well?'

'Since I came here there've been four warders and one trustee who disappeared in weird circumstances – oh, and sixteen prisoners. All of them just vanished. Sure, there'll be a missing shuttle in the dock sometimes, or we'll find a wrecked skimmer out on the surface, but look a little closer and you find the facts just don't fit.'

'And the Governor knows about this?'

'He doesn't *want* to know. He's told me we don't need to bother the Executives, sweeping it all under the carpet so it won't look bad on him.' He grimaced. 'You can see the effect the strain's been having on him. He's a mental and physical wreck. And I can't say I'm surprised – the Executive should have cottoned on to the fact that *something*'s rotten here by now. Instead they're sending *more* prisoners!'

'Well, what about the people who sent you? What are they doing?'

'What the hell *are* they doing?' Norris agreed bitterly. 'When I was sent here it was arranged that someone would contact me four months later. Well, I waited for that someone and – nothing. Nothing ever since, either.'

'Well… can't *you* get in touch with *them*?'

'On a deep-cover op?' Norris snorted. 'And here was me thinking maybe you knew something. But if you're asking dumb questions like that, you really don't know jack, do you?'

Rose shrugged. 'So what do you think… The people who put you here have left you to it?'

'I don't know what to think.' He looked at her again, imploringly. 'You swear you don't know anything? Only you've been acting kind of weird for a regular girl, and this alien stuff…'

'I came here with a friend,' said Rose. 'And I know he could help you, if we could only find out where he was…'

Norris shook his head. 'I can't help you, girlie. I can't even help myself.'

The cell door swung suddenly open. 'You're dead right there, Norris.'

Blanc stood in the doorway.

Norris scrambled to his feet. 'OK, Tyler,' he said quickly, forcing gruffness into his voice. 'I've tried the nice guy approach and you still won't play ball. Now Blanc's gonna teach you a lesson.'

'You have no idea,' said Blanc.

She reached out her arm and hooked it round his neck. Norris was a big man, he should have been able to shake her off with ease. But his eyes bulged, and a thick, throttling noise built in the back of his throat as Blanc tightened her armlock.

'Get off him!' Rose shouted, throwing herself forwards. But Blanc kicked her back against the bench.

With a noise like cracking eggshells, Norris's head lolled forwards. One last rattling breath bubbled up from his crushed throat as he slumped to the floor.

Rose stared at her, appalled. 'You've killed him!'

Blanc shrugged. 'Kinder that way. The people he's hoping will contact him are dead or replaced by now. He was all alone, poor thing.' Her eyes twinkled. 'Now he's gone to join them.'

'You evil –'

'Yes, why *am* I so evil and twisted?' said Blanc in mock consternation. 'Was I abused as a child? Was I bullied and beaten at school?' She belched. 'Or am I a mean old thing stuck in a ridiculous human body who'd do *anything* for a few laughs to pass the time?'

'Oh no,' said Rose, as the smell of bad breath wafted past her nostrils.

Blanc grinned. 'Oh *yeah*.'

And she parted her scraped-back hair to reveal a tiny golden zip in the centre, running vertically across her head.

'But you're too thin!' Rose protested. 'How do you fit in there? I thought –' Then she realised. She'd met the Slitheen back in her own time – and now she was hundreds of years in the future. Who was to say that Slitheen in this day and age weren't more advanced?

Whatever, Blanc ignored her. 'We're too close to pulling this off to let a weird little miss who knows the Slitheen steam in out of nowhere to screw everything up. So, I've scared you and scared you till you stink like the pretty little piggy you are… and now I'm going to have me some happy hunting.'

Rose charged at Blanc. It was like running at a wall. Her shoulder jarred with the impact, but she managed to knock the woman aside long enough to squeeze through the doorway.

'I want you to run, Tyler,' called Blanc mockingly. 'You'll only make it sweeter!'

Rose skidded to a halt at the end of the corridor, looked back. The warder was just standing there. Then her hand moved to her forehead and tugged on the zipper. Blue and yellow light started to crackle and flicker from the split in her head. Her smooth complexion slid away like a rubber mask as something big and glistening and alien started to hoick itself free from its human disguise. Its head was long and broad, with wet black eyes the size of bowling balls. Its hide was knobbled and greeny-grey. The long arms ended in three enormous, twitching claws. Its chest and belly sagged and quivered as it stepped from foot to oversized foot. A gleaming, tubular device was strapped tight to its thick, crusty neck.

It was the phantom that had haunted her since her experience in the Governor's office, finally made flesh: sticky, horrible, alien flesh, and *metres* of it.

There was no mistaking it. It was a Slitheen.

Swearing under her breath, Rose turned and ran as the creature gave a cackle of pleasure and triumph. 'Naked, I… am… *magnificent!*' it preened, swinging its massive head from side to side. Then it started thumping down the corridor after her.

Rose's heart was racing, but her mind raced faster. Didn't take a genius to work out where the missing warders and inmates had got to. Not with a psychotic Slitheen on the loose, hunting and killing to pass the long nights inside. But what was it even doing here? How could taking over some lousy prison in the back of beyond help their plans? It had to be something to do with money – Rose knew that Slitheen pursued profits as relentlessly as their prey.

Right now, she knew that better than anyone.

She skidded to a stop as she rounded the next corner. There was a barred door ahead of her. She was trapped.

'Oh, little human girl,' called the Slitheen from somewhere behind her, like a mother putting on a spooky voice to amuse her child. 'I can smell how scared you are… such a pretty stink. So much adrenalin pulsing round your juicy body…'

In desperation, Rose yanked on the door. It opened without a sound.

For a few moments she was elated. Then she realised – Blanc must have left it unlocked deliberately. Slitheen loved to hunt, to prolong the agony of their victims.

She heaved the door shut behind her and ran on. This wing was dilapidated, deserted. Maybe solitary wasn't used much any more. Maybe Blanc had insisted she be placed here, a nice, quiet place to get rid of her. One more missing person.

After what she had seen, Rose knew Blanc could not allow her to live. Another greedy cackle echoed around the dull corridors. The monster was gaining on her.

And finally, she ran up against a door that wouldn't open. She hammered on it, skinning her knuckles, shouting till she was hoarse for someone to open it up, to let her out.

'Pretty, pretty,' said the Slitheen as it padded around the corner. 'You're bleeding…'

'Stay away from me,' Rose warned it, panting for breath.

Again, it giggled, and clicked its monstrous claws together. 'Let me kiss those sore little knuckles better…'

Nostrils twitching, sticky drool stringing from its grisly, puckered mouth, the monster crept closer.

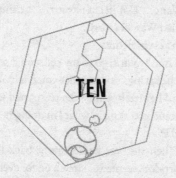

TEN

Rose turned away, banged harder on the door. There was still a chance someone might hear.

She could hear the heavy slap-slap-slap of alien feet pounding down on the tiles towards her.

Tears squeezing themselves out from behind her eyes, she slammed her raw, ringing fists into the metal still harder; it sang like some sick dinner gong.

'Little huuuuuumaaaaaaaaan…'

The door banged back at her. Repeated thuds from the other side. And a gruff male voice, 'Who's there?'

'Rose Tyler!' she yelled. 'There's something here, it's after me, please –'

The door clicked loudly as a key turned. The door started to open and she turned back to face the Slitheen, arm raised in an obscene and hugely satisfying gesture.

But the creature had cut and run. The corridor was empty.

Suddenly Rose was seized from behind, slammed up against the wall.

'How'd you escape from your cell?' A woman was holding her, twisting her arm up behind her back.

'Warder Blanc... Not her, a *monster*... it came for me,' she gasped. 'It killed Warder Norris.'

'Norris ain't even on duty.'

'She killed him – quick, go to my cell, you'll see –'

'She must be raving,' said another voice, a bloke this time.

Rose gritted her teeth against the pain, tried to calm down. 'Well, how would you explain what I'm doing here? I didn't let *myself* out, did I?'

A pause. Then she was hauled away, back the way she'd taken. The corridors seemed to stretch on for ever. How did she manage to run so far?

'Come on, faster!' she urged her guards. 'Blanc's gone back there ahead of us. She'll be disposing of the body. Quick, she mustn't get away with it.'

But when they arrived, the cell was empty save for the spattered remains of her untouched meal on the floor.

'She got away with it,' said Rose numbly.

She saw one of her warders for the first time as he crossed to the door and removed a large ring of keys. He was tall and slim with short ginger hair. 'I'll check the ident on these,' he said. His accent was funny, somewhere between New York and Scouse. 'We'll soon know who let her go.'

'I can tell you for nothing right now, those are Warder Norris's keys,' said Rose hoarsely. 'He came to me because... Well, let's not go into that right now, but Blanc wants you to think he came to let me go free, and now he's run away or whatever, which is kind of a lame story but since Norris is dead you're never going to hear the truth from him, or even see him –'

'Will you listen to yourself?' said the woman.

'You've got to find Blanc, *now*, before she can... Oh, what's the use.' Rose let her body sag in the female warder's grip. 'Can't you see? If I was going to lie to you why would I make up such a crazy, stupid story?'

'Beats me,' said the warder, still holding her arm behind her back. 'But then it beats me what all the fuss is about you. Beats me why the Governor wants to see you in his office this time of night.'

'Go easy on her, Jamini,' the man said. 'You can see she's scared.'

'What are you like?' sighed Jamini. But she relaxed her grip just the same. 'John Robsen, the prisoners' sweetheart.'

So this was Riz's star warder. From the frown lines on his forehead and the smooth skin round his eyes, he worried a lot and smiled just a little. But Rose sensed there was a kindness about him.

'We'd better take her to the Governor right now.'

Then again… she thought.

Jamini marched Rose from the room, and Robsen slouched after her. No one noticed the figure watching them go, half hidden by the pooling shadows at the turn in the corridor.

'Get up,' whispered a voice in the Doctor's head. He blinked, suddenly awake in the darkness – it was the implant, he supposed. 'Proceed to the meeting room you attended earlier. Flowers will be waiting for you.'

'Why?' he whispered. But no one answered.

The Doctor got up cautiously. The cell door opened.

And a massive claw closed around his leg, holding him still.

'Going somewhere, Doctor?' hissed Ecktosca Fel Fotch.

'Implant just told me. I've been summoned.'

'Oh yes? By whom?'

'Flowers, I think.'

'He's going to see Issabel,' came Dram's angry snarl. 'He'll betray us!'

'Course I won't,' said the Doctor crossly. 'I don't know what this is about. The door opened by itself. I didn't do it, did I?'

'The globs took you last time,' said Ecktosca.

'Yeah, so now I can find the way myself.'

'He's going to make a deal for himself by selling us out,' Dram fumed. 'I would in his shoes.'

'Well, you're not in my shoes, are you?' said the Doctor. The claw was like slimy stone, tight around his ankle. 'Trust me. I won't grass you up.'

The claw tightened around his calf, and he gasped with pain. In the darkness, he heard the thuds of descending globules as they fell from their high, invisible holding place to immobilise Ecktosca. The claw snapped back open and the Doctor hopped away, rubbing his bruised shin.

'A tiny taste, Doctor,' the Slitheen whispered, 'of what informants can expect.'

'You'd have to be quick to beat the globs.'

'I would let nothing stop me, Doctor. Nothing.'

The fetid atmosphere in the cell felt suddenly stifling. The Doctor turned and walked away, glad for the corridor's clean air.

Flowers was waiting for him in the forum room. She looked tired and crumpled, but jubilant.

'What's going on?' he asked.

'I know it's kind of late, but when Consul Issabel reaches a decision, she hops to it,' said Flowers. 'She's okayed a discussion with your expert.'

He stared at her in disbelief, then whooped and clapped his hands. 'When does she get here?'

'She doesn't. You'll be talking over videolink.'

'That's not fair,' he complained.

'Take it or leave it.'

He grinned. 'I'll take it.'

'Now, you said Rose Tyler is an astrophysicist and expert in gravity wave mechanics…'

'Did I?' he said. 'Well, yeah, she is – among other things.'

'Well, I have a teeny tiny grasp of them myself,' said Flowers, looking up at him over the top of her pink glasses. 'And I can see how it would apply to what you were saying.'

'What *was* I saying?'

'All those marvellous ideas you had on how to provide us with the required volume of gravity.'

'Oh yeah. Them.'

She gave him a long-suffering look. 'Come on. Issabel's meeting us in the lecture theatre in one hour. You may not be bothered about how impressive she finds you. But unless your friend can convince us that she's a genius,' Flowers went on, 'you may never see her again.'

Robsen hated the night shift. Hated the sobbing in the cells, the long trudge through the dark corridors, the time to think of what he was missing back home. His kids growing up. His mum growing old. He felt as much a prisoner as the poor swines he watched over.

Usually he wandered round half asleep, longing for the morning bell to chime so he could get some sleep or grab breakfast at the officers' mall. But tonight he was wide awake and worried. Very worried.

The keys in the cell *did* belong to Norris, just as the girl had said. If he had been trying to get to her – or at her – for whatever dodgy reason, why would he leave his keys behind? Why incriminate himself?

The sound of quiet crying carried to him as he turned down another corridor. After a year here he could tell you precisely who was weeping from a single sob. But not this time.

He frowned. These tears were coming from Kazta's cell. And the only way Kazta showed emotion was with her knuckles. Could she have someone in there?

Robsen unlocked her door and looked inside. Kazta was lying hunched up on her bed, staring at him through mistrustful, red-rimmed eyes. Her face was streaked with tears.

'What's up?' he enquired, not expecting much of an answer.

'Nothing,' she said. 'I'm all right. Warder Blanc just looked in on me to check.'

Robsen frowned. He'd never known Kazta volunteer information. 'She did?'

'Yeah.' She looked down. 'She's been in a couple of times the last two hours.'

'So she was patrolling this block?'

Her tearful eyes flashed. 'Told you, didn't I?'

'Well, if you're OK – keep the noise down.' Robsen left her to it, locking the door behind him. He should be getting back to Jamini in the Governor's office, tell them about Norris's keys.

But first he would pay a visit to Blanc.

God, he hated the night shift.

The lecture theatre was vast and echoing, its ochre walls stretching up to the tall and shadowy ceilings. Tiers of padded chairs filled the front half of the sizeable auditorium, while at the back the seating was a bit more fluid to accommodate those more unusual life forms who might attend. A vast rectangular screen formed the focus for the hall, shimmering with light.

Flowers took off her specs and rubbed her eyes. She was exhausted, but still buoyed up on a wave of euphoria, not only by the new and unexpected direction her accelerated gravity project had taken, but by the seeming success of the solar flare containment programme. She'd imagined such a break-through was miles off, but the Slitheen had got results at incredible speed.

Her mind kept niggling excitedly at what would come next, like a child fiddling with the wrappings of a big, bright parcel. Tomorrow morning there was the meeting of the Senate – and suddenly there was so much to show off about. During the next few weeks she could fully test and refine the containment process and then hand it over to the Executive on Justice Delta for more rigorous testing...

Jolting herself back to the present, she called up a schematic of the Justicia system. It showed the six planets orbiting their three suns and their various masses.

The Doctor was slumped in the front row, staring up at the screen. 'Needs something,' he informed her.

'I can adjust the clarity, or the focusing?'

'Nah. Something else.' He grinned. 'Got any popcorn?'

'Pay attention. We don't have long.' Flowers had no idea what he was talking about and she couldn't afford to be beguiled by that smile of his right now. 'Obviously, if we're playing with gravity on such a massive scale, we need to make sure we're not affecting any of the other system planets. So I thought as an exercise, your friend could –'

'Is that map to scale?' wondered the Doctor.

'The positioning of these planets means something to you,

doesn't it?' she said. 'Did Nesshalop bring them up on screen this morning?'

He nodded. 'Are those orbits true?'

'This system chart,' said Flowers proudly, 'was created from my own observations, just two years ago. It's all my own work. Not *everything* you see here is leeched from our illustrious inmates.'

'Go on, though, you've kiddified it, haven't you? Except for ours, the orbits are drawn as perfect circles.'

'That's because they are, near enough.'

'Yeah?' The Doctor raised his eyebrows. 'And the distances between the planets – they look to be exactly the same.'

'More or less. Justice Alpha is the closest, orbits at approximately 100 million miles from the suns, Justice Beta orbits at 148 million, Justice Gamma at 201 million…'

He laughed. 'You're joking!'

'If you won't take it from me…' She called up the exact figures for him on the schematic.

'Well, well,' he was forced to concede. 'Nature's not often so neat and tidy. What are the chances of that?'

'Billions to one!' She smiled. 'It's actually one of the reasons Justicia set up here – that amazing balance, good for publicity. You know, with the scales of justice thing, blah blah…'

The Doctor pulled a face. 'Cheesy.'

'Justice Prime is the only rebel of the group, with an elliptical orbit that takes it way, way out from the others. Probably the result of some great collision in the early days of the system.'

'And its freewheeling spirit lives on in you,' said the Doctor, tongue in cheek.

'So *anyway*,' said Flowers. 'Do you think your genius friend could work out how far we can safely accelerate local gravity without influencing the other planets in the system?'

'Without computers, right?'

Flowers stared in surprise. 'Well, if you don't think she'll need them.'

'Shouldn't do,' he said, smiling again. 'The answers might be a bit ballpark, but it'll give Issabel a bit more wow, won't it? A bit more X-factor.'

'Well, *we'll* need to use the computer to predict the figures, anyway,' said Flowers. She looked at him shrewdly. 'Or how do we know your friend isn't simply making up anything she likes?'

'Thanks for giving her this chance,' he said.

Flowers blushed a little. 'I'm not being kind,' she said stiffly. 'I want you well motivated for this project, and since this girl clearly means a lot to you…'

'Right, let your computer do its stuff,' said the Doctor, smiling back at her agreeably. Under his breath he added, 'And let's see if I can do mine.'

A quick check on the duty roster told Robsen that Blanc *was* supposed to be on patrol in Kazta's block, and that Norris had put in for a night off. But since there was no sign of Blanc anywhere, he decided to try to find Norris instead. May as well hear his side of the story – could someone have taken his keys?

He traipsed across to the officers' dorm, a fair-quality hotel staffed by robots on the fringes of the borstal grounds, decorated in pale pastel colours.

Norris's quarters were unlocked and empty. After a brief look inside, Robsen was satisfied that the man's bed hadn't been slept in.

Another one right for Rose Tyler.

But Warder Blanc had been on duty. She'd called in on Kazta twice.

Robsen had never seen Blanc as the caring type. And he couldn't imagine Kazta crying on a screw's shoulder.

Since he couldn't find Blanc on duty, he decided to try her rooms. The cream carpet softened his footfalls as he approached.

Voices carried from inside her room.

'You were careless and undisciplined, my daughter,' a woman was saying. She had an austere voice, shot through with age. 'We cannot afford to draw attention to ourselves now.'

'I have acquired an alibi. She would not dare to give me away.' Robsen would have said it was Blanc until he heard the woman giggle: a joyful sound that he would never associate with her. 'I nearly scared her to death.'

'Await my commands, child,' said the first woman. 'You will find further support here shortly.'

Robsen crept nearer to the door. As he did so, the ground seemed to thrum beneath his feet, like some powerful tremor was building, just for a few seconds. Then it was gone. What the hell…?

Frowning, he knocked quickly on the door. 'Blanc? It's Robsen. Everything OK?'

Silence. He couldn't hear a thing.

Then the door opened. Blanc stared at him expectantly.

'You're supposed to be on duty. I've been trying to find you.' He pushed inside her room. 'I thought you had someone in here?'

Blanc gestured round the empty room, and Robsen peered

into the one adjoining. It was empty.

'I was listening to a recording.' Blanc smiled and held up a gleaming audio disc. 'I've just come from Kazta's cell. She's disturbed – reckons someone has it in for her, that she's being threatened. She said she recorded them on her sound pad. So I came back here to listen for myself.'

'And?'

She looked dismissive. 'I think it's staged. She's making it up. Attention-seeking.'

Robsen thought back to the voices he'd heard. 'I'd like to listen.'

She shrugged and inserted the disc.

'Breathe a word about this and I'll make you sorry…' The voice was low and guttural. It spoke over a backdrop of Kazta's terrified sobbing. *'No one will believe a fat liar like you, anyway. And if you say something, I'll get to hear. You know I will. And I'll show you the monster in me again…'*

Robsen shifted uneasily as she turned it off.

'You see?' said Blanc quietly, a smile flickering round her thin lips. 'It's nonsense. Has to be staged… don't you think?'

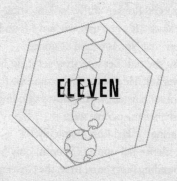

ELEVEN

At last, thought Rose, as Warder Jamini marched her inside the Governor's office. Jamini was a bit rough – in every sense – but Rose was glad of the willowy, long-faced woman's presence. She still didn't trust the Governor. She'd been looking for the zip in his head in the wrong place – he could well be Slitheen too. But if that was true, why would he save her from Blanc by calling her to his office in the dead of night?

At least there were no spooky lights in his office this time – though from the smell of things he was still cracking one off every now and then. He was sitting behind his desk in a smart peacock-blue suit and black tie; this transformation from his usual scruffy state was presumably one of the reasons she'd been kept waiting.

Robsen knocked on the door and entered. 'No doubt about it, sir,' he told the Governor. 'The keys are Norris's. And –'

'– he's gone missing,' Rose cut in. 'Nowhere to be found?'

'That's right,' said Robsen. He looked uneasy. 'Not a sign of him.'

Rose nodded. 'You found Blanc, though, right?'

'I am conducting this inquiry,' thundered the Governor.

'Sorry, sir,' said Robsen stiffly, looking straight ahead like a soldier on parade. 'It's just that when we found Tyler, she did seem to know that Norris would be gone.'

'Of course she did! Because they set it up between them!' said the Governor. 'He had to run because we foiled their little plan! Oh, I never trusted Norris. Always finding fault. Always trying to convince me people were –'

'Disappearing?' asked Rose pointedly.

A heavy silence fell upon the room, only broken when a loud, wet-sounding burp burst from the Governor's throat. He opened the drawer to his desk and swigged from a bottle of milky fluid. 'Stress,' he muttered. 'All I get is stress.'

'Should we perhaps speak with Warder Blanc?' mooted Jamini.

Again, Robsen opened his mouth to speak.

'You mean you believe that ludicrous rubbish about Blanc being some enormous killer monster?' spluttered the Governor.

'If you take a close look at her head you'll see there's a little golden zip, like a centre parting under her hair,' Rose said.

'And when you attacked me, that was what you were looking for?'

She blushed. 'Back then, I thought the zip would be in your forehead.'

The Governor stared at her as if she was fruit-loops. 'Well, if it will help disabuse you of this absurd fantasy…' The Governor combed his fringe neatly this way and that. Rose had to admit that there was no telltale glint of metal in his scalp.

Robsen glanced over awkwardly at Jamini, then cleared his throat. 'What should we do about Norris?'

'I'm sure he will turn up in time,' snapped the Governor.

'Now, Robsen, return to your patrol. I'm not prepared to listen to another word of this fantastical nonsense!' Robsen walked out, and the Governor advanced slowly on Rose. 'However, it seems the same cannot be said for Consul Issabel, Technocrat Major of Justice Prime. She is so insistent that she must speak with you at once, Tyler, she's seen fit to ruin my rest period, demanding you be prepared for an audience.'

'Why? What have I done?'

'We shall see.' He threw some fresh clothes at her, and what looked like a bag of cosmetics. 'Jamini, take her to the executive washrooms and see that she smartens herself up.' He paused. 'Issabel is a prime mover in Justicia. I want her to be given a good impression of this prison.'

'And never mind the reality,' Rose muttered, as Jamini marched her away.

The Doctor passed Flowers a printout hot from the computer feed. 'Here you go. Projected safety levels. That's what Rose should come up with.'

Flowers nodded and pulled out a small, boxy device. 'I'll check the figures on this. The gravometer.'

'The what?'

'Blista's been working on it,' she explained. 'Internal scanner picks up real-time data on planets and stars, and their gravity fields. If it really works it could take years off his sentence.' She frowned. 'I've dialled up Justicia. But I'm getting a different reading.'

The Doctor frowned and took the gravometer. 'Try the computer – it uses the planets' orbits as you calculated them two years ago, right?'

'Right.' She did as he suggested. 'Aha. Now the figures

match. Poor Blista. Must be a bug in his programming.'

The Doctor frowned at the data scrolling down the gravometer's screen. 'Yeah. Suppose there must be.'

Suddenly, Flowers jumped up. A slightly hunched woman threw open the doors and stormed into the lecture theatre. She was dressed all in black, which only made her pale, gaunt face seem whiter still. Her thin grey hair was ruffled, as if she'd raced here from wherever she'd sprung from.

'Consul Issabel, this is the Doctor,' said Flowers.

'Should I salute?' the Doctor wondered.

'I suggest you do not provoke me,' said Issabel tightly. 'I am going to a good deal of trouble because of you.'

'Only cos you know I'm worth it.'

'But *are* you?' Issabel studied him appraisingly. 'How do you propose to send gravity waves faster than light without a disruption engine the size of a small planet?'

'By using the six big planets you've got already.'

She stared at him. 'Explain.'

'It's an amazing coincidence – but get this. Justicia's planets are evenly spaced in proportion to each other, right? All spinning about, all whirling around their three suns in a perfect circular orbit...' He shrugged. 'Well, seems to me it's like some giant cosmic centrifuge waiting to happen, isn't it?'

Flowers gave a strangled gasp behind him. 'Of course! An ordinary centrifuge can simulate the effects of gravity or acceleration on humans or animals... but if you could somehow harness the energy of the entire planetary system...'

But Issabel was harder to impress. She didn't seem surprised in the least. 'And how *would* you harness that power, Doctor?'

He shrugged. 'I'd build a gravity amplifier.'

Flowers was fiddling excitedly with the hem of her grey top.

'And if you amplified the natural gravity into faster-than-light gravity waves, you could open up those short cuts through space we were talking about.'

'Yeah. Of course, you'd only need to go to work on a small part of space. Use the amplified gravity to open up a warp-hole big enough to send a ship through.'

She clapped her hands together. 'A tunnel through time and space! Gateways to interstellar travel! The more you amplify the waves, the further you can travel through the warp-holes!'

'What do you think, Consul Issabel?' the Doctor enquired. 'Do I win a coconut?'

'It's a brilliant theory!' Flowers said dreamily.

'But it is *only* a theory, Doctor,' said Issabel, still quite unruffled. 'I'd be interested to know the limits of such an amplifier.'

'There *are* no limits, in theory.'

'Prove it!'

'Wouldn't take long. That Blista fella has already done the groundwork with his experiments. They just need some adapting.'

'You're serious?'

He shrugged. 'Well, when you transfer my friend over here, perhaps we'll show you.'

'You'll do exactly as we want, Doctor,' Issabel hissed. 'I promise you that.' There was something dark and murderous in her eyes. 'Now, if Flowers has prepared the test for your "friend"... I suggest we begin.'

When Rose was washed and ready, Jamini escorted her back to the Governor's office. He indicated that she should sit in a high-backed chair. The chair faced a blank wall, but as Rose took a seat, a woman came into focus.

She was knocking on a bit with pinched, worried features. She stood slightly hunched, not making full eye contact.

'Greetings, Consul Issabel,' said the Governor behind her. 'I have done as you've asked. It is a pleasure, of course, to receive your image.'

'This is the prisoner?' demanded Issabel. 'Rose Tyler?'

'Yeah,' said Rose. 'What do you want?'

'To be impressed,' said the woman, with the ghost of a smile. 'Very well, Doctor.'

'Doctor!' yelled Rose. She jumped up from her chair with delight but Jamini was there to wrestle her back into it. 'Doctor, are you there?'

'Yeah! I'm here!' His grinning face pushed into view on the screen.

Rose could have sobbed with relief. 'I thought I'd never see you again.'

'Are they treating you OK?'

'There's a *Slitheen* here –'

'That's enough,' hissed the Governor.

'Slitheen?' That was Consul Issabel, out of shot; she sounded shocked. 'Governor…?'

'You mean…' The Governor gulped. 'Forgive me, Consul Issabel, but – but you've actually heard of these… Slitheen things?'

'I'm sharing a cell with two of them,' said the Doctor brightly. 'Not bad company once they get used to not being able to kill you.'

'What would a Slitheen be doing in a jail for human juveniles?' asked another woman, outside the circle.

'Trying to slaughter me for one thing!' said Rose.

The Doctor's face darkened. 'What kind of a prison are you

running, Governor, where alien creatures can threaten the people in your care?'

The Governor actually quivered. 'The girl's delusional!' he protested.

'Yes,' said Issabel, with sudden certainty in her voice. 'She is wrong.' Seconds ago she'd seemed genuinely alarmed – so why was she now dismissing Rose's story out of hand? 'Doctor, you have a point to prove. I suggest you attempt to do so at once.'

'Point to prove?' Rose frowned.

'They don't believe you're a genius,' said the Doctor. She caught the playful light dancing in his blue eyes. 'They don't reckon I need you, and they're so, so wrong. So, anyway, I'm sorry, but they want to test you.'

'Genius. Test. OK.' Rose kept herself composed, though there were some heavy-duty alarm bells ringing inside her right now. 'Whatever. Go for it.'

'It's a question of gravity wave mechanics…' said the Doctor, and he started rabbiting on about relative densities of planets and orbital inclinations and God only knew what. He usually preferred to gloss over the techy stuff, so Rose guessed he was attempting to impress Issabel and whoever else he was with. She glanced up at Jamini and saw the warder's eyes glazing over. The Doctor was scoring around eleven out of ten on the scientific waffle-ometer, and clearly Rose the genius was meant to get exactly what he was talking about.

'I get the picture,' she said carefully. 'You want me to solve this gravity problem. Without any help.'

'That's right,' he said, shaking his head almost imperceptibly. 'With no help at all.'

A small, down-at-heel woman nudged into view, coming up to chest height on the Doctor. 'Rose?' She smiled a little self-consciously. 'I'm Senator Flowers, the Doctor's overseer and in charge of the gravity wave project.'

'Hi,' said Rose evenly, and managed a smile back. She'd take Flowers over Blanc and the Governor any day.

'The Doctor's outlined the situation and detailed the relative orbits. Assuming a gravity bend of 96 per cent in system space, what would the tangential warp offset register?'

Rose swore she could feel the colour draining from her cheeks.

'Hey, Rose, it's worth your while to answer,' said the Doctor. He leaned a little closer. 'If this project comes off we get a royalty that could bring in a lot of cash – and we're talking telephone numbers, right, Flowers?'

'Be silent, Doctor,' snapped Issabel.

'Sorry!' he looked at Rose again. 'Mum's the word.'

Flowers frowned at her. 'Well, Rose?'

Rose adopted her most studious expression. The Doctor was cheating somehow. Her mind raced. Telephone numbers... Mum's the...

Her *mum's* telephone number? Was that what she was supposed to reel off here?

All eyes were on her. She had one shot at this.

A thick trickle of sweat squirmed down between her shoulder blades. What about the 020? Was that part of the deal?

She cleared her throat. 'I'm not surprised Consul Issabel wants you to stay quiet, Doctor. She might think you're sending me a *coded* message.'

He laughed as if at the very preposterousness of the idea. 'No. No codes.'

Rose thought she might join the Governor in letting one rip as she reeled off the number: '7... 398...'

Flowers smiled once Rose had finished. 'She's close, Consul, considering that's a mental calculation. All right then, what about the warp overlap?'

Rose's buoyant heart started sinking again, and fast.

The Doctor was frowning, fidgeting. 'She's already taken the test, Flowers.'

Flowers glanced up at him in mild surprise. 'Shouldn't be hard for her, Doctor, considering the mental agility she's just demonstrated.'

'Yes, Doctor, don't fuss,' Rose said coolly, trying to buy time. 'It's not a problem.'

'It is,' the Doctor insisted. 'These people always want more proof, I'm sick of it. It's like when I brought Pauline, Martin and Sonia in-house –'

'Be silent, Doctor,' snapped Issabel.

'– so many stupid questions they had to address –'

'Be *silent*.'

Rose looked at him, uncomprehending. Why was he babbling on about the Fowlers from *EastEnders*? She'd made him spend a day off watching old episodes on video in her flat a while back, catching up on some storylines she'd missed. Think, think...

'Can't we all just talk face to face?' the Doctor asked hopefully. 'If you look at a screen like this for too long, your eyes go square, I'll bet.'

Except he said the last words oddly so they sounded like "Albert".

Albert Square – the Fowlers – bringing them in-house. In *a* house? Questions they had to address...

'Address!' she blurted, wide-eyed.

'I'm sorry?' blinked Flowers.

'Nothing.' Rose racked her brains for the Fowlers' address in Albert Square. *The Queen Vic is 46...*

'Answer her question, Tyler,' said the Governor warningly.

'Oh yes. Sorry. You want to know about the warp overlap.'

'That's right,' said Flowers, watching her carefully.

Number 43 – no, that's Sharon's old flat, come on, come on...

'An overlap of 45!' she declared.

Flowers smiled. 'Yes, that's exactly right.'

The Doctor grinned wolfishly at her. But then Issabel pushed past him, came into the centre of the screen.

'Forty-five what?' she enquired icily.

Rose copped a deaf 'un. ''Scuse me?'

'An overlap of 45 *what*?'

But then, to her planet-sized relief, she was saved by the bell. Or rather, by the strange wailing warbling noise that seemed to tear out of the screen. It was some kind of klaxon.

'Fire drill?' the Governor wondered.

'Code One alarm,' snapped Issabel, forgetting Rose and rounding on Flowers. 'Attempted breakout.'

'It seems you have a situation on your hands, Consul,' said the Governor. His concerned look did nothing to disguise the smugness in his voice.

Issabel had to raise her voice over the racket of the siren. 'Arrange for the girl to be sent to me here immediately.'

'I'll send her on the next shuttle out.'

'I said immediately,' Issabel snapped.

'Very well,' said the Governor quickly, 'I'll arrange a shuttle right away.'

Issabel didn't seem appeased. 'This session is terminated.'

The white light illuminating the screen sputtered and died. The alarm's insistence hushed to silence.

The Governor seemed quite baffled. 'Extraordinary woman.'

'They shoot, they score.' Rose sighed happily.

Flowers had flapped into a fully fledged panic. 'What's happening?'

Consul Issabel crossed to the computer bank beneath the main screen. She muted the local alarm and linked through to the security processors. 'The Slitheen. They've gone missing.'

'Made a break for it?' The Doctor looked at Flowers. 'Thought that was impossible.'

'They won't get far,' Issabel barked. She approached the Doctor. 'You've shared their cell. Have you noticed anything suspicious?'

'Nothing,' he said flatly. 'Perhaps they thought I smell. Do you reckon I smell?'

'I smell a rat, Doctor,' said Issabel. 'But the truth will out. Globules! Escort the Doctor back to his cell.'

The Doctor held out his arms resignedly. A crowd of globs plummeted from out of the shadowy sky and perched there like misshapen pigeons. He was ushered out of the lecture theatre at the double.

'Get to your quarters, Flowers,' said Issabel. 'I'll speak to system security and issue updates as and when.'

Flowers nodded and ran off at once.

'Well, this is excellent news,' the Governor announced to the room at large as both the screen and the siren cut out. 'Not only am I authorised to get rid of this Tyler troublemaker post-haste, but Issabel has a breakout to contend with.'

'How is that excellent, sir?' asked Jamini haltingly.

'Use your noodle, Warder. An insurrection will make *her* a bigger target for an Executive inquiry than me!'

Rose frowned. 'What do you mean?'

'The Executive on Justice Delta. Those who study us, organise us, help determine our policies…' His big chest puffed up with pride. 'Our prison here has maintained a clean bill of health for seven months running. Despite these spurious claims of yours.'

Seven months… Norris had said how the Executive had gone as suddenly silent as his covert bosses, back in their shadowy branch of Earth Government. Blanc the Slitheen had said that those bosses were dead…

'Have you spoken to any of the Executive lately?' asked Rose, wondering if they could have gone the same way.

'They communicate their wishes to me through Consul Jakkson, Detention Centre Chief Overseer, you silly girl,' said the Governor. 'Now, Jamini, arrange for a shuttle to take her to Justice Prime and wait with her in the holding area till she's ready to board. Goodbye, Rose Tyler.' He belched. 'I'm glad to be shot of you.'

Jamini hauled her up by the arm and led her across the office.

'Just check on Blanc like I told you,' Rose pleaded. 'If you don't then she'll –'

'I said, goodbye!' the Governor snapped.

'Why don't you just drop that bull, Tyler?' said Jamini gruffly once they were out of the office. 'What use is it to you now? You're getting out of here.'

'Everything I've told you has been totally true,' said Rose fiercely.

Jamini shook her head wearily. 'Sooner you're out of here

the better.' But Rose could see the disquiet in her eyes as the two of them marched on through the darkened corridors.

The Doctor felt a wave of gloom overtake him as he reached his now-empty cell. The Slitheen must have believed he'd told Flowers and Issabel their secret about the home-made compressors after all – and put whatever plan they had into action.

Well, good luck to them. Whether they were successful or not made little difference to three fundamentals.

One, that when Rose arrived, the two of them could no longer piggyback the Slitheen's escape attempt.

Two, security would doubtless now be stepped up, making it still harder to get away.

Three, being stuck here, powerless, was an all-round royal pain in the...

The Doctor kicked his mattress in frustration. At least Rose was on her way here now. At least they would be together. But he had seen the cold, malevolent look in the eyes of that Issabel woman when she'd questioned Rose at the end. What would happen when the Consul saw that she was no genius astrophysicist? Send her back? Punish her? Worse?

And what was this about a Slitheen in Rose's borstal? Aliens were sent *here*, Flowers had been adamant on that when he'd first arrived. And yet Issabel had seemed alarmed at the possibility at first, before suddenly dismissing it out of hand. Rose was wrong, she'd said. Just *wrong*.

He remembered Ecktosca Fel Fotch's words before lights-out. *It is not only the globules that watch over us on Justice Prime...*

Consul Issabel returned to her office and sat herself wearily behind the desk. A barrage of inconclusive reports scrolled across her computer screen. It seemed the Slitheen had well and truly escaped. Loathsome creatures. Thorns in her flesh.

Still, even at large, for all their posturing they could pose little threat to her plans. Especially now it seemed that the Doctor and his friend would be able to move things along so quickly. The datacore from the console that his mental acrobatics had scrambled lay on her desk, singed and oily. She picked it up, contemplated it for a few moments.

She pressed a button under her desk and a small screen warmed into existence on the wall beside her. A familiar figure appeared, huge and surrounded by stubby, smoking candles.

'It's me,' she said. 'I've met with the Doctor myself now and I've studied his thought impulses. His mind is undisciplined and unorthodox, but highly advanced – he's already worked out how the positioning of the planets in their orbits may prove significant. The girl may be valuable too – I'm less convinced by her, but a man of the Doctor's intelligence is unlikely to associate with fools.'

'So why are you bothering me?' rasped the shadowy shape.

'I think we should speed up the operation. The door's been opened for us. We should go through it at once.'

'About time too,' said the figure on the screen. 'We'll proceed to the final phase.'

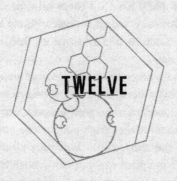

TWELVE

You got so attached to people here, Flowers reflected on her way to the meeting of the Senate the next morning. Hardly surprising, when you were more or less a prisoner yourself.

Issabel had turned down her last three requests for leave on one of the local pleasure satellites, insisting that too many of her projects were at a 'critical' stage. She supposed she hadn't been too bothered – you weren't even allowed to leave the confines of Justicia in case you were trying to leak secrets or do private deals with techno-corporations. Just for a change of environs she'd asked for a brief transfer to Justice Delta. But according to Issabel, the Executive Consuls had no time to receive her. This was a story they'd stuck to for some months, and it was starting to rankle – especially given the quite excellent work Flowers had passed to them over the last seven years.

Another three years and her contract would expire. She'd be forty, then. *Life begins at forty* the old saying went, and in Flowers's case it was true. For a start, by then she'd have earned an absolute mint from her ten-year attachment through wages, royalties and patents – which ought to lead to more success with men, or at the very least a more comfortable independence. She'd have had hands-on experience of state-of-the-art technology, and an enviable working knowledge of scores of alien cultures and intelligences, worth a fortune to military agencies.

Oh no, she'd never been bothered by the ethics of her employers. Obviously, it was a shame that most funding for hard science came from weapons research, but Flowers had always liked to think she was, if nothing else, practical. If she didn't accept the army dollar, there were a hundred others poised to take her place – all of them probably taller, better-looking and generally more glam than she was, the cows, so they could stuff it. Besides, the military might pioneer new technology, but it filtered through to everyday life in the end – so that was all right, wasn't it?

Trouble was, 'everyday life' on Justicia was something that had been slowly eating away at Flowers's resolve these last years. She had honestly thought she could crawl into Justicia as if it was a chrysalis and give up ten years of her life to become the woman she always meant to be – mature, buoyant and set up for life. Now it seemed to Flowers that the girl she'd been seven years ago was the one who'd been set up, with promises that could never be delivered.

It was a horrible, humbling crashdown. On days like yesterday, with major breakthroughs on two projects, she'd felt as if graceful wings could strike out from this ungainly, lumpy body she'd been saddled with. But then, nights like last night made her realise that the SCAT-house was not so much a cocoon as a tomb. A place that saw new arrivals now and again, but never new *life*.

At least, not until the Doctor had turned up.

Someone passed her swiftly in the corridor. A stooped

black man, smartly dressed and with a pointed, greying beard, passed by without comment. Flowers thought she recognised him as one of the Executive's senior diagnostic chiefs. He must be here for the meeting of the Senate.

'Dr Meldow,' she called after him. 'Dr Meldow, I, er, think you'll find the meeting is this way…'

He didn't turn or acknowledge her in any way. He just shuffled into the aquaculture compound, the main door sliding smoothly open and closed to accommodate him – which was weird, since Issabel had ordered the hydroponics experiments postponed while they prioritised the gravity projects. Still, he *was* a VIP. Perhaps he wanted a quick look round at them before the meeting began.

For a moment, she wondered if she should warn him about the Slitheen. They had not been found anywhere in the SCAT-house, though their means of escape and how they overpowered their implants remained a mystery. Flowers knew she would miss them. Their banter, their strange grace, their ferocious intellects… She felt a little warm ache in her ribs. At least they'd perfected control of the solar flares before they'd gone – as a thank-you to her, perhaps, for all she had tried to do for them on the inside? It was a pleasing thought, and she dwelled on it all the way to the Senate meeting.

Only when she got there, she found the meeting room was empty. Puzzled, she contacted Issabel on the video link.

Issabel appeared on the glowing screen and almost bit her head off. 'I cancelled the meeting! Didn't you check your mail?'

'No, I –'

'We're on a state of maximum emergency, I've got escaped prisoners on the loose – and you expect me to play show and tell?'

'But I've just passed Dr Meldow in the corridor, surely if he's here –'

'He's *not* here. You are mistaken, Flowers.'

'Excuse me, Consul, but with respect, I know what I –'

'You are mistaken.' An icy smile passed over Issabel's face. 'You may check the shuttle logs if you do not believe me. No shuttle has arrived, nor is any *due* to arrive until that which is carrying the Doctor's prisoner friend.'

'I… I'm sorry, Consul. Do please forgive my incompetence.'

'That's better. Now, I want you to arrange a secure cell for her. Put her to work with the Doctor on the gravity wave amplifiers the moment she arrives.'

'Of course, Consul Issabel,' said Flowers, scarlet-cheeked, a tingle of fear travelling down her spine.

It was an unpleasant reminder that somewhere deep inside she must have a backbone after all.

The sitting around, the pacing, the endless waiting were over. Now Rose sat in a shuttle cabin identical to the one she'd arrived in, only this time her mood was one of cautious optimism. On her journey to Justice Beta, only the unknown had awaited her. Now, the Doctor was waiting at the other end of the journey, and together the two of them might just stand a chance of striking out for the TARDIS –

Always assuming she got there. Her nose was twitching. Smoke.

It was seeping out from under a bulkhead door in the centre of the far wall, clouding the air in sinister spirals.

Rose marched up to the other end of the cabin and started banging on the door that led to what she assumed was the cockpit. 'Hey! Anyone in there? I think something's on fire.'

There was silence.

'Look, I don't blame you for thinking this could be a trick or whatever, but it's not!' The smoke was getting thicker, darker, and Rose beat on the door more urgently. 'And I don't know what you keep the other side of that door, but something's definitely caught fire, OK? I mean, if you only had smoke detectors on this crummy ship you'd –' A high-pitched beeping started up at ear-splitting volume. 'OK, so you do. Now will you listen?'

The door abruptly opened to reveal a male, swarthy pilot the other side. 'Back up,' he snarled, jabbing a small, nasty-looking gun in her face.

Rose quickly did as he ordered. Once the pilot had stepped through to the cabin, the door closed behind him. He crossed to the bulkhead. 'Something in the hold,' he muttered, and placed his palm on a metal square beside the broad doorway. The door hummed open. A load more smoke belched out from the hold.

While the pilot was dragged *into* it.

Rose heard his frantic shout – then silence. She backed away to the cockpit door, but she had no way to open it. She started to choke on the smoke now filling the cabin.

There was a clattering noise from inside the hold. A rushing, whooshing noise – a fire extinguisher maybe. The alarm cut off abruptly.

'Who's there?' Rose said in alarm, looking around with streaming eyes for something she could use to defend herself. There was nothing. 'I said, who's there?'

Then a dark figure loomed out through the smoke.

'Just your friendly neighbourhood block-walker,' said Dennel with a bashful grin.

'Dennel!' Rose stared at him in horror. 'What the hell are you doing here?'

He frowned. 'Duh! Rescuing you! I had to hide when Norris came for you. I overheard what he said, and I saw what that creature inside Blanc did to him. Saw her chase after you…'

'Oh, terrific.' She threw up her hands in the air. 'I didn't need rescuing from this ship, thanks very much! It's taking me where I want to go!' She choked again on the smoke. 'Justice Prime, where the Doctor is!'

Dennel looked crestfallen. 'But… I thought you'd be pleased. We can get away now!'

'I can't go anywhere without the Doctor or the TARDIS.' She peered past him into the smoky hold. 'Now, what have you done to that pilot?'

'Hit him on the head with an extinguisher. He's out cold.'

Rose held her breath, ducked into the hold and re-emerged, pulling on the pilot's prone body. 'Help me, then!'

Dennel saw what she was doing and together they raised the pilot's hand up to the touch pad beside the cockpit door. It buzzed open smoothly and they collapsed inside the small control room, breathing the clear air gratefully. Through the wraparound window, she looked out over the star-speckled blackness of space and the bright baubles of nearby planets. The vista was a lot easier on the eye than the cockpit controls – all nameless clumps of lights and switches and blinking screens, gaudy and incomprehensible.

'Cheer me up,' said Rose. 'Tell me you can fly this thing.'

Dennel looked at the controls. 'Most of it will be automatic. When the pilot wakes up we can force him to give us control.'

'I don't want control! I want to go where I was going!'

'But – they'll throw away the key if they catch me now.'

Dennel looked crumpled and miserable, a big smear of soot on one cheek. 'I thought you were in danger. Thought you'd be pleased to see me.'

Rose sighed and patted his leg. 'Look, I am glad to see you, OK?' She smiled despite herself. 'You Muppet! How'd you even get on-board here?'

'When Blanc chased after you, I saw Norris was dead. So I took his ID-scan from his body before she could get rid of it.' He grinned at her despite himself. 'And suddenly it's, like, access all areas. So when I heard Robsen would be setting up the shuttle for you, I hid myself on-board.'

'To rescue me… and to get right away from that big ugly monster you saw, right?'

There was a guilty look in Dennel's eyes. 'What *was* it?'

'I've seen things like it before. They were called Slitheen.' She shuddered. 'They're killers. Speaking of which, you could have killed *us* with that dumb fire!'

'Nah. I'm good with flames.' Dennel produced a slim silver lighter from his pocket. 'Fire's what I do, see?' He scraped the flints and a small flame flickered up, its dance holding him transfixed. 'I was an arsonist, Rose. That's why they put me inside.'

Rose watched him studying the flame and felt suddenly cold. She remembered Riz teasing her back in the borstal, knowing what she didn't – *He's hot all right. You're playing with fire there, Rose.*

'Did you hurt anyone?'

'No. I only torched empty places.' He flicked off the flame and flicked it on again. 'A distraction, for my dad, see? While I sent somewhere up in smoke and caused a fuss, he was knocking off the bank round the corner or whatever.'

'Good role model, then.'

'He's the best,' said Dennel fiercely. 'When the police caught me, he gave himself up to try and get me off. They stitched him up, of course. Stitched us both up.'

'What happened to him?'

'They put him on Justice Epsilon. He writes sometimes, but…' He shrugged, wiped his nose. 'I miss him.'

Rose nodded. 'I know how tough it is, growing up without a dad. But at least my mum's always been there for me.' She smiled. 'Right there in my face yelling, most of the –'

She broke off as the console suddenly parped very loudly.

PILOT CONFIRM was the message on every screen, flashing red and black. PILOT CONFIRM.

'What's that about, d'you reckon?' wondered Rose. 'Confirm what?'

'I dunno.' Dennel looked at her. 'Should we see if the pilot's awake now?'

'Yeah,' she said as the console parped again. 'And quickly.'

Riz Mani slipped back to her cell after breakfast so no one would see her crying.

The breakfast hall had been filled with the whispers and rumours that Rose Tyler was gone – shipped out as quickly as she arrived. She caused too much trouble, some said. She'd even broken out of solitary. Now she was being sent to one of the really bad prisons on Justice Gamma. Or off to build pyramids and row galleys on Alpha. Some said she might even be sent to the plantations on Epsilon. But all agreed, nowhere on Justicia would be able to hold her.

To the inmates of Detention Centre Six, Rose Tyler was a legend.

But to Riz, she'd been company. The only person she'd seen in years whose smile was real and warm, who had some life about her. Now she'd been taken away, just like that, and Riz was all alone again.

Except, she found, as she turned from her mirror, for Kazta standing in the doorway to her cell.

Riz grabbed her henna paintbrush and swiped the air with the pointed end. 'Get out.'

Kazta ignored her, looked at Rose's unmade bed. 'So Tyler's really gone?'

'You've got eyes, ain't you?'

'Yeah. But they can play tricks on you.' Kazta stepped inside and closed the door behind her.

'I'm warning you –'

Kazta strode forwards and twisted the little brush from Riz's grip. Then she held on to Riz's hand.

The big girl was shaking and she looked to be on the verge of tears.

'Did Tyler say anything to you about the monsters?' hissed Kazta. 'Only they're real. I've seen one. It lives inside Blanc.'

'You're joking,' said Riz. 'Or you're crazy.'

But she was watching Kazta's eyes carefully. She'd seen crazy eyes before; Sally, her last cellmate, had them. And she'd seen frightened eyes, too; in her reflection, most days, when there was no one about. She could tell the difference.

And a chill went through her as she saw that Kazta's eyes were terrified.

Rose and Dennel entered the smoky cabin to find the pilot was still slumped in a heap.

'How hard did you hit him?' Rose complained.

The parp changed to an intermittent beeping. The message on the screens changed so it now read: CONTROL LOCK COUNTDOWN BEGINNING. PILOT CONFIRM OVERRIDE. She noticed that a metal pad at the side of the console, similar to the palm-print plates beside the doors, was glowing a warning red.

80… 79… 78…

Rose bit her lip. 'Now I get it. The ship's computer must realise the pilot's been out of the room for a while, that he's not touched anything.'

Dennel swore. 'They're going to lock down the controls. We won't be able to fly anywhere, we'll just drift till they come to pick us up!'

'Sitting ducks.' Rose dashed out and grabbed hold of the pilot by his wrists. 'God, he weighs a ton. Give me a hand with him – so he can give *us* a hand.' She heaved as hard as she could. 'If we can get his palm print on to that plate, maybe it'll…'

Her voice died in her throat. The pilot's hands were coming away, the skin stretching like elastic. Rose let go and they slapped back into shape.

Dennel whimpered.

'Oh God…' Gingerly, Rose crept forwards and parted the pilot's bushy hair.

A fleshy furrow ran from the back of his neck to the top of his forehead – where a golden zipper peeped out.

'It's another monster,' Dennel whimpered. 'It could wake up any moment.'

Rose nodded. 'And we're trapped up here with it – with nowhere to run.'

In the cockpit, the bleeps blasted down each passing precious second as the countdown continued: *61… 60… 59…*

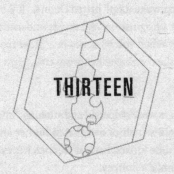

THIRTEEN

'What – what do we do?' stammered Dennel as the beeping of the shuttle's computer went on. His fringe was plastered to his forehead with sweat. 'What the hell do we do?'

'We don't panic for a start,' said Rose grimly. 'OK, we might wake him by moving him. But maybe we can shift a bit of him.'

'What are you on about?'

It occurred to her that Dennel's question was the sort of thing she'd ask of the Doctor. She wondered with a pang of guilt if he ever found *her* so annoying.

But it was the computer's bleeping that was really driving her mad: 47... 46...

'Do you have a knife?' she asked him.

'No. What are you going to do, slit its throat?'

'Don't be so gross! All right, give me your lighter.' He passed it to her. It felt warm and slippery in her hand as she ground the flints and the oily flame blossomed. 'I hope this works... and that I don't throw up!'

She pulled on the pilot's wrist and the skin sucked upwards like PVC. She held the flame to it and, after a few seconds, it started to blacken and tear.

'*That's* gonna wake it up!' hissed Dennel. 'It'll be in agony!'

'This is just a disguise, its real skin is underneath. You must have got lucky when you whacked it…' Rose frowned in concentration as she continued her grisly task. 'How long have we got?'

'It's 33… 32…'

Rose's fingers were reddened and stinging. Smoke blew into her eyes. Then a stench of bad breath hit her and she almost gagged. 'Ugh!' She looked back at Dennel, her eyes streaming. 'That would choke a donkey!'

'Look out!' he hissed.

The hand she was pulling on suddenly inflated like a fleshy balloon, then ripped open as the huge Slitheen claw burst through it. The flesh on the arm tore too as the alien flesh beneath swelled up and outwards.

'Omigod, omigod, omigod!' Rose skittered away. 'Must be the flame, I've made the gas exchange go funny.'

'The what?'

19… 18…

'That's how it crams its real shape into a human body.' She snatched up the pilot's hand from where it lay on the floor like a ripped rubber glove, and hurried over to the bleeping controls. 'The compression field creates a gas exchange that…' God, now she was even *sounding* like the Doctor. 'Never mind.' She slapped the scrap of skin down against the metal pad at the side of the console.

13… 12… COUNTDOWN ABORTED.

'Yes!' cried Rose.

'You did it!' Dennel grinned at her and grabbed her in a clumsy hug.

'I didn't do it,' she said, wriggling free a little awkwardly. '*He* did.' She dangled the scrap of human disguise by one deflated finger. 'Palm Pilot. Get it?'

From the puzzled frown on Dennel's face, she guessed he didn't.

And from the Slitheen's sudden roar, she supposed it just didn't think the joke was very funny.

Rose and Dennel jumped and yelled as the last scraps of the human outfit ripped away and the Slitheen was revealed in all its hideous, glistening glory. It shambled up, its enormous bulk filling the gangway between the seats, its oversized claws scraping and shredding the fabric on the chairs.

Rose lunged for the pad by the door, knocking Dennel aside. She slapped the scrap of wet palm against the metal and the door slid swiftly shut, shielding the monster from view.

Then the shuttle lurched violently to one side and she was thrown against the wall. 'What's the ship doing? What's the ship doing?' she gasped.

'I think it's *me* doing it!' She'd knocked him against the console, his back was crushing buttons and switches.

'Well, get off!' She quickly helped him down. 'What are you even *doing* there?'

'You shoved me here!' he complained. 'That thing – is it the same monster who was inside Blanc?'

'Depends.'

'On what?'

'There might be loads of them.'

The shuttle lurched again and Rose's stomach with it. COURSE DEVIATION, was the message on the screen. INPUT PARAMETERS. INPUT PARAMETERS.

'If I throw you on there again, do you think it might put things right?' said Rose wearily.

'We've changed course,' said Dennel. 'We're flying blind!'

A smashing, crashing noise started up behind them, as the Slitheen began to knock down the door.

The Doctor had wasted no time, and in the gravity workshop, the core of the amplifier was already under construction. With a mixture of deft hand signals and encouraging noises he had directed his team to different tasks, and the work seemed to be going well.

Nesshalop was sitting in a slowly spreading puddle, constructing a series of power focusers. Yahoomer was constructing a delicate crystal-core lattice, his four trunks twisting and unfurling like sea creatures among sparkling coral. Blista was checking and rechecking a billion improbable equations, making sure they would hold true.

'Nice one, mate.' The Doctor patted the reptile on his knobbly back. 'You know, it's criminal that you lot are inside.'

Sensing someone behind him he turned to see Flowers. She was white as snow, her pink glasses drawing attention to her red-rimmed eyes, and she was holding the gravometer in her hand.

'Here to tell Blista about the bugs in his clever little box?'

'Yes.'

'I wouldn't just yet.' He took it from her and started scanning the Justicia system. 'My sonic screwdriver would be useful too. Any chance I can have that back?'

'I'll... I'll ask Consul Issabel. When I next see her.'

'Thanks. Oh, and we'll be connecting the calibrating crystal into the central core later on – it'd be much easier in zero gravity.'

'Of course. We can generate a local zero-gravity field.' She snorted softly. 'We could generate one all through the SCAT-house if we wanted to.'

'Aha. Thought the gravity was way too Earth-normal for a little planet like this. So, you fake it!'

'I think it would be nice sometimes,' Flowers said quietly, 'not to feel so weighed down.' She sighed, made an effort to pull herself together. 'Right. Give me a full briefing on what you've been doing this morning.'

'Oh, just bossing people about, getting stuff done...' He watched her closely. 'How about you? Boss giving you a hard time?'

'I asked you for a progress report, Doctor.'

'Well, that answers my question. And no sign of the Slitheen?'

She turned away. 'That's none of your business.'

'While that answers *that* one.' The gravometer beeped and shunted figures down its screen. The Doctor nodded to himself. 'Thought so. You want a chat? Fine. That side room's free.'

'I give the orders,' she insisted, then faltered. 'Er, yes. We'll go in that side room.'

He followed her inside. 'Well, Senator Flowers, the work's going well. It should be a doddle. Especially since we're being helped.'

She frowned. 'Helped?'

'Yeah. By forces unknown.' He gave her a big grin and held up the gravometer. 'There's no bug in this. I checked this morning on the workshop scanners. The orbits of the planets in this system have been *changed*.'

'That's impossible,' said Flowers.

He passed her back the gravometer. 'These *are* the real-time positions of those planets. And if you check them against the orbits you calculated for that diagram of yours two years back, you'll see there's a big difference.'

Flowers studied the figures. 'There *must* be a fault…'

'Either that or some massive gravitational force has messed with the orbit of every planet in this system. You know how the orbits were almost perfect circles? They've become *entirely* perfect. Justice Alpha now orbits at precisely 100 million miles from the suns, right the way round. Justice Beta at exactly 150 million miles. And on it goes.'

'Not enough difference to trigger a climate change…'

'No. Although Gamma and Delta have got a little way to go till they make a perfect circle. Whatever's doing this hasn't finished moving them yet.'

'But this is unbelievable,' said Flowers. 'What – what about us, on Justice Prime?'

'Oh, us.' The Doctor took a step closer. 'We're different. We're being pushed further *away* from the suns. A fair old way, too – maybe fifteen, twenty million miles? I can't tell you exactly cos it's still going on. Under your noses. Under your very feet. And none of you have noticed – not even your bean counters on Justice Delta.'

'It – it must be some kind of a natural phenomenon.'

'Whatever it is, it's a godsend for us lot on the fast gravity project. It's gonna make everything easier, more efficient, more effective. We're now so far from the other planets that we can harness and boost their energy from here without worrying about being caught up in the effect at all. And we can create those warp-holes in space you want so badly.' He fixed her with a look. 'You know, it's almost as if someone had this brilliant idea to use the planets in this system as a centrifuge ahead of us. And they've been working towards it for some time.'

'In which case…' She stared back at him. 'We're just finishing things off for them.'

'Or making it possible for them to take their work to the next level.'

'What do you mean?'

He smiled suddenly. 'When can I expect Rose to arrive?'

'A few hours,' said Flowers, distracted now. 'Excuse me. I – I think I need to speak to Consul Issabel.'

'And if you *could* ask her about the sonic screwdriver…' he called after her. Then he sighed. He should get back to work. Not *real* work, of course – but his own little project.

The planets were being dragged off course. That would require some pretty heavy-duty equipment. Lodestones in space. But where could such lodestones be hidden? They'd have to be huge, and where could you possibly hide them without attracting suspicion?

One, or rather, several possible answers occurred to the Doctor at once. But the implications weren't nice.

He took the gravometer and plugged it into the workshop's computer bank. He stabbed at the buttons with some reluctance – almost afraid to see if he was right.

'We're out of control,' shouted Rose, as the shuttle bucked and swung like a fish on the end of a line. She and Dennel were thrown this way and that, but the heavy pounding of the Slitheen fist on the door kept up steadily regardless. The uncertain, protesting climb of the ship's engines didn't come close to drowning it out. Not yet.

'Look!' yelled Dennel, clinging on to the pilot's seat. 'Where did *that* come from?'

As Rose wedged herself between the console and the wall,

she saw an emerald planet had swung into view through the cockpit window, frighteningly close. 'Maybe we won't crash into it. Maybe we'll get tugged into its orbit.'

'Great. And then our troubles really begin.' Dennel gulped. Behind them the door had started to buckle inwards. 'The big bad wolf's ready to blow our house down.'

'He may not get the chance,' muttered Rose. 'It may not be standing for much longer.' She saw the scratches of dull cloud on the world's surface, the vast craggy continents beneath it, rushing closer at sickening speed.

Then finally the door was smashed open. The Slitheen stood framed in the doorway, the great, sticky oval of its head swinging this way and that. It looked like some terrible giant staring round for children to eat.

'What a lovely stink of adrenalin,' it declared in its grating, gravelly voice. The black saucer eyes narrowed as it fixed on Dennel, grabbed hold of him in a single claw and slammed him up against the roof.

'You hit my head, I'll hit yours,' the creature hissed.

'Don't kill him!' Rose yelled over the rising roar of the engines. 'You haven't got time! We were going to open that door anyway – we're going to crash and you're the only one who can stop it!'

The Slitheen stared at the emerald mass on the screen. Then it swore, tossed Dennel aside and bundled itself into the pilot's seat, its three gruesome fingers flicking over the controls.

'You hopeless, spineless little human fools,' it gurgled, sparing Rose a malevolent look. 'And you're supposed to be the smart one. I'm not allowed to hurt you.'

Rose frowned. 'What?'

'I'm smart too,' whimpered Dennel.

'Shut it,' the Slitheen snarled. The ship had dipped down through the cloud cover. Detail was starting to emerge from the shapeless olive green of the ground far below them. 'Just hope I can save our skins…'

The engines got louder, the rattling and bucking grew worse. *Great,* thought Rose. *My life depends on a bug-eyed killer alien monster. Who may or may not have passed its driving test.*

Dennel scurried over to join Rose, and the two clung together. A wide forest of conical trees had resolved itself below them. If they dipped any lower she could probably lean out and touch them.

'We're still losing altitude,' she shouted.

'Like I hadn't noticed.' The Slitheen was too big to fit in the seat, so its work with the controls was hampered. It lurched between the different systems, breathing heavily, its slimy carapace dripping with foul-smelling sweat. But slowly, painfully slowly, it brought the shuttle back under something approaching control and their flight levelled off.

'Yes!' cried Rose. 'You did it!'

The pilot gave Rose and Dennel a superior look as it punched in a new course and the ship veered upwards to star-board. 'Don't get too excited. Now it's time to finish what I –'

'Look out!' Rose yelled, pointing through the window. 'Quick!'

The Slitheen folded its cumbersome arms. 'You don't expect me to fall for –'

Some kind of miniature metal building was floating in the sky, directly in their path. With a sickening smash, they collided. The Slitheen let out a high-pitched roar of agony as the cockpit windows shattered over him and the controls exploded in flame. The lights went out, a cold, biting wind blew in, fanning the flames, squalling round the ruined control room.

'Hang on!' Rose shouted, clutching hold of Dennel, her hair gusting over her eyes, hiding from them the horror of the scene. 'We're really going down this time!'

The ship dropped from the sky like a stone. With a noise like thunder it began to char a crazy swathe through the tree-tops.

As the siren sounded for end of shift, Flowers walked with grave purpose back to Issabel's office. She had carefully rehearsed what she would say. She had checked and double-checked the figures and prepared a set of notes to demonstrate to Issabel what the Doctor had shown her.

She shuddered. He'd been right, of course. Something *was* manipulating the planets in the heavens. But what did that 'something' want? What were its plans for the SCAT-house, being shunted further and further from the warmth of the suns?

But Flowers told herself firmly that she would not be flustered. She would be efficient and cool. And she imagined that the import of what she had to say would make even the Consul sit up and take notice of her for once.

But as she neared Issabel's office, a terrible cry of pain sounded from inside.

Her first instinct was to run to her, to see if Issabel was all right. But just outside the door, she hesitated. There had been a strange, feral note to the scream of pain. Something almost… inhuman.

Issabel was sobbing inside now. 'My cousin,' she wailed. 'My poor, sweet cousin…'

Flowers felt the hairs rise on the back of her neck. What was she hearing? The door was open just a fraction and so she peeped inside. She'd never imagined Issabel had much of a heart beating away in that hunched body, but to look at her now, wringing her hands, pulling at her hair…

It seemed she had found something there – a tangle or a knot perhaps. Her fingers closed on whatever it was and tugged.

'Clem Sel Hetch,' she said thickly. 'Oh, my sweet cousin… I must feel you fully. This hateful body is choking me…'

Flowers stared on in terror as a pale electric light started sparking around Issabel's shoulders in shades of blue and yellow. The top of her head had split open and now a sluglike mass of flesh was pushing itself out through the rupture. The thin, pinched body was shucked off like a rubbery husk as the light faded.

And the creature inside Consul Issabel revealed itself at last.

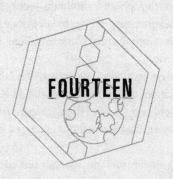

FOURTEEN

Issabel's true massive, muscular frame rippled with power. The sticky flesh was the colour of maggots. The swollen black eyes leaked a milky slime, tears that dropped sizzling to the desktop. Then it started raging, smashing its great three-fingered fists against the walls, kicking in cabinets with its waxen legs in the mother of all tantrums. It was bigger and paler than either Ecktosca or Dram Fel Fotch, and its face was scored with thick black wrinkles.

Run, you idiot, Flowers told herself. *Run before it sees you.*

But then the creature pressed something under Issabel's desk and a square of light appeared in the wall, a shadowy shape in its centre, shielded in part by a swathe of smoke. Flowers felt with a dreadful calm that she had to stay. There were too many mysteries here. She had to try to learn what was happening.

'My cousin is close to death, Don Arco,' the wrinkled Slitheen hissed at the screen. 'I felt it. I felt his pain. What has happened?'

'The shuttle en route to you with the genius girl on board has encountered difficulties, Ermenshrew,' came an alien voice – by the rough and rumbling tones, it was another Raxacoricofallapatorian. 'It diverted to Justice Delta, where it collided with a monitoring platform. Clem Sel Hetch was piloting the craft.'

'I should have insisted he use the pathways to reach us,' said Issabel – or rather, this Ermenshrew who'd been living inside that stooped old body. 'Uncle Hipp Sel Hetch travelled here this morning to assimilate the equations I salvaged from the ruined datacore –'

'– and he's already told me that they suit our purpose,' said Don Arco, the creature on the screen. 'But you know full well that while our glorious bodies may brave the pathways, these human animals are less robust.'

'Yes.' Ermenshrew sniggered. 'I have witnessed the results of my daughter's cavalier experiments.'

'A search is being mounted for the vessel. While Clem Sel Hetch still lives, there is hope.' A pause, as Don Arco shifted closer. 'Now to business. If the Doctor's expert is dead, will it now delay the operation?'

'I will not tolerate delays,' she said darkly.

'Well said. You've all waited long enough in those hateful little bodies. Final-phase replication is now in progress.'

'Oh good,' she purred.

'My second cousins are ready to replace the plantation managers on Justice Epsilon. On Beta, the Governors of all borstals are to be replaced by my youngest stepsons – great kids but a little wild, the responsibility will be good for them. On Gamma...'

Flowers listened with mounting horror as the litany of replacements went on. There were impostors in positions of power all over Justicia, on every world – and had been for some time, it seemed. Her head crowded with questions. Just how far did this alien corruption spread? What were these 'pathways' Ermenshrew had mentioned, and where did they lead? And as for this 'operation' that was stepping up a gear…

She looked at the figures in her hand, and realised with a cold dread that the proof she had so painstakingly acquired was unlikely to come as a surprise to her erstwhile boss.

The Doctor. She had to get to the Doctor.

As she turned, terrified, the tiniest squeak of a fart escaped her cheeks. But the effect on Ermenshrew was electric.

'Wait, Don Arco,' she snapped, sniffing the air with her poky little nostrils. 'I have let my grief mask my other senses. I can smell a spy. An ugly, big-boned human who now knows too much.'

Flowers crept away from the door. 'Don't faint,' she told herself weakly. 'Don't faint, don't faint.'

'Can you dispose of it?' she heard Don Arco growl.

'We're in the final phase now,' Ermenshrew rumbled. 'Its usefulness is ended.'

'Then enjoy your hunt,' hissed Don Arco. 'If the work goes well, I shall be seeing you very soon.'

Flowers broke into a run. The papers slipped from her hand. Behind her, she heard the office door as it was flung open, and heavy footsteps squelching on the tiled floor behind her.

As she fled down the corridors she felt tears building up, tears of fear and frustration and disbelief. It was hard to run when your world had been turned upside down. Especially when you had a really nasty stitch as well.

And then, as she skidded round the corner, she saw the Doctor. He raised his eyebrows at the sight of her. Globs clustered around his neck and shoulders, steering him back to his cell.

'I wanted to stay working but these things called time on me,' he sighed. 'I'm close to a breakthrough, there's no time to stop now!'

Gasping for breath, lungs on fire, Flowers couldn't speak. She tried to mime a Slitheen with massive claws.

He grinned at her as the globs shuffled him onwards. 'You been hitting the sauce, Flowers?'

She shook her head, staggered towards him, clutching the stitch in her side, struggling for the breath to tell him. 'Globs off,' she croaked, and they whooshed off to the shadowy ceiling.

'Is this a keep-fit thing?' he tried again.

Then Ermenshrew thundered round the corner, drool stringing from her jaws. When she saw Flowers with the Doctor, her wrinkles deepened in anger.

'Ah,' said the Doctor.

'Issabel,' gasped Flowers. 'That's Issabel!'

He groaned. 'Oh, *terrific.*'

Robsen woke to the sound of construction work outside his bedroom window. He opened the curtains, shrinking like a vampire from the blazing sunlight. There were cranes and 'dozers trundling over the pale green marshland of the planet's surface.

Once he'd dressed and gone down to the diner for brunch, he found Jamini sitting alone, stuffing her grumpy face with coffee and croissants.

He pulled up a chair beside her. 'You couldn't sleep with all that racket going on either, huh?'

She grunted.

He swigged from her coffee. 'Suppose they've got to put the new prisoners somewhere…'

'They're putting a load of them in here, till the new accommodation is built,' said Jamini. 'The Governor said so in his a.m. briefing. It's crazy…' She scowled. 'You didn't hear?'

Robsen shook his head.

'To make room there has to be a sharp increase in prisoners sharing cells. That's males and females sharing the *same* cells.'

'But… that's crazy!' Robsen protested. 'It's not just asking for trouble, it's begging for it. What's the Governor playing at?'

'New directive from on high, he says.' Jamini washed down another doughy mouthful with some coffee. 'You know him, anything for a quiet life. No wonder Norris has pushed off. Probably saw it coming.'

'Probably,' said Robsen faintly. Through the windows he watched as the construction crew scuttled about, setting down the prison colony's new foundations.

'Come on!'

The Doctor grabbed Flowers by the hand and hauled her back the way he'd come. Legs cramping, ribs burning, she tried her best to keep up with him. The thumping squelch of Ermenshrew as she ran was like some terrifying heartbeat echoing through the corridors. Flowers wondered what the prisoners would make of it, safely locked away in their cells.

'There's – no – where – we – can – go,' she panted.

The Doctor ducked into a side corridor. But the globs whooshed down once more to stop him. He gasped with pain as they began to glow sickly yellow, draining his energy.

'Off,' Flowers said huskily, struggling to push out the words. 'Get off! He has auth… authorisation.'

Almost reluctantly, the globs detached themselves and spiralled back to where they came from.

'There's *somewhere* we can go,' the Doctor said thickly, wiping his mouth. 'But I'll need the sonic screwdriver.'

She patted the pocket of her tunic. He reached in and fished out the screwdriver.

'So you *were* going to ask her if I could have it back!' he beamed.

'Soft… touch,' she agreed.

The stamping behind them was getting louder.

'Right, now, where's your systems hub?'

'Systems… hub…?' She slumped against the wall and waved an arm in the general direction of the power room. He grabbed the arm and towed her along after him.

Ermenshrew was gaining on them. Giant claws were clacking together in excitement.

'Where now?' the Doctor asked as they found themselves at a T-junction. 'Quick, tell me!'

She pointed left. 'She's hunting me… Needs you. Won't… won't kill you.'

'You've got to get more exercise, Flowers,' the Doctor chided, yanking her along again. 'Job like yours, lots of sitting around, no fresh air, it's very bad for you…'

The whole corridor was shaking with Ermenshrew's pursuit. 'Systems hub's down here,' she wheezed, waving at a narrow side corridor with black and yellow decals on the walls.

'Access designed for humans only,' he said approvingly, slipping inside sideways so the two of them would fit. 'She should have a job to get to us.'

A grey bulkhead loomed ahead of them. 'What are you going to do?'

'Keep my fingers crossed you weren't exaggerating.'

'What?'

He set her down and brandished the screwdriver. The door slid open sideways to reveal a dark chamber beyond – but at once the globs were dropping on to him, clustering round him like giant leeches, sucking greedily. The Doctor cried out in pain again.

'I authorise this prisoner... to undertake emergency work... on the systems!' Flowers beat ineffectually at the pseudo-creatures, trying to knock them loose from his shoulders. 'Release him!' But this was a serious cautioning offence, and the globs seemed intent on draining him dry. They pulsed and glowed and fattened, the folds in their gummy bodies smoothing out.

As the Doctor sank to his knees he thrust the sonic screwdriver into Flowers's sweaty hands. Only then did the globs move sluggishly back up towards the ceiling shadows.

'You needn't have bothered,' she said, flashing her passcard under his nose. 'I have access.'

'Now you tell me,' he muttered, shaking with pain. 'That glob on my wrist. It's had me before, back in the projects room.'

'You recognise a *glob*?'

'Trust me. It has a very distinctive bite.' He grinned weakly. 'Know what? I think that's a good thing.' He nodded to the dark room that had opened up to them. 'You'd better do it.'

'Do what?' she said desperately. 'Doctor, you haven't told me what –'

She broke off as a long shadow fell over them. Ermenshrew had appeared at the end of the corridor behind them. She gave an exultant shriek at the sight of them and her wide, sticky baby face twisted into a leer of malevolence.

Flowers felt like a mouse cowering in a mouse hole.

Trapped.

And the cat wasn't about to give up.

Carefully, Ermenshrew squeezed into the corridor sideways and started scrabbling towards them.

Rose woke up feeling as if a giant had shoved her into a sack full of rocks and then swung her over his head for half an hour.

She was sprawled in a darkened wreck, with Dennel lying slumped face down over her legs and a Slitheen's smouldering foot crushing her chest. The shuttle must have crashed through half a forest on its way down – not great for the environment, but enough to slow them to a halt. She wriggled out from under Dennel's dead weight and the huge, smoking foot and checked her body for bruises or breaks.

Still just about in one piece, Rose stood unsteadily. Green fronds and exotic flowers crowded in through the shattered windows, blotting out most of the sunlight. She could hear the weird chirrups and chitters of alien critters outside and shivered. Just her luck if she came through all this and then got bitten by a poisonous ant or something.

Stooping, she checked up on Dennel. He was still breathing, though he had a nasty purple bruise over his temple.

'You're alive, then.'

The low rumble of words made Rose jump and spin round. The Slitheen had raised his blackened, crispy head to regard her. Thick yellow pus dripped from a puncture in his left eye. He looked to be in a bad way.

The Slitheen propped itself up on one lumpen elbow. Rose backed away against the console. It hummed mournfully into some semblance of life.

'We crashed into a monitoring platform – one of the eyes

and ears of Justice Delta,' said the pilot. 'We've reached Justicia's administration centre, the heart of the system. You can call for help.'

Rose frowned. 'What do you care?'

'I don't want to die,' he said frankly. 'I can't move. Call for help, you *must*.'

'Why so keen? If humans find you in your real form –'

'They will make me well again so they can put me in prison.' The creature chuckled, its one good eye agleam. 'The prison we were heading for. I expect they will take us straight there!'

Rose chewed her lip. A distress call might suit her, and even the Slitheen. But the Executive would put Dennel back in borstal and chuck away the key.

'I'll call for help,' she agreed. 'On one condition. You don't mention Dennel to anyone, yeah? We hide him and let him stay behind. When I get out with the Doctor we'll pick him up, get him out of here.'

'Fine,' hissed the creature without argument. 'Now, hurry.'

Between heavy, laboured breaths it gave her the pilot's code so she could work the console, told her which buttons to press.

'Mayday – or SOS, or… Well, whatever,' she said, feeling a bit self-conscious now she was talking into a microphone with a big monster hanging on her every word. 'This is Rose Tyler, you were holding me in a detention centre on Justice Beta. I was being transferred, now I've crash-landed. My location is –' She squinted at a small read-out – 'north quad, seven by eight alpha.'

The screen on the console buzzed with lines of static.

'Look, this is actually pretty urgent. The pilot turned out to be a Slitheen, and there was a bit of a fight and we –'

'Slitheen?' hissed the pilot, almost choking on the word.

'How dare you call me Slitheen!'

'Well, sorry.' Rose frowned. 'But I figured since there were Slitheen on Justice Prime…'

'Slitheen are dunderhead scum. Worthless, unimaginative, old-fashioned –'

Rose gritted her teeth. 'Well, OK, sorry about that, whoever's out there, but the pilot's *not* a Slitheen – he's some other ugly monster thing that looks the same and comes from the same impossible-to-pronounce planet –'

'We are Blathereen,' hissed the creature.

'Blathereen?' Rose frowned. 'Well, excuse me, but what's with the royal we thing?'

The Blathereen's eyelids were drooping but it managed a sinister chuckle. It seemed to be looking behind her.

Rose turned and jumped.

On the monitor screen, a horrible image had resolved from the static. A dozen creatures identical to the pilot were crowding together, grinning widely and jostling to look out at her.

'This is the Executive Centre on Justice Delta,' giggled one of the creatures.

'Currently under Blathereen control,' chortled another.

Rose covered her hands with her mouth, rounded on the pilot. 'You tricked me!'

'Easy… peasy…' it croaked, before passing out.

'Thank you for your message and for your location fix, tiny human creature,' the first Blathereen went on, while its buddies burst out into belly laughs. It pushed its hideous head up close to the screen as if trying to smell her. 'We shall be coming for you very soon.'

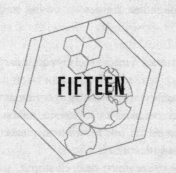

FIFTEEN

The Doctor was still weak and pale. He indicated the systems hub. 'Get in there, quick! We want the environment controls. Work out what's what.'

Flowers pushed past him and into the dark chamber. Soft white lighting clicked on and she stared round, trying to familiarise herself with the systems.

'Oh, little fat Flowers, my plump fool!' Ermenshrew was giggling, reaching slowly, steadily towards them.

'She's alien! Why don't the globs get her?' cried Flowers.

'No implant,' the Doctor reminded her, struggling up from his knees. 'Besides, she must *control* the globs.'

'Time to die, my little one!' the creature called.

'Hurt her and I'll do nothing for your precious project, hear me?' snapped the Doctor. 'I won't lift a finger.'

Ermenshrew shrugged her massive, glutinous shoulders. The movement allowed her to creep a little closer. 'If you won't lift a finger, I'll pluck them from your little girlfriend's hands instead, one by one. Provided she's still alive, of course.'

Flowers heard the Doctor's voice catch. 'What do you mean?'

'I mean the shuttle she was aboard has crashed on Justice Delta.'

'*What?*'

'Never mind *her*! A member of my family has been hurt, and frankly I hope he used your friend for a soft landing. He has invested so many years pretending to be human that for him to die now, when our plans are so close to fruition…'

Flowers bit her lip, told herself to stop eavesdropping and start fathoming the controls.

'Whatever you're doing here, I'll stop it,' said the Doctor calmly.

'Oh?' Ermenshrew's big black eyes widened further in amusement. 'And what can you do? You are my prisoner.'

'I'll expose you,' he promised. 'Tell the others who you really are. They might be less keen to work for you –'

'– knowing I'm from Raxacoricofallapatorius and not Earth?' She snuffled with mirth. 'Even if they believed you, I imagine they might be rather happy to hear that the human trash that sought to incarcerate them has been… removed.'

'Removed?'

'We have been moving behind the scenes here for so long now,' she rumbled. 'But finally the need for secrecy is ended.' Her black eyes glinted with malice. 'With only middling minds to exploit, the work towards our ultimate ends has gone slowly and in secret. But your excellent work, Doctor, has allowed us to advance our plans.'

'It's true,' piped Flowers. 'I heard her talking to another one – they're replacing people in all kinds of positions, all over the system.'

'The family gathers, my dears,' she slobbered. 'Soon Justicia will fall entirely under our control.'

'And then what?' The Doctor watched her wriggle that bit nearer. 'What do you want it for? Why have you been trying to turn the Justicia system into an enormous fast-gravity centrifuge?'

'You geniuses are all the same. You can never see the possibilities in your own work...' Ermenshrew breathed in, sucking in her sagging stomach so she could squeeze more quickly down the passage. 'Justicia has long profited from the exploitation of alien minds. Under our control it will profit from whole planets!' She lunged forwards, claws outstretched – but her sinewy body snagged once more in the small corridor, her talons inches away from the Doctor's chest. 'No one and nothing can protect you, Flowers.'

Flowers was forcing back tears. 'What are we going to do, Doctor?'

'The gravity regulator!'

'What about it?'

'You said you could make it zero gravity all through the SCAT-house.'

'Well, in theory,' she flapped. 'But the power required would be –'

'*Do it!*' he thundered.

Flowers started to alter the settings, hoping it would work.

Then she shrieked as her body lurched up into the air.

The Doctor was rising with her. Ermenshrew stared impotently up at them, wedged stickily in the narrow shaft of the corridor as her prey floated up and away. With a bellow of anger, she swiped for Flowers's feet with her long, raking claws. But she was a fraction too slow; Flowers had nudged herself just out of reach.

'You asked for this,' she screamed. 'I'll put the others to work in your place, Doctor. Oh, *how* I'll work them. Kindness gets you nowhere, Flowers!'

'Ignore her. Kick out with your legs!' the Doctor ordered, swimming through the air. 'We've got to move fast. How long can the systems keep this up?'

'It's a big drain on the power cells.' Flowers turned a slow somersault and looked at him anxiously. 'They'll default to Earth gravity in a few minutes, maximum.'

A frisson of fear ran through her as she realised they were about to breach the thick shadows that cloaked the high ceiling. She realised that although she'd lived in the SCAT-house for years she had no idea what actually lay up here, out of view. The globs were part and parcel of the place. She'd always taken them for granted.

And yet this was their lair, the dark place where Justicia's guardians hovered, vigilant and vengeful, on the lookout for trouble down below.

'Where are we going?' she hissed urgently.

'To test a theory,' he said, as the blackness swallowed them.

'And if you're wrong?'

'We die.'

'You don't sound very bothered.' She shut her eyes. 'Oh dear, you're not suicidal after your friend –?'

'Shut up,' he growled. 'She's fine. Shuttle crash? Nothing.'

She couldn't even see him now in the thick gloom, and her hands flew to her glasses to check they weren't floating away. Below her she saw Ermenshrew trying to free herself from the confines of the corridor. If she fell now, she'd impale herself on those long, clacking claws…

'Switch on the screwdriver,' the Doctor told her. 'We need the light.'

Flowers did so, and had to stifle a gasp. In the ghostly blue light she saw that they had drifted right up into a nest of globs. There had to be twenty of the creatures up here, perched on a shelf cut into the dry, rocky roof.

'Why don't they react to us?' she whispered.

'They can't have programming for intruders up here,' the Doctor suggested, peering into the soupy blackness ahead of him. 'They're designed to watch over the world below – ah!'

'What is it?'

'At first I thought the globs were grouped in strategic places all around the SCAT-house. But what if you've got a riot going on – a small flock of globs may not be enough. So! They have to be able to move about, right?' He started swimming through the squid-ink air with smooth strokes. 'Like that one I recognised out in the corridor – he'd moved from his little patch in the projects room. So what does that suggest to you?'

'That if there's trouble they have to get there fast, and in numbers.' Flowers couldn't stop looking down. 'Look, Doctor, the zero-G will cut out at any moment –'

'And did you ever see a glob dip down through a doorway?'

'No. Which implies some kind of…' Now she got what he was driving at, and nodded furiously. 'Some kind of tunnel network up above in the roofing. It must link all the rooms and walkways together!'

'Right. So there should be one at the end of this ledge they're sat on!' cried the Doctor, bobbing in the darkness up ahead of her. 'Quick, grab my coat-tails.'

Flowers held on and allowed herself to be pulled after him. She was gently drifting in to perch when Earth gravity reasserted itself, and she fell the last few inches. Waving round the screwdriver she saw a pitch-black hole ahead of them, bored out smoothly through the rock – and the Doctor grinning like a maniac.

'That was close, wasn't it?' he said gleefully.

'Do you suppose they have ledges like this along every wall in the place?' she said shakily.

'Be a waste of energy to have the globs hovering around the whole time, wouldn't it? So they sit up here out the way to keep themselves fully charged.' He started shuffling along the ledge. 'Come on. Should just be wide enough for us if we lay on our fronts and wriggle.'

'I've got more front than you,' Flowers complained as she shunted herself along after him. 'Anyway, where are we going? We can't stay hiding up here for ever. Issabel – I mean, Ermenshrew – will soon figure out where we've gone!'

'There's somewhere we have to get to,' the Doctor told her.

'Where?'

'Justice Delta. I have to know that Rose is really OK.'

'Doctor, I'm sorry about your friend, but I hardly think it's likely that one of these tunnels leads to another planet hundreds of millions of miles away!'

'Not one of *these* tunnels, no,' he answered.

'Dennel!' hissed Rose. 'Come on, snap out of it!'

At his first semi-conscious groan she grabbed hold of him and pulled him to his feet. Dennel stared round, terrified at what he must have lived through.

'We've got to get out of here and fast.' She glared at the Blathereen. 'Things like that are on their way to hunt us down.'

'Oh,' said Dennel, who still seemed kind of shell-shocked. 'We don't stand a chance, do we?'

'We have to try.'

He nodded. Rose took him by the hand and led him past the fallen, smouldering body of the Blathereen, towards the exit.

The Governor stared at the blank screen on his wall. He'd been trying to contact his superiors. None of them were responding.

The relaxing blue lamp started to flicker again. He switched it off in annoyance, let the darkness soothe his eyes. He'd heard the grumblings from his staff at the new directives, even when he'd tried so hard to pronounce the new decrees with conviction, to assure them that everything was for the best.

Truth was, even the Governor was beginning to wonder.

He'd done so much to appease the Executive these last years, taken all policy decisions on-board without protest no matter how strange they seemed, hoping that if he did so, the rumoured wrongdoings taking place here would remain overlooked. That's just what they were, after all. Only rumours. Not a shred of real evidence.

But no one had come looking at all. And now, after wasting a day trying to track down any of the Area Governors, he was beginning to think the Executive had ceased to exist altogether.

Suddenly his door slid open. He couldn't see who was there, so he switched on the blue light again.

Warder Blanc.

'I didn't hear you knock.' He frowned as she stepped inside. 'And I never said you could enter!'

'Sorry, sir,' said Blanc, with a small smile. 'But I needed to see you.'

'Yes, well. As it happened, I wanted to see you too.' He smiled stiffly. 'That troublemaker – the girl, Rose Tyler – made some very odd complaints about you.'

Blanc raised an eyebrow. Her smile grew broader. 'Oh?'

The Governor snorted. 'Some nonsense about you being a monster! Even so –'

'That *is* nonsense.' Blanc giggled. Then she whistled to someone standing just outside the door. 'This is the monster.'

A huge, glistening, grey-green creature lumbered into the Governor's office, its eyes black and gleaming, terrifying claws flexing and quivering at the end of its oversized arms.

'That Tyler human had the nerve to think that you were one of us, Governor,' said Blanc. 'Crazy.'

The Governor stared at them in the flickering blue light, struck dumb with terror.

'This is the person you're going to be,' Blanc told the monster. 'A pathetic, ineffectual animal, I know – that's why we didn't replace him sooner. But there you go. The rabble here quite like him. They think he's… *fair.*' She pronounced the word like it tasted of sick. 'Don Arco reckons they'll do a lot for him, if he asks them right. We'll get better results than if we drug the prisoners into compliance.'

'What…' The Governor finally teased a word on to his tongue. 'What is the meaning of this, Blanc? What joke are you trying to play on me?'

'It's a knock-knock joke,' Blanc giggled.

The Governor stared at her blankly.

'Knock, knock,' said the monster. It lashed out with its fist and thumped twice on the governor's head.

The second blow crushed his skull against the mahogany desk, and splintered both. The blue light toppled over and fizzled out in a pool of his blood.

'Do you think he got it?' chuckled the monster, and Blanc fell about laughing.

* * *

At the same time, all over Justicia, the final substitutions took place.

The colonial government on Justice Epsilon met to discuss the radical new laws regarding the death penalty proposed by their president. She planned to conscript all fit men and women on the planet over the age of twenty-one to a heavy labour programme. Those who refused would be executed. The politicians were in uproar. They didn't even understand why this heavy labour should be necessary.

But the Blathereen did. And once they'd barged in, slaughtered the ministers and taken their places, a unanimous vote saw the new policies agreed and ratified without delay, to be implemented in time for the first great burn-up.

On Justice Alpha, members of the Executive informed the last of the galley masters that his branch of historical punishment was being shut down. All slave workers would be diverted to the pyramid-building programme. At the same time, the general overseer for pyramids was hunted down and brutally murdered. A Blathereen wriggled into his skin and announced that, from now on, slaves would work to erect a more useful form of storage facility...

In the penal settlements of Justice Gamma, the last remaining human governors were executed by their Blathereen replacements. Liberal regimes would soon be a thing of the past, but so too would the bloody extremes of the harsher prison camps. Their human prisoners would no longer be subjected to a diverse range of experiments. Instead they would be worked like beasts of burden, drugged only should it be necessary to quell any resistance.

Soon, these humans' work would begin. Hard, dangerous work that would kill hundreds if not thousands of people.

But the Blathereen knew they had enough livestock to turn a very tidy profit in the first three years of the new operation. And by carefully keeping up appearances, new prisoners would continue to arrive to replenish their labour stock. They wouldn't need to raise a single, sticky claw themselves.

Flowers had been trailing the Doctor's feet along the ledges and through the tunnels for some time. Her limbs were aching, her elbows and knees scraped sore, and it was dark and claustrophobic. To conserve the sonic screwdriver's power they were pressing on in the dark. Sometimes they would chance upon a glob, wet and springy like a ball of turf, but it would meekly roll out of the way and hover in the air until they had passed.

'What do you suppose Ermenshrew is doing right now?' asked Flowers.

'If I were her I'd be busy trying to get the globs to attack us up here,' came his cheerless reply.

'What about Ecktosca and Dram Fel Fotch?' she asked.

'If I were *them* I'd be swigging a ginger beer and toasting freedom.'

'No, I mean, why did they even want to escape? If the Slitheen have taken control of the prison, they must have known.' She gasped. 'Maybe the whole thing was staged! Maybe Ermenshrew needed to press them into service somewhere else, and smuggled them out!'

'No, that doesn't fit,' he told her. 'Ecktosca and Dram had put together home-made compression fields. I found them in the cell.'

'They can't have!'

'Well, they did. They're incredibly crafty. But why would they go to all that trouble if a quick word with Issabel could get them out in a moment? She put them here in the first place –'

Flowers shushed him. Her nose started twitching, and in a moment, her body flushed with adrenalin. 'Doctor, I can smell Slitheen!'

The Doctor stopped wriggling forward. 'There are globs blocking the way too.'

'It's Ermenshrew!' said Flowers desperately. 'She's waiting the other end for us. She's going to get us!'

The Doctor took a long noisy sniff. 'There's someone up ahead of us all right… Who's there?' he called.

Flowers held her breath, straining to catch the faintest noise.

A quiet fart noise penetrated from the blackness ahead of them.

'Screwdriver,' hissed the Doctor.

She activated it with trembling fingers. In the eerie blue light, beyond the Doctor's silhouette, she saw two globs were blocking the way ahead of them.

But no ordinary globs.

These two had zippers stretching from end to end.

'So you didn't escape,' Flowers whispered. 'Ecktosca Fel Fotch? Dram?'

'Senator Flowers, I never dreamed you'd go to such lengths to find us,' rumbled the nearest glob – in the voice of Ecktosca.

'We weren't looking for you,' the Doctor told him. 'We're on the run from one of your kind, and this is the only place she can't get us.'

Ecktosca's glob tried to nod thoughtfully. 'So you've learned the truth about Consul Issabel – or rather, that harpy Ermenshrew.'

'You knew?' breathed Flowers.

'Oh yes, all along.'

'And you didn't try to warn me?'

'Slitheen do not share family business with *aliens*,' the glob informed her tartly. 'The Blathereen are *our* problem, and one we shall deal with. One day.'

'Blathereen! Ha!' The Doctor seemed delighted. 'I *knew* Ermenshrew had to be from a different family! That explains why "Consul Issabel" dismissed Rose's claim that there was a Slitheen on Justice Beta.'

'Your friend said that?' hissed Dram quickly.

'Yeah – but what she'd *really* seen was a Blathereen.'

'One of a whole pack of them,' said Ecktosca distastefully. 'The Blathereen have been infesting Justicia for years.'

'They're working on some big master plan,' the Doctor agreed. 'But *what*?'

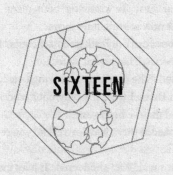

SIXTEEN

Riz had never imagined she would one day find herself sitting with Kazta in the social hall. But here they were, together in the smoky fug at the back of the room, just the two of them.

Members of a secret club that believed in monsters.

Kaz had abandoned her cronies for now. Like everyone else, they were fixating on the idea of mixed-sex cellmates; this, aside from some speculation as to Rose's whereabouts, was the sole topic of conversation. The prettier prisoners were working on cool chat-up lines. The more pragmatic were practising strangleholds and coercion tactics.

Then Maggi came up to Kaz. With her lank orange hair and gormless expression, she had always been rated by Riz as one of the less scary members of Kaz's gang – and the most stupid.

'Kaz, I want to talk to you about the monsters,' said Maggi.

'You believe me?'

'I do. Honest.'

She scowled. 'If that cow Blanc hadn't twigged I was taping her I'd have all the proof anyone would need.'

'I tried to get the others to believe you.' Maggi pulled up a stool. 'Told them that the monsters are real. Told them Rose

Tyler got sent away for knowing 'bout them. But all they're talking about now is boys, boys, boys.'

'And the boys can only talk girls, girls, girls,' Riz agreed. 'It's distraction tactics. That's what *we* reckon.'

Kaz nodded. 'The monsters are taking over.'

'Rose and Dennel were the only ones who knew about it,' said Riz. 'And they've both gone.'

Maggi looked at them wide-eyed. 'Did you really see one for real, Kaz?'

'You bet it's real.' Kaz shuddered. 'It lives inside Blanc. She came to my cell. Said she'd kill me if I didn't back up her story that she was with me the night Norris and Rose and Dennel disappeared. Unzipped her head and…' Kaz wiped her eyes furtively, not wanting anyone to see her tears. 'This *thing* just sort of… wriggled out. It was horrible. Big. Slimy. These boggly black eyes…'

Maggi stared, chewing on a ginger strand of hair. 'Go on.'

'What could I do? When Robsen came in, I said I'd been with her.' She looked down on the floor. 'What else could I do?'

'I reckon maybe we should go and tell Robsen what really happened that night,' said Maggi.

'Yeah, like he'd believe us!' snorted Riz.

'He's one of the better ones,' Kaz admitted.

'A screw's a screw,' Riz insisted. 'If it got out that we talked, we'd *all* disappear.'

'Well, I'm not waiting around till some monster sneaks into *my* cell in the middle of the night,' said Maggi with unexpected determination. 'You do what you like. I'm gonna see Robsen.'

Riz watched her go, gallumphing off across the social hall.

'What's got into her?' wondered Kaz.

* * *

Rose led Dennel out of the ruined, smoking ship and into the mint-smelling jungle. The light from the three suns dazzled her, made everything seem overexposed. But it was wide open and springtime out here, a total contrast from the cramped, sweaty grey of the borstal. Fibrous leaves and stalks burst up from the ground in a frenzy of green. Rose and Dennel hadn't gone far before the vegetation masked all trace of the wrecked shuttle.

'What can we do?' said Dennel helplessly. 'Those things are gonna catch us and eat us.'

'The Blathereen won't eat us,' she assured him.

'They won't?'

'Nope. They'll just kill us.' She pulled aside a tangle of branches so that he could clamber through. 'Which is why we're looking for that monitoring station we crashed into. If it's not a total write-off, we might be able to find out how many there are and which way they're coming from.'

'Then we can run in the opposite direction.'

'Or try to sneak past them.'

'Well, how're we going to find it?' He produced his lighter. 'Maybe I could burn down some jungle.'

'And lead them straight to us?' Rose began scrambling up a chocolate-brown tree trunk. 'Let's try an aerial view.'

Halfway up, she could see it, some distance off in a clearing – like a large turret of blackened metal, rocking on its side. A flattened path stretched away behind it – not so much a turret then, as a big silver slug, nudging forwards through the foliage. Beyond it, looming over the trees, she could see a big white high-rise. It was uglier than anything you'd see back on her council estate, which was saying something. One of the admin centres, she supposed – it figured that the Blathereen pilot would try to put them down somewhere close to its buddies.

'We've been going more or less the right way,' she reported, shinning back down. 'Come on, let's check it out.'

Dennel took the lead. She decided there were worse bums than his to be stuck behind while trekking for her life through an alien jungle, pursued by monsters.

But suddenly he stopped dead in his tracks.

'Come on,' she said, 'you can't be tired yet. We've got miles to…'

Her mouth went horribly dry as she saw what he was staring at. They had come to a large, natural clearing.

It was strewn with bodies and skeletons, all clad in borstal uniform.

'Ronika,' breathed Dennel, staring down at the corpse of a dark-haired girl who might have been pretty once, her rotting lips bared in a horrified grimace, tiny green bugs pouring in and out of her open mouth. He stumbled forwards, towards two more bodies lying in twisted, unnatural poses. 'Malc… Dix…' He swung back round to Rose. 'All these kids who went missing inside. Transferred, they said.'

'But it was Blanc,' said Rose, covering her mouth. 'Look.'

Propped up against the tree was the staring cadaver of Warder Norris.

Dennel took some deep breaths, looking pale and sick. 'No wonder they never found no trace of these people. She's been dumping them out here.'

'But how did she get them here?' Rose wondered. 'She couldn't have taken a shuttle or whatever each time, could she? How'd she get Norris here so fast?'

'Does it matter?' he snapped. 'These people are dead, and all you care about is how they wound up here!'

'I don't!' she protested, took a step towards him – and trod in something sticky. She looked down and blanched. 'For instance, I also care about how come this person here... seems to have been turned inside out.'

Her foot had snapped through a ribcage into the lining of a uniform caked in powdery red detritus. Gingerly, she lifted her leg clear.

'I'm glad I put my foot in my mouth *before* I stepped in that,' she told him.

It was a fairly feeble line, and it only raised a feeble smile. But when she held out her hand for Dennel to take, he took it, and she led the way on through the spearmint jungle.

Flowers lay uncomfortably, flat on her face on her gloomy, smelly perch, wishing the Doctor might take his conversation with Ecktosca and Dram on the move. If Ermenshrew *was* working on a way to get them back into her clawing clutches...

'So come on then,' he demanded of the bogus globs. 'We may not know what the Blathereen are up to, but what about you lot? Why are *you* here?'

'We explained –'

'All that guff about being family historians...' The Doctor shook his head. 'I saw your picture on the cell wall – the Slitheen family business is still going strong, isn't it?'

'You merely saw a historical re-enactment. I always dress up for an auction, the punters love it.' He leaned forward and jiggled his zipper. 'The fuel-sale business *had* to be wound up – because the Blathereen undercut us and stole all our customers. They were better organised, more streamlined and had lower overheads...'

'So you're yesterday's men,' the Doctor surmised. 'And with your noses put out of joint. So you came along here –'

'To get our ancestors' belongings,' he insisted. 'I mean, yes, we knew the Blathereen were sneaking about Justicia – but who cares? Humans deserve all they get, if you ask me.' The shrunken Slitheen gave a loud belch. 'Then that ratbag Ermenshrew had us banged up because she needed our brainpower!'

'And she got it, too, didn't she?'

'We didn't want her getting suspicious while we worked on our escape,' said Dram.

'I'm amazed she didn't cotton on,' Ecktosca admitted. 'I mean, if our genius allows us to compress the powers of a solar eruption, it follows that we can compress ourselves quite spectacularly too – for a limited time, anyway. And you were right, Doctor, it sorts out that silly implant good and proper.'

Dram giggled and let loose an enormous fart. 'Although it does push the gas exchange to the limit.'

'I hadn't noticed,' said Flowers politely, trying not to gag.

'But how'd you get up here…?' The Doctor clicked his fingers. 'Easy! You start a fight while you're full size, wait for the globs to come down and get you, set off your compression fields and hang on when they float back up to the rafters.'

'Very good, Doctor,' said Ecktosca drily. 'If this thing had hands I'd be clapping.'

'But why? I mean, now you're prisoners up here instead of down there. Not much to choose between, is there?'

'Your discovery of our compression fields forced us to move sooner than we would have liked,' he said. 'We've not yet located the only way out.'

'But *no one* can get in or out of Justicia,' said Flowers. 'Unless…'

The Doctor craned his neck to look round at her. 'Go on.'

'I overheard Issabel – Ermenshrew, I mean – talking

about… pathways. Passages that must exist between here and one of the other worlds.'

'Not just *one* of the other worlds,' said Ecktosca. 'There are pathways joining *all* the worlds in Justicia.'

Flowers reacted. 'All of them?'

'Not pathways – warp-holes.' The Doctor rolled over, perilously near the edge of the ledge, to look back at Flowers properly in the dim blue light. 'The very thing you've been hoping to use for space travel. Only the Blathereen have already got them. They've used them to travel between the worlds of Justicia without arousing suspicion.'

'And we're going to use them to get out of here,' hissed Dram determinedly.

'But if the Blathereen already have these warp-holes, why would they want us to keep working on the gravity amplifier?' Flowers wondered.

'To make little warp-holes into big warp-holes, perhaps. Increase the power of the centrifuge.' The Doctor nodded. 'That's why the Blathereen have been trying to move the planets into different orbits with exact measurements, to improve the system. Imperfections lead to instabilities.'

'And Justice Prime, with its irregular orbit, gets shoved right outside the system.' A shiver ran through her. 'But the power you'd need to shift planets…'

'Wake up and smell the Arkellis sap, Flowers!' the Doctor roared. 'Thanks to your little chain gangs slaving away on the problem, they've *got* that power! All your research, your findings, your inventions…'

'All along, they've been using us for their own ends,' Flowers realised. 'Leading us by the nose, steering our studies.'

The Doctor nodded. 'While I was working on the amplifier

today, the computer picked up some interference. So I checked it out, and what did I find? Three enormous gravity warp generators – not only drawing the planets off their natural course but powering their warp-holes, keeping them open. There's one hidden here somewhere on Justice Prime. Another on Justice Alpha – must be what drew my ship there in the first place. And there's a third out in deep space. But there's also a whole load of tiny little disturbances scattered all over Justicia.'

'Each one of them must be a point where you can enter or leave the warp-holes,' Flower realised. 'A sort of portal.'

'It's through one of those we're hoping help will come,' said Ecktosca quietly. 'They'll be hidden in all key locations. Quiet places, so no one sees you coming or going.'

'Yeah, that figures. But what about the third major warp, outside the Justicia system altogether? Where's that based?' The Doctor looked between Flowers and the globs. 'Come on, anyone got any ideas?'

'It'll be on-board their mothership!' Ecktosca suppressed a burp. 'That's how the Blathereen have swelled their numbers here. They've used the warp-holes to smuggle whole armies into Justicia, one at a time!'

'One of the girls wants to talk with you. And only you.'

Robsen looked up at Jamini, who was smirking in the common-room doorway, and raised an eyebrow. 'Who says?'

'Tiller, coming off shift. It's that Maggi Jalovitch. Friend of Kazta's.' Jamini pulled a face. 'None too bright, of course. But then why else would she want to see *you*?'

'Ha, ha.' Robsen frowned. He'd never had any personal requests for audiences before. If it had been anyone other than a friend of Kazta's...

Jamini turned suddenly serious . 'Kazta's not been the same since you said Blanc called in on her. Think it's linked?'

'Could be. I'll go and see Maggi later.'

'Want me to come with you?'

Robsen considered. 'Nah, it's OK. She might open up more if she thinks it's one on one.'

'Could be a set-up, or a trick.'

He smiled to see the concern on her long, chiselled face. 'I'll let you know.'

'Is it just me,' said Flowers, 'or is the light getting fainter?' She shook the sonic screwdriver, clamped tight in her clammy hand.

The Doctor rolled back on to his stomach. 'Battery's running down. Better switch off, save the power.' She did so, and his grim voice floated out of the darkness. 'We *have* to find the portal. I need to get to Justice Delta and rescue Rose.'

'I know where the portal must be,' said Flowers with sudden certainty. 'I saw one of the Executive senators walking about this morning. I thought he was here for a meeting but it had been cancelled – and no shuttle had arrived. Issabel tried to convince me I'd made a mistake, but I *saw* him. He went into the aquaculture compound.'

'Did you see him come out?' hissed the Doctor.

'No – I mean, I didn't stay around to look, but what would he have been doing in there by himself?'

'It's quiet, deserted?'

'The experiments were scaled down some months ago,' said Ecktosca.

'Then postponed, by Issabel herself,' Flowers added, 'and she never did explain why.'

'How fast can we get there?' hissed the Doctor.

Dram and Ecktosca rolled away nimbly through the tunnel.

They pressed on. Somehow, the Doctor seemed to know when she was flagging in the pitch-blackness. 'Come on, Flowers,' he'd whisper. 'This is the last push. All downhill from here…'

And then things really did go downhill.

'Doctor,' hissed Flowers. 'There's something on my leg.'

'What?'

'There's something –'

'I know what you said, what is it?'

Something else squidged on to the side of her arm, like a big bit of chewing gum being pressed against her.

'Globs!' she hissed. 'They're – they're all over me!'

She heard a squelching noise up ahead. 'Yeah, taking a bit of an interest, aren't they? Quick, Dram! How close are we?'

'Not far to –' He broke off, gave a surprisingly shrill shriek of pain. 'One's got me! It's got me!'

Flowers cringed as a glob squelched softly on to the back of her neck. 'Ermenshrew must have reprogrammed them to attack anything up here!'

'Thanks very much,' huffed Ecktosca. 'We were perfectly safe up here till you came along!'

'Shut up and keep moving,' snapped the Doctor. 'They're sluggish. Getting a feel for their new programming. There's still time… Look, we must nearly be there! There's light at the end of the tunnel!'

Flowers wasn't sure if he was speaking in metaphor or if he could really see it – because a glob was pressing itself into her face like a bad kisser. She tried to pull it free, but she needed her elbows to keep herself moving. Any minute now the globs would start sponging off her energy… draining her dry…

'We're here!' gasped Dram. 'Aquaculture compound.'

'Too far to jump,' the Doctor realised. 'Way too far.'

Flowers clawed the glob on her face to one side, squirming as it latched on to her hair instead – just in time to see the Doctor throw himself from the rocky perch…

'Of course,' breathed Ecktosca. And like a bouncy ball he hopped and jumped out through the hole after the Doctor. Dram followed him without hesitation.

Suddenly, Flowers understood. Summoning all her strength, she wriggled sluglike to the opening and propelled herself off the edge.

At once the globs kicked into action – and held her in midair. Presumably the Doctor had reckoned on the fact they couldn't let any of them die. They were programmed to punish, not to kill.

That was Ermenshrew's job.

Flowers stared down over the aquaculture compound. It was a big, circular chamber. Around the perimeter, and in a large circle in the middle of the room, trees and plants stood in bays awash with nutrients. They were fed through ribbed pipes that hung down around them like vines from occasional metal silos. The white walls behind them glowed with simulated sunlight.

There was no one else here besides the Doctor, who was staggering about with two globs on his shoulder and one on his leg. Flowers found her own globs to be quite obliging as they swooped her down over the centrepiece of bushy plants then deposited her gently on the ground beside him.

Then, to her surprise, they hopped straight off her and on to the Doctor.

'Out of their lair, out of their hair.' He spoke through gritted teeth, forcing his limbs to move him along. 'You don't have the implant.'

'Ermenshrew was hoping they'd hold us up there?'

'Then herd us off to wherever she's waiting,' the Doctor agreed. 'Get them off me!'

'Globs, leave him,' she commanded. Nothing happened. 'Let him go!'

'No good. She's taken away your control. Don't waste time. Find the portal. Only chance.'

'Where are the Slitheen?' she asked, looking round frantically. 'They could help!'

'Might already have gone.' Another four blobs swooped down from the darkness and thudded into his torso, slurping greedily. He gasped and sank to his knees. 'Portal. *Quick!*'

SEVENTEEN

Flowers started haring about the aquaculture compound in a flap. What would the gateway to a tunnel through space look like, anyway?

'What's this?' she heard the Doctor croak.

She turned back to him, and gasped with horror. The globs were swarming over him – thirty of them at least, glowing and throbbing darkly. His hand stuck out of the mass, pointing to the nearest metal pillar.

'It – it's a nitrogen feed,' she told him. Two more globs plopped down to join the scrum, one on his thigh, one slap bang on his face. 'Don't worry, Doctor, I'll find the portal –'

'Thought it was a nitrogen feed. Feeding from where?'

'The planet's surface. There's a pipeline that stretches right up. Now let me go and –'

'The atmosphere's nitrogen?'

Flowers wrung her hands, feeling utterly helpless. 'Almost all of it. As we reach the furthest point from the suns, it freezes and falls as nitrogen snow. It's processed in the silo here, combined with ammonia and fed to the plants –'

'Open the feed,' he gasped, dragging himself towards it.

'What?'

'Sonic screwdriver! Inspection plate, there!' Five more globs gathered over him; he was all but buried. 'Hurry! Ermenshrew will be on her way!'

Flowers pointed the device at the inspection plate. The screwdriver whirred but the energy released was feeble. The pinhead screws barely jostled in their housings.

'Give it a thwack!'

Flowers whacked the shaft of the screwdriver against the silo. The blue energy waves gave a sudden crackle and the inspection plate burst open. Flowers screamed and leaped back as a lethal blizzard of nitrogen escaped at high pressure.

It sprayed out into the walkway and all over the Doctor.

Or rather, over the globs that smothered him. With an unpleasant squealing noise, they wobbled off him like lumpy icicles, fell and cracked on the floor. The Doctor struggled clear of the freeze. A pattern of hard frost rimed his jacket, but aside from a few red patches on his face and forehead he seemed unharmed.

'Well done,' he said to her, kicking aside the dead globs and crossing to help her up. 'I meant to say, get out of the way.'

'How did you know that would happen?'

The Doctor started looking around. 'This planet's been moved 20 million miles further out from the suns, remember? That's frozen more of the atmosphere into nitrogen ice, brought it twinkling down to the ground ready for processing – far more than that thing was built to cope with.'

Flowers wasn't satisfied. 'There must be something more to it than that.'

He scrutinised a nearby tomato plant. 'You explain it, then.'

'The thing they're using to make the space tunnels – the

gravity warp!' cried Flowers. 'They've built it up on the planet surface, haven't they? Where no one would ever see it!'

'What, and you reckon the short-wave gravity field forced that near-liquid nitrogen out at high pressure?' He looked at her and smiled. 'Oh, so *that's* what happened!'

Flowers own smile was stifled by a sudden sharp tang in the air. 'What's that smell?'

He sniffed the air himself. 'Ammonia. We must have ruptured the nutrient tank, it's escaping into – ah!' Abruptly, he gripped the trunk of a tall, graceful sapling, littered with burgundy leaves. 'And on the subject of escaping…'

Flowers clutched his arm. 'You've found the portal?'

'This is a poppito tree. Native only to the Slitheen planet.' He gripped it, pulled it, peered all around it. 'Got to be a clue, right?'

'What a genius you truly are, Doctor.'

Flowers looked up in alarm at the grating alien voice.

Ermenshrew, still in her true and slavering form, had entered the compound. She was watching them now through black and narrowed eyes.

The thought that Maggi Jalovitch was desperate to see him filled Robsen with disquiet. It was probably nothing – probably a wind-up. He knew he already had a reputation as a bit of a soft touch. But Maggi was friends with Kazta, and there was always the chance that she could know something he didn't. Something that Kazta would never dream of telling a screw.

Something about Blanc.

He kept thinking back to the voices he'd heard coming from Blanc's room, and the gloating look on her face when she'd played him the recording. He'd been forced to accept her argument that *those* were the voices he'd heard. But deep down he knew she'd been having a conversation with someone *in the room with her.* So where had that person gone?

He kept thinking back to Rose Tyler's crazy talk about monsters...

Maggi had an extra kitchen shift today; it was Sunday, and the usual circus of full-block dinner awaited them all, even the Governor. In the meantime, Robsen decided he would go to see Blanc, and ask her a few more questions, now that he'd time to think things through.

He checked the roster in the canteen. She was on shift in the washrooms. Perhaps he could sneak into her room and have a quiet poke about...

If he were caught he'd be sacked and shipped back home with a six-month pay penalty. He was crazy. He'd only signed up for the money, and now he was ready to blow the whole point of his coming here. All those months away from his kids, leaving them in the foster home...

But when he reached Blanc's door, still fretting over how he might break inside, he found it a fraction ajar.

A gift. Now he was doing nothing wrong. He was *investigating* – wasn't Blanc meant to be on shift? If so, why had she left her door open?

Warily, he pushed it open.

Maggi was inside.

'What the –' Robsen's hand went for his baton, but there was no need. The girl was red-faced and quivering with fear. 'Jalovitch! What are *you* doing here?'

'Oh, Warder Robsen,' she babbled, a big tear starting down her face. 'Blanc knew I was gonna tell you stuff about the monsters so she took me here.'

'*She* took you here? When?'

'Just an hour ago, tied me up.'

There were signs of a possible struggle, Robsen supposed – a spindly plant with russet leaves had been knocked over. 'Where is she now?'

'Dunno, sir. Said she'd get me later.'

'She marched you here in full view of everyone?'

'We never passed no one, sir,' said Maggi wretchedly. 'She tied me up but I got free, see! I had to – she's a monster, sir! She's got this zip in her head –'

'This crazy talk about monsters,' said Robsen, shaking his head. 'You've put each other up to it, haven't you? It's a pack of lies, isn't it?'

He so wanted to believe he was right.

'Ask yourself, then,' Maggi protested. 'Why would *she* bring me here?'

Robsen didn't have an answer. Then he saw that Maggi was crouched in front of a large black disc.

'She brings other people here too,' whispered Maggi. 'Other monsters. I'm not making it up, honest. This disc makes people appear from nowhere. And when they tread on it, they go back there too.'

'All right,' said Robsen. 'Come on, we'll go to the Governor. We'll get Blanc there too. We'll get this sorted out.'

'But – the Governor's one of them now!' She looked wide-eyed, terrified. 'He is!'

'Just calm down, Jalovitch, or I'll have you restrained –'

She threw her arms round him. 'I'll make you believe me!'

He was trying to pull himself free when she suddenly let go, and he staggered back on to the black disc.

There was a quick, greedy hum of power.

And with the sound of his own screams ringing and echoing in his ears, Robsen felt himself start to burn away, clutching the hot and shifting air with dissolving fingers until he fell away into nothingness.

Finally, panting and sweaty, Rose and Dennel reached the monitoring station. It was the size of a small bungalow and lay rocking feebly like some great wounded creature.

'Anti-gravs,' said Dennel. 'Still trying to lift it up in the air.'

'Nice to know we've all got something in common,' she sighed as she clambered in through the gaping doorway. 'Hopeless optimism.'

It may have been a monitoring platform once, but now it was more like a funfair ride. After their grisly find on the way over here, Rose fought to keep the contents of her stomach as well as her balance as it shifted from side to side. A hum of power whirred erratically through the air around her, and in the soft shine of fluorescent lights she saw that the floor – once a wide, curved wall – was filled with TV screens.

She tapped an 'on' button with her foot and a screen glowed into life. She tried another – nothing. But the one beside it snapped into life like an eye winking open.

Rose grinned, kept switching on sets.

And then she realised what the monitors were showing.

She supposed the humans round here had used this place Big Brother style, spying on the poor people trapped in their various prisons. But it seemed the Blathereen were using them to check up on their own kind. Little subtitles on the screens helpfully informed her of the various locations:

Justice Epsilon, High Minister's office: a Blathereen sat in a big leather chair with its feet up on the desk.

Justice Alpha, Overseers' Station: three Blathereen stood with their backs to the camera, stubby tails wagging as they looked out over distant pyramids. But there were other buildings under construction in the foreground, vast, graceless rectangles of heavy stone. What the hell were they…?

Then her eyes fell on the screen by her right foot. Justice Beta, Detention Centre Six, Governor's office. 'Dennel, look at this,' she whispered.

He joined her, silently staring at a Blathereen as it wriggled inside a cosy, fleshy sack. As it zipped itself into the Governor's skin, pulling at the flabby folds on the neck and the cheeks. Straightening itself out, ready for duty.

'Oh no…' breathed Dennel.

'Why are the Blathereen doing this? What do they want?'

'They want us dead!' snapped Dennel. 'Like Ronika, Malc – all of them out there!'

'No. Not all of us. They must need some of the people here alive, or why bother with the whole stealth thing?'

'Doesn't matter,' said Dennel dully. 'We can't hide from them now. There's nowhere to go.' He stared at her. 'They've taken over everything.'

Flowers quailed as Ermenshrew took a sticky step closer.

'What d'you want *now*?' The Doctor sighed, looking quite affronted at the Blathereen's sudden presence.

'How did you free yourself of the globs?' she hissed.

He shrugged. 'Gave them the cold shoulder.'

'I have had more than enough of your pathetic attempts to stave off the inevitable.'

'Well, we were just off anyway,' said the Doctor. 'About to jump down your warren in space.'

'And it is *only* ours,' she hissed. 'Our carapaces are strong enough to travel the warp-holes with no ill effects. Humans are not so hardy. It's very inconvenient – if we could have risked bringing your pretty little human piggy through the portal, my cousin would still be well.'

'But you're not making these tunnels just for convenient travel, are you? With the gravity amplifier magnifying the energy of the warp-hole network, you can create tunnels through space a billion times bigger.' The Doctor stared at Ermenshrew. 'But why? Why d'you need such a big hole?'

'You'll find out for yourself soon enough.' Her dark eyes glittered. 'Your team are progressing so very nicely without you on the late shift, Doctor. Construction of the amplifier will soon be complete.' Ermenshrew cocked her enormous head to one side. 'Now that I've shown them what happens if they fail me.'

She threw something down on the floor. It landed with a wet slop.

Flowers stared, appalled, at a thick yellow puddle in which floated a single, sugar-frosted eye.

'Oh, Nesshalop,' she whispered.

'And now, Flowers, I think it's time you were dead.'

'No.' The Doctor was trembling with anger. 'Before you do anything else, I should take a sniff with that supersnout of yours.'

And Ermenshrew did. 'Ammonia?'

''S right.' He gestured to the gaping inspection panel. 'I programmed a hyper-destronic pulse into the nitrogen feeder. The ammonia's acting as a carrier. Every passing second it's transmuting the energy as we speak – ready to send it shooting up into your gravity warp above.'

'You're lying.' She took a step forwards, raised her claws.

'You've not got long to disconnect it. Any minute now, that warp's gonna be scattered over half the frozen surface of this planet. And that'll make a mess of *anyone* who tries to go through one of your warp-holes, won't it?'

Ermenshrew turned to a patch of glowing wall and hissed in anger. It slid smoothly aside to reveal a vertical access shaft studded with meaty metal rungs. 'For the record, I know this is a trick, OK?'

'Sure you do.'

'Just remember, there's nowhere you can go to escape me.' She ducked inside and started to climb. Her voice floated down to them in eerie echoes. 'Even if you dared risk the portal, the controls can't be primed by *aliens*. I'll be seeing you very soon.'

The Doctor dashed to scoop up Nesshalop's eye in its sticky fluid. It winked at him sadly, and he pressed a kiss against its wrinkled, frosted lid. 'We'll leave this in a nutrients tray. If it doesn't dry out she may be able to reabsorb it.'

'What's the use?' moaned Flowers. 'That evil *thing*! She'll kill Nesshalop, all of us! How can we possibly stop the Blathereen doing whatever it is they're doing?'

'How can I find Rose?' He gently placed the eye at the base of a tomato plant. 'Not by sitting here and crying.'

She wiped her eyes. 'That's the ammonia,' she muttered, her throat starting to burn. 'Leak's getting worse.'

Suddenly the ground either side of her seemed to explode in a blinding charge of electric blue light. She jumped in alarm as, in the wink of an eye, two Slitheen were coughing their guts up beside her.

'Thought you'd scarpered,' grinned the Doctor, slapping them both heartily on the back.

'Waiting for you lot to push off out of it,' Dram growled.

'You should try coping with that level of ammonia when your lungs are the size of a pig's nipple,' added Ecktosca. 'Filthy stuff.' Still coughing, he clamped a claw around the poppito tree's golden trunk. It glowed and vanished – to reveal a large black disc in the bottom of the plant tray.

'Can't be primed by an alien, but *will* respond to their own kind,' grinned the Doctor.

'After what we've been through, we're not about to get locked up by Ermenshrew, poisoned by gas or blown to bits by the back-blast of your hyper-destronic pulse!' Ecktosca scrambled on to the disc.

'My what?' The Doctor frowned. 'Oh, yeah, that!'

'Come on, Dram,' said Ecktosca. 'Anywhere's got to be better than here.'

Dram joined him. Their images blurred and faded.

The Doctor took Flowers by the hand. 'We must follow.'

She coughed, her throat still burning with ammonia. 'But we don't know where the tunnel leads!'

'We won't be there long – we'll be going straight on to Justice Delta. Unless it *leads* to Justice Delta, of course.'

'But you heard her, it's not safe for us.'

'You think it is *here*?' He placed his hands on her shoulders, and his eyes looked into hers. 'You saw the gravometer. The planets are now in their most efficient and balanced positions. Should be a smooth enough ride.'

'Should be?' Flowers pulled at the collar of her tunic.

From somewhere up the access tunnel, a deep cry of rage was building.

'D'you think she's found out I was bluffing?' The Doctor jumped on to the platform and hauled Flowers after him.

She huddled beside him on the disc. Slowly, a feeling of pins and needles stretched out through her body. Her ears popped. She found she couldn't breathe. It was as if some prickling, invisible fist was squeezing her like dough.

Then the world seemed to fade away and Flowers fell screaming into a searing, crackling void.

EIGHTEEN

Rose had found one bank of screens marked Justice Delta, showing scenes that had to be local. There were a number of offices, clearly built for humans, now Blathereen squats. One screen showed a room piled high with broken swivel chairs, not built to accommodate alien backsides. Another showed a dark and sinister place with a big blobby shape shifting about at its centre, masked by a blurry yellow light and loads of smoke.

But just as she and Dennel were about to leave the lurching platform in despair, they saw one of the screens was showing the dumping ground for bodies they'd stumbled upon earlier.

'We should stay put,' Dennel sighed. 'At least if the Blathereen come the same way we did, we'll see them and *know* we've only got ten minutes left to live.'

Rose gave him a gentle shove. 'It's not over till it's over.' Then she frowned. 'Hang on – why would the Blathereen want to set a camera *there*?'

'Maybe they like gloating over dead humans.'

Just then a grey swirling shape marshmallowed out from nowhere. Rose blinked as the shape resolved itself into –

'Robsen! It's Warder Robsen!' Dennel stared in bafflement. 'How did he – where did he –'

'We know the where, don't we? From the borstal!' Rose watched the screen as Robsen took a slow, shaky look around. 'As for how – well, it's not magic, is it?'

Dennel pushed back his fringe. 'It isn't?'

'It must be, I dunno, some sort of transport. They must film it to keep an eye on who goes through!' She clutched his arm, a wild grin on her face. 'Maybe *we* can use it to get out of here!'

Dennel clutched her back grimly. 'And maybe, if *we've* just watched him come through – so have the Blathereen!'

'They might have seen us passing that way too!' Rose scrambled outside into the humid mint of daylight. 'We've got to get to Robsen and clear the area, fast!'

Flowers opened her eyes and gasped. A Blathereen face was glaring down at her, filling her vision. She opened her mouth to scream, but a heavy, slimy claw slapped down over her face.

'It's Ecktosca,' hissed a familiar voice. 'You've already jeopardised our lives by coming after us, at least have the good grace not to shriek like a child and bring every guard in the place down here.'

Flowers nodded, and he removed his claw. She saw that she was lying in a gloomy, windowless room. By the familiar black and yellow decor it had to be an Executive conference room. She felt dreadful, but at least she'd survived the journey. Which meant that the planets were more or less in perfect position for whatever the Blathereen were planning.

She had a hunch that her own position right now might be less agreeable.

'Where's the Doctor?' she whispered.

Ecktosca gestured behind her. She rolled over groggily to see him crouched over a black disc identical to the one they had stepped on in the aquaculture compound, wielding the sonic screwdriver, pausing every few moments to give it a good shake before continuing.

'It's not wise, using these things when they're almost out of batteries,' the Doctor said with a sigh. 'The beam's not fully focused. It's probably exciting all sorts of stray molecules.'

'I'm glad something's excited,' grumbled Dram.

'What are you doing?' said Flowers.

He turned to her with a big smile. 'Oh, there you are. It's Justice Delta! Are we jammy or what?'

'I feel like my insides are jam.'

'Not that bad, was it?'

'It was the most horrible thing that's ever happened to me.'

'So far.' The Doctor returned to his work. 'Hang on. I'm just trying to stop Ermenshrew coming straight after us.'

'How?'

Ecktosca filled the ensuing silence: 'By feeding in an offset gravity pulse to the warp relay.'

'Yeah, what he said,' the Doctor murmured, waving an arm vaguely. 'They won't come through here, they'll get shunted that way a bit...'

Flowers left him to it and turned to Dram and Ecktosca. 'Why are you two still here?'

'Because there are guards outside the door,' hissed Ecktosca. 'We've heard them moving about.'

'But we don't know how many there are,' Dram added. 'We need to be really stealthy, strike them down – maybe take the skins of a couple of them.'

Ecktosca nodded. 'Then perhaps we can bluff our way –'

'Done it!' yelled the Doctor happily. 'That ought to –'

'Shhhhhhhhh!' He was nearly drenched in saliva as everyone hushed him at once.

Then the door swung open and a Blathereen with a gun in its claw barged into the room. Closely followed by another. And another. On instinct, Flowers stared round for somewhere to run or to hide, but they were already coming for her. She squirmed as a claw tightened like slippery steel around her wrist, forcing her to her knees. Dram clenched his claws as if ready to try to fight his way out, but Ecktosca shook his head and raised his arms in surrender.

The Doctor pulled a rueful face. 'Well, at least that's one question answered. There are *lots* of guards outside the door.' He made no protest as a Blathereen grabbed his shoulders in its colossal claws and lifted him a good metre off the ground.

'Hello,' said the Doctor brightly. 'Take me to your leader!'

Riz and Kazta sat together at dinner, a pathetic attempt at strength in numbers. Talk was still going round the tables about the stunt Rose Tyler had pulled two nights previously, and Riz found one or two admiring glances thrown her way by association. Kaz was oblivious to all this. Her eyes were fixed on the Governor as he came in with Blanc.

Riz knew why. There was something in the way he walked, a little spring in his step, which seemed out of keeping. His face, too, looked a little fleshier. And he and Blanc were as thick as thieves.

Kazta had noticed too. Riz could see her knuckles had whitened around her plastic spoon.

Maggi joined them at her table, white-faced.

'Where've you been?' asked Kaz. 'I heard some of the girls

saying you bunked your shift.'

'I was in Blanc's room,' said Maggi simply. 'She thought you'd been talking to me and she hauled me up on it.'

Riz and Kaz swapped *no way!* glances.

'She took you to her *room*?' Riz almost yelled, and Kaz kicked her under the table to keep the noise down.

Blanc looked over, but her face was impassive.

'She thinks she's scared me into shutting up,' said Maggi. 'It was horrible. I wouldn't have got out alive, except Robsen…'

'Robsen?' Kaz pulled a face.

'Oh, my God!' Riz felt a little twinge of jealousy. 'He rescued you?'

'It – it wasn't really like that,' Maggi said shakily. There was a haunted, glassy look about her eyes, as if she was in some kind of shock. 'Look, I found stuff out. Stuff you won't believe.'

Riz glanced around, to check no warder was about to come and hassle them. 'Try us.'

'Don't have to. I'm gonna prove it. To everyone.' Abruptly she gave that slightly hopeless smile of hers. 'And when I do, Kaz, you gotta take charge. You gotta make sure stuff happens.'

Kaz gave her a weary look. 'What you talking about *now*?'

But her eyes widened, just as Riz's did, when Maggi sneakily showed them a gleaming white key card.

Riz felt like her jaw had dropped down to the table. 'Is it Robsen's?'

Maggi nodded. 'I don't think he'll be needing it where he's gone.'

Robsen came to on a bed of fragrant grass. The smell mingled with rotting flesh and turned his stomach. The sky was a bilious green, which matched the way he felt perfectly.

191

Then he saw Block-walker Dennel and the girl, Rose Tyler. His brain ground through the pieces of this poser, but found no answer.

'You're on Justice Delta,' said Rose. 'How d'you get here?'

'Maggi Jalovitch pushed me...'

Rose gave him a hand up. 'She's a big girl, but that's still one hell of a shove.'

'Norris...' Robsen couldn't stop staring at the big man's body, his dark and lifeless eyes. 'Then Blanc *did* kill him?'

Dennel nodded. 'And hid him out here with the rest of her victims.'

Robsen joined in with the nodding, speechless.

'At last he sees the light. Oh, and you know those monsters I tried telling you about? I think there's a load more of them on the way.' Rose peered around behind him. 'Now, you seemed to pop right out of thin air, somewhere over there...'

He rubbed his tender head. 'It's all mixed up. Maggi – Jalovitch, I mean – was in Blanc's room, and there was this sort of disc thing...'

'Like *this* disc thing?' called Dennel.

Rose helped Robsen up and saw Dennel was gesturing at a dark, round platform, like a swish set of bathroom scales, half hidden by the undergrowth.

'So if we stand on that, we end up in Blanc's room?' Dennel looked hopeful. 'Home!'

'Prison,' Rose reminded him. 'Back to square one.'

Dennel shook his head. 'Freedom's well overrated. I wanna go back. I don't know nothing else.'

'You'll know Blanc's claws round your throat if you go back,' Rose told him. 'It's no safer for us there –'

'Of course it is!'

'All right, enough!' Self-consciously, Robsen pulled himself free. 'Dennel's right. We've got to go back.'

Rose folded her arms. 'Oh yeah? Well, let's see you work it.'

Robsen stiffened. 'Well, before, I just sort of…' He staggered on to the disc.

Absolutely nothing happened.

He and Dennel peered around the area for any workings, but there was no sign.

'Blanc could send humans through –' Rose waved around the corpse-strewn area – 'but she wouldn't exactly want them coming back, would she? Not that they were in any state to.'

'I know I'm supposed to be your warder, but…' Robsen held his face in his hands. 'What do we do? I mean, are there *really* monsters here?'

Rose glanced about nervously. 'If we wait round here much longer, you'll find out when they come to kill us.'

Even as she spoke, a distant, tremendous crashing sound carried through the fresh mint forest.

'Waiting's over,' said Dennel.

Flowers, Ecktosca and Dram were marched down the corridor behind the Doctor. They must have covered fifty metres before the Blathereen called them to a stop by a set of double doors.

'No wonder that portal's so heavily guarded,' said the Doctor. 'We're on the big man's doorstep!'

'Don Arco,' muttered Dram.

Flowers frowned. 'That's who Ermenshrew was talking to in her office!'

'The Blathereen Patriarch. May plaque brown his belly.' Ecktosca earned himself a cuff round the back of the head. 'So this is where he's set up shop.'

'It's the Executive's prime lecture theatre,' said Flowers.

The Doctor shook his head. 'Not any more.'

Justicia's new management had made one or two changes.

Inside it was oppressively dark. The stale, rank air was so thick you could chew it. The ornately designed windows had been smeared with a brown, gooey slime as if to keep out the light. The seats had all been ripped out and an uneven, glassy material secreted over the floor in their place. Flowers felt as if she was standing on the carapace of some enormous, sleeping creature.

And there was another creature that sat in the middle of this nightmare landscape. She could see it from here, shrouded in spice-rich smoke from the hundreds of burning candles that encircled it.

The guards held back, apparently reluctant to continue into the ruined theatre, and the Doctor turned to Ecktosca. 'Why all the vapours?'

But it was Dram who answered, with ghoulish enthusiasm. 'Don Arco's escaped execution twice. The second time he had to hide out in a toxic dump for a year. Wrecked his lungs.'

'The fumes from the salve-candles are meant to ease his breathing,' said Ecktosca. 'Though if you ask *me*, he's just posing. There's nothing wrong with him at all.'

'Approach,' boomed a gravelly voice through the swirls of smog.

Flowers recognised it from her eavesdropping on Ermenshrew. She and the others were pushed on into the gloom, their feet sticking on the syrupy surface. Flowers choked on the smoke. Then, out of the flickering, shifting shadows, the shape of an enormous, obese Blathereen resolved itself, wheezing for breath. Its stomach spilled over its lap, almost reaching its waxen knees. Its neck was a swollen sac, and rippled as it swept its head from side to side, until it came to fix its bulbous, watery eyes on the Doctor.

'Don Arco, right?' The Doctor nodded in greeting. 'The big cheese. The head honcho. The Patriarch.'

The leathery lips cracked open in a smile. 'Welcome to my worlds.'

Riz was staring at the bowl of gloop in front of her, too nervous to eat, despite Kaz urging her to keep up her strength for the struggles ahead.

They had a warder key – a passcard that could get her and Kaz and Maggi anywhere in the prison. A last kindness from Robsen. She hoped he was OK, wherever he'd ended up.

Now they could grab a shuttle, force someone to take them away from here. Forget this place. Escape. Start again somewhere, be *free*…

But Maggi Jalovitch was famous as the thickest girl in the block – and *she* was calling the shots. What if she messed up?

Suddenly Maggi started moaning and groaning and clutching her stomach. 'I'm gonna be sick! I am!'

Riz stared at Kaz. What was Maggi doing? Already a pair of warders was heading her way, while Blanc and the Governor looked over and frowned from the top table.

'Give me the key card,' Kaz hissed. 'Maggi, if they search you…'

But it was too late. Maggi meekly allowed the warders to take her away, out through the canteen doors.

'She bottled it,' whispered Kaz hoarsely.

Staring down at her steaming plate, Riz didn't see what happened next. But somehow Maggi had got free and sneaked back inside. Because a few seconds later, she was standing right behind Blanc and the Governor, shouting at the top of her lungs.

'You don't believe in monsters?' She slapped one hand down on Blanc's head and another one down on the Governor's. Shocked, they tried to turn to face her, but as they did she yanked something in their hair. 'Look who we got in charge here!'

The canteen fell silent as a blue crackle of energy erupted in front of Maggi. Blanc was up on her feet now. Through the unearthly glow, something was pushing out of her head like thick waxy pus from a zit. The Governor, too, was thrashing about as something alien, something far bigger than he was, fought for release.

"'S what I saw,' whimpered Kazta. 'What Blanc showed me.'

Riz watched in horror as the monsters crawled out of their human hiding places. People started to scream, to be sick, to burst out in tears.

Blanc lunged at Maggi with massive, muscular arms, but she was too slow. Instead, her claws connected with a panicking warder. He collapsed over the table, his head twisted at an unnatural angle.

Maggi pushed aside the Governor and scrambled over the warder's body, standing on the table. 'You all got a choice!' she bellowed over the racket in the hall. 'Stay here and let the monsters kill you – or kill them first!'

'So, you're the esteemed Doctor.' Don Arco heaved a noisy breath, nodded approvingly. 'The man who showed us the light. We were so close to the breakthrough we needed, we just couldn't see it.'

The Doctor peered at the grotesque creature. 'Can't see

much in this fog, can you?'

'I can see you have two Slitheen with you.' He chuckled, a noise like rubble shifting. 'Bad luck, boys. You were full of big words at the start. But you couldn't stop us.'

'We're not through yet,' sneered Ecktosca. The guard behind him kicked the back of his leg, forced him down on one knee.

'Hey, I may be recruiting. You want a job, Slitheen?' He laughed again, phlegm rattling in his labouring lungs. 'Only I got this big butt, see? And it needs kissing nice and regular. Think you can pucker up for me, Slitheen? Huh?'

'May your mother boil in the cauldron of atonement, Arco,' Ecktosca hissed. His guard struck him. The blow sounded like the first bite into a toffee apple.

'You're little people,' said Don Arco, peering down at the Slitheen. 'Look at you. Your family used to be respected. Used to prosper. You held the outer archipelagos in your dirty claws. But it all went wrong for you, didn't it…?' He leaned forwards in his chair, causing the candle flames around him to gust alarmingly. 'When did you go so soft, Slitheen?'

Dram struggled in the hold of his guard, but he too was forced down to his knees.

'So these schmucks have got you on side, huh, Doc?' Arco stretched out his wobbling neck to scrutinise the Doctor more closely. 'Got you as their scientific advisor?'

'What are you on about?'

'For their big comeback.' Again, the Blathereen laughed nastily. 'You're gonna help them get back on top of their planet-frying game, right?'

The Doctor looked at Ecktosca and Dram, the disappointment on his face clear. 'So much for antiques and dressing up.'

The Slitheen said nothing, but Don Arco was happy to fill their silence. 'They came here snooping for their old relics. And in the process they found out *we* were here. They really thought they could take over our operation. Thought they were big enough to cope.' He laughed again, big dribbling gasps of laughter as he turned his attentions on the Slitheen. 'Know what? I don't even get pleasure from seeing you beg. You're nothing to me. I think maybe I should just kill you now.'

'Never mind them. Why don't you tell me what *you're* doing here? What I've helped you to achieve?' The Doctor smiled. 'What I could go on to help you achieve.' Flowers stared at him, appalled, but he just shrugged. 'Time to think about other plans.'

A furious bellowing carried from beyond the blacked-out windows. Don Arco gestured, and the guard holding Flowers went over to see, dragging her with him. He wiped his claw against the mucky glass and she caught a glimpse of overgrown lawns, of straggly topiaries: a magnificent garden gone to pot.

And in the middle of a bush, the legs of a Blathereen pedalling the air. There was another shriek of rage.

'It's Ermenshrew,' the guard reported. 'Upside down in a bush. Should I go help her?'

'She's blown up worlds. She's massacred millions. She's run a talent agency on Hastus Minor.' Don Arco glared at the guard. 'You think she can't get herself out of a bush?'

Flowers looked away as Ermenshrew dragged herself out of the bush and started stomping towards the building. The Doctor's sabotage had worked after all – not that it made much difference.

Don Arco stared at the Doctor. 'How come there's a

problem with the portal? *You* got through OK.'

'These little warp-holes in space can play up a bit,' said the Doctor. 'What are you using them for, anyway – saving on taxi fares?'

'They've made a useful little travel system for getting around Justicia. But once your gravity amplifier is up and running –'

'You can enlarge them. That's what you've been planning all along.'

Don Arco sniggered, a sound like elephants dancing in a skip full of gravel. 'We knew you alien schmucks would make the breakthrough some day. So we've been busy preparing…'

'So, now you can join all the holes together to create a whacking great portal in the fabric of space.'

'Precisely.'

'But *why?*'

The Patriarch smiled round at them all, even at the Slitheen still kneeling before him. 'The super-portal we're going to create is for the entire Justicia system to pass through. The planets, the suns – all of it!'

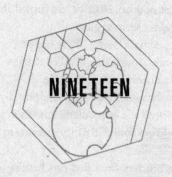

NINETEEN

Rose led Dennel and Robsen in the charge away from the relentless crashing sound. They were moving towards the big buildings she'd seen; the thick forest was impenetrable in all other directions.

'There must be about fifty of them coming after us!' panted Dennel.

Robsen nodded. 'We don't stand a chance.'

'Shhh!' Rose stopped running, held out her arms to slow down the others. 'I think I heard something up ahead. Give me a bunk-up.'

With a worried look behind him, Robsen offered his hand as a stirrup and helped Rose shin up the nearest tree. Then he clambered up after her.

'Hurry up!' Dennel urged her, as the crashing and cracking of branches got still louder. 'They're almost on us!'

But the news was no better this way. Crowded in a small clearing about 100 metres away were six Blathereen, alert and listening – and an injured one on the end who could barely stand. He had to be the pilot.

'There are your monsters,' Rose whispered.

Robsen just nodded. His face had turned so white it made his ginger freckles seem to glow.

Rose dropped back down. 'We're trapped.'

'Can we circle around them?' asked Robsen.

'If we had a dozen machetes maybe.'

'Or a flamethrower,' said Dennel mournfully.

Robsen winced at a particularly loud thud and crack from behind them. 'They sound like they're trying to run *through* the trees.'

'Making as much noise as they can, herding us on in a panic so we run slap into their mates *this* way,' Rose reasoned.

Then, with a tearing, cracking sound, a massive tree toppled towards them.

Robsen cowered back. 'What the –'

'They've caught us up!' cried Dennel.

'No,' said Rose, gaping as something huge and steel and shiny pushed gracelessly through the gap in the treeline. 'No, look!'

Like some bizarre missile, the entire monitoring platform was slithering towards them. It rocked on its side, ploughing a steady, inexorable path through the forest.

'Must be the grav motors,' said Dennel, staring in bewilderment, 'malfunctioning or something. Pushing it along.'

'It's our only chance,' said Rose. 'Door's open. We can get inside.'

'And get past those monsters,' Robsen agreed. He ran alongside the monitoring platform and then swung himself through the doorway. 'Come on!'

'Quick, Dennel!' Rose grabbed him by the hand and dragged him after her.

They threw themselves inside just as the capsule struck

another tree and rattled them around like beans in a tin can. Rose fell head first into the bank of TV screens. She clung on, praying the glass wouldn't break beneath her.

'Warder Robsen,' said Dennel as the platform ground its way onwards, 'when we get back to the detention centre, will you lock me up and never let me out again, please?'

'We've got to get the door closed,' shouted Robsen. 'Before the Blathereen —'

Rose heard a clanging sound and a hoarse alien cry, caught a twisted glimpse of two of the creatures staggering past the gaping doorway, horribly injured.

'OK, never mind,' he concluded. 'You think they saw us?'

'If not, they'll have smelled us,' said Rose.

Dennel clutched his head in his hands. 'They'll be coming after us madder than ever now!'

Suddenly the monitoring platform started to rotate clockwise as it pressed onwards. Rose felt like a hamster in a wheel, trying to keep the right way up. She didn't manage it and fell on to the screens again. When the platform stopped shifting, the doorway was now more of a skylight.

'Well, that'll make it harder for them to get in,' said Robsen.

Dennel nodded, wiping a cut to his head with his snotty sleeve. 'But how do we get out!'

'Shut it, both of you,' hissed Rose. The screens were still working, and one in particular had caught her attention. The dark and sinister scene she'd seen earlier... Up close she could see that the blurry yellow light was coming from candles, *they* were making the smoke.

And the Doctor was there.

'It's him!' Rose pressed her hand against the screen. 'I need volume. Now.'

Robsen found the controls for her. The three of them clung on desperately, staring and straining to listen as their transport bludgeoned its way through the dense forest.

They were already up to their necks in dog-doo. Now, as the truth squawked out through the few speakers still functioning, Rose could feel it rising over their heads.

Pandemonium kicked off in the borstal canteen as the monsters finally broke out of their human hiding places. Riz watched, frozen in fear, as a gang of hard lads, real bruisers, advanced warily on the monster Blanc had become. The thing rounded on one boy who was wielding a chair, swiped it away with her claws and took most of his arm with it.

But his cries, and the blood, seemed to turn a tide in the panicking crowd. Scary monsters killing a screw was one thing – but now it had maimed one of their own. People stopped yelling in panic. Instead they started picking up chairs, heaving at table legs, trying to break them off. The group of boys, at least twenty-strong, started laying into the creature, and more were joining in – Kaz included. She helped to pin down one of its claws, while two boys smashed down chairs on its gruesome skull. Soon the creature was lost from Riz's sight through sheer weight of numbers.

The other monster almost reached the doors. But it was still half caught in its human disguise, it couldn't move or fight back freely. The mob wrestled it to the ground, smothered it, meted out the same crazed punishment.

Maggi worked her way between the two scrums, grinning like a maniac. 'Yeah, hit it! Kill the alien freak!'

'We're in control now!' Kaz shrieked, triumphant, alien blood dripping down her cheek.

'And we can all bust out of here!' cried Maggi, waving her key card in the air. 'See this? Follow me, and I'll get you out of here. All of you!'

The mob roared its agreement. Riz watched Kaz and Maggi lead the march from the hall. She saw a couple of screws, Jamini and Tiller, cowering behind tables, powerless, as the inmates crowded out and left them behind with the twitching, broken bodies of the monsters.

Maggi had created a *new* monster, an unstoppable force that was busting out of this dump after all these years. And as she joined the mass exodus, Riz felt a real rush at the thought that now she was a part of it too.

Flowers stared slack-jawed at Don Arco in the wake of his words. 'It's impossible. Can't be done. The force you'd need to shift suns out of their orbit, together with their family of planets –'

'We *can* do it,' Don Arco assured her.

'But you *can't* fly an entire solar system through space!'

'Can so too.' Don Arco nodded happily, setting his chins wobbling. 'It's taken me thirty years of research, and eight more in the field here while we've slowly taken over this whole place. We've turned your Executive's headquarters into one big calculating machine, working out the quantum mechanics involved. And thanks to some inspired work from your team on the hardware side, Senator Flowers, we're almost good to go. We'll control the whole thing remotely from Justice Prime, well away from the powers of the centrifuge.'

'The whole *thing's* impossible.' Flowers just couldn't take it in. She took off her glasses and started polishing them furiously. 'It's a ludicrous notion.'

'Ludicrous!' the Doctor agreed. 'Unlikely. Preposterous.

Couldn't happen.' He took a step closer to Don Arco, somehow dragging his towering guard along with him. 'Suppose that's what you want the judge to think, isn't it, when the law comes looking for you? You know, after you've committed whatever perfect crime you're planning.'

'Oh, come on,' said Ecktosca suddenly. 'Dirty great solar system whizzing through space? Hardly the least conspicuous getaway vehicle.'

'No one's gonna see a thing, Slitheen,' said Don Arco. 'The space-warps provide instant travel, right? So, we open us a hole in space – and Justicia jumps through it. We pop out close to another solar system.'

The Doctor stared at him. 'But you'll destroy it. You'll start a gravity-quake, knock that system's planets out of orbit.'

'Nah,' said Don Arco. 'The three suns will incinerate them before then.' He patted Dram on the head. 'These guys built us a solar flare compressor. Reverse the circuits and you've got the biggest flamethrower in the universe. We can use it to burn up any number of worlds anywhere… Then pop back through the hole and into Justicia's native space like nothing's happened.'

'So you bombard other worlds with nuclear radiation from Justicia's suns,' said Flowers, 'leave them burnt-out cinders – but why?'

'Because one person's burnt-out cinder is a space mer-chant's stockpile of fissile material,' said the Doctor. 'The Blathereen can sell off the chunks to any dodgy dealer with a nuclear space fleet to power.'

'But you're missing the true genius of our plan,' huffed Don Arco. 'It's not just the unique positioning of Justicia's planets that makes it perfect for our needs. And it's not just having access to brilliant alien minds.'

'The rest of Justicia's worlds?' the Doctor breathed. 'What are you gonna do with them?'

Don Arco clapped his slimy claws together with joy. 'Nothing shall be wasted! On Justice Epsilon, the colonies will be put to work processing the fissile material we collect from the burnt-up planets.'

'They won't live long exposed to that much radiation.'

'Which is why, on Justice Beta, we have instructed that young male prisoners will mingle freely with young female prisoners in the borstals.' He sniggered. 'They will breed a new labour force for me. And of course, the good planets of Earth's empire will continue to send their unwanted louts, crooks and murderers to Justicia.' His bulk throbbed with mirth. '*We* want them very much. *We* shall put them to excellent use.'

'And you don't think anyone in EarthGov will notice?' Flowers challenged.

'Oh, I'm sure those humans on the secret monitoring committees would soon notice something.' He chuckled. 'If I hadn't already replaced them all with my godchildren!' He quivered with giggles, thick saliva dribbling down his fat neck. 'So, no worries there.'

Flowers felt her stomach twist and tighten another notch. 'But Justicia is in the business of selling punishment solutions to colonies all over the Empire – and you've messed up all the experiments!'

Don Arco waved a dismissive hand. 'So, some of us stay in human character and report back to Earth now and then to sell them some faked results. Why not? Another little cash flow coming in.'

'These are people you're talking about,' the Doctor said furiously. 'Human lives you're playing with!'

'If they can't do the time, they shouldn't do the crime.' Don Arco clicked his claws together. 'And, as I say, they'll serve a useful purpose. Those historical punishments dished out on Justice Alpha, for instance – building pyramids and the like? Not any more. Now those lucky people will be building store-houses for our processed fissile material, where it can be kept until it's ready for collection.'

'Poisoning the planet, poisoning the people –'

'So what? When one part of Justicia gets too polluted I can use the portals to relocate the entire labour force to another of its worlds.' Don Arco giggled. 'That's the wonderful thing about taking over a whole solar system: room for expansion. Important for any business, don't you think?'

'The scale of it!' Dram actually sounded impressed. 'The *nerve* of it!'

Ecktosca agreed. 'We thought you were maybe planning to nuke the suns or something for increased fuel yield, but *this* –'

'Oh, yeah,' said the Doctor. 'It's incredible, audacious... all of that. *If* you pull it off.' He stared up fearlessly at the hideous creature. 'But you won't. No way. Because I'm gonna stop you.'

At that moment, the doors to the Blathereen's lair slid open and Ermenshrew thundered in. The candles flickered, alarming Don Arco.

'Gently, half-sister, gently!' He retched up a spluttering cough. 'You'll give me a turn!'

'Kill the Doctor, Don Arco!' she howled. 'Kill him! The trouble he's put me to today!'

The Doctor turned and grinned. 'Oh, it was no trouble, honest!'

'You're too hasty,' rumbled Don Arco. 'We can still use his brain.'

'Yes – as a chamois leather!' rasped Ermenshrew. 'I'll have Flowers polish the gravity accelerator with it – before I break her back!'

Flowers shuddered, and the Doctor must have noticed. 'It's OK,' he said soothingly. 'She won't really make you polish with my brain. Think of the mess.'

'Calm yourself in my presence, half-sister!' Don Arco commanded.

'Forgive me,' she said. 'But… it's my daughter. On Justice Beta. Something terrible has happened to her, I can feel it.'

'Well, we'll check it out,' Don Arco assured her. 'Soon, OK? Now, don't let yourself get distracted. We need focus. How long before we're ready to take this system for a test drive?'

'A matter of hours,' she said hollowly. 'Your atmosphere is prepared in the SCAT-house, my dear.'

His bulk shuddered with satisfaction. 'Then we shall go there shortly.'

Flowers turned away, feeling the spike of her Blathereen guard's claws in her shoulders. She stared at the patch of sunlit garden she could see through the smeared window.

A dark shadow was sliding over the lawn.

Flowers craned her neck upwards to see what was coming. She blinked.

It looked like a monitoring platform.

A split second later, the building rocked as the platform smashed into the floors above them. Flowers was jolted free of the guard's grip. The windows shattered, shards of glass spitting from the frames, and the guard cried out as wreckage from the ceiling collapsed on top of him. A slab of masonry landed close to her head, and she rolled aside, trembling.

'What's happening?' shrieked Don Arco. At once, his

guards rushed to encircle him. 'Ugh! That's fresh air coming in through those windows!'

'We're under attack!' shouted Ermenshrew.

The Doctor was staring round in bewilderment too, but clearly he wasn't about to waste a good distraction. Freed from his guard's grip, he dashed over to where Flowers was cowering beneath the window.

'What hit us?' he demanded. 'A great big floating tower thing?'

Flowers dusted off her glasses and stared up at him. 'A monitoring platform, yes. How did you –'

'There's another one coming straight for us!'

He yanked Flowers up from the floor just in time for an enormous blast to knock her down again. But somehow the Doctor kept his balance. As he dragged her back up, heading for the main doors, a big crack in the glass-mottled floor appeared in front of them. Swiftly, he bundled Flowers across to the other side, just before the crack widened into a minor chasm.

Ermenshrew was lumbering towards him, eyes narrowed with malice. 'You're going *nowhere*.'

'The air!' gasped Don Arco. Through his protective circle of Blathereen, he was flapping about like a fat fish out of water. 'Leave them, Ermenshrew. We must evacuate! Regroup! Reassess! *Retaliate!*'

'Re-*eally* does go on, doesn't he?' beamed the Doctor. He turned and leaped across the divide, landing with a clumsy flourish. To Flowers's relief, the crack widened further. 'I think perhaps you'd better go to him.'

With an impotent hiss of rage, Ermenshrew stomped back towards her half-brother.

The Doctor hauled up Flowers as the ructions went on between floor, walls and ceiling. 'Quick, before the whole place falls down.'

'What about Ecktosca Fel Fotch? And Dram?'

The Doctor gave a cursory look round. 'Already cleared out. So let's get after them.'

'But you heard Don Arco and Ermenshrew. They're going to the SCAT-house, they're going to use the amplifier!'

'We can't stop them if this lot comes down on us – come *on*!'

Rose heard the explosions in the Blathereen lair in stereo – for real as well as from the tinny monitor speakers. She'd seen the ceiling crashing down around the Doctor's ears, and through the capsule's doorway – or rather, their improvised skylight – she could see a plume of black smoke darkening the sky.

'What was that?' shouted Dennel.

'I don't know,' said Rose, 'but we've got to get to the Doctor.'

'No. We've got to get away from Justicia and warn EarthGov,' Robsen insisted. 'To think that those things have been manipulating us… using us.'

'Believe me, the Doctor's our best bet for getting out of here.'

'Look, Rose, I'm the warder here –'

'You're *not* a warder!' she stormed. 'You haven't been for months. To the Blathereen, you're just another inmate! That makes us equal, yeah? And wherever we head for, first things first. We need to get out of this thing!'

Robsen opened his mouth to protest, but no words came. The capsule bounced off something, shook them to the floor.

'The engines aren't pushing us,' Dennel reported. 'It's like we're being dragged along by some giant magnet!'

With a last splintering crack, they finally ran out of things to knock into. The monitoring platform was slithering over a smooth surface now, and picking up speed.

'I think we're out of the forest,' said Robsen.

'But not out of the woods,' said Rose. 'We're still accelerating. If we hit something now –'

The capsule hit a bump and lurched dramatically. It spun anticlockwise, bringing the doorway back within reach.

'I think I'm gonna be sick,' Dennel groaned.

Robsen grimaced at Rose. 'Let's jump for it before he adds his guts to the mess we're in.'

Rose scrambled over to the doorway and leaned outside. The grass was rushing by beneath her. The crumpled monitoring platform was moving like a missile now, ploughing a deep groove through a massive, overgrown garden. The wind lashed her hair around her face as she squinted dead ahead.

And swore.

'That high-rise I saw before,' she shouted back through the doorway. 'Something's crashed into the top of it. And we're about to crash into the bottom! Move yourself, qui…'

Rose stopped talking as two figures emerged from a doorway in the glass and steel base of the building. They stood frozen as the wreck of the monitoring platform bore down on them, closing fast.

Rose started waving manically. 'Doctor!' she shrieked. It *was* him. There he was with that Flowers woman she'd seen on the screen in the Governor's office. 'Doctor!'

'Rose?' First he stared, gobsmacked. Then he started whooping and jumping in the air, his long leather jacket flapping around his lanky frame. 'Rose!'

Behind her, she felt Robsen push past through the doorway.

He hit the ground and rolled over and over.

'Get out of the way, Doctor!' she yelled.

Flowers pelted off, but the Doctor stayed put. 'You all right?' he called, grinning madly.

'Yeah!' Rose shouted, grinning back despite herself. 'But get out of the way!'

'Come on!' yelled Dennel, as he too dived from the capsule.

'Yeah, jump for it!' The Doctor started running towards the slithering platform. 'Jump! I'll –'

Rose took a deep breath and jumped from the platform, just as it hit a raised flowerbed. She went whooshing through the air. For a second she was a kid back on the estate, jumping from a swing after a really big push, pretending she could fly.

And though she came down with a bang, she landed in the Doctor's arms, and inside she was still flying.

But he couldn't hold her, not at that speed. They went down together in a tangle of arms and legs, falling winded to the grass. Then the capsule collided with the side of the building. A fierce heat swept across Rose's skin and the ground shook with another colossal explosion.

A plume of fire a mile high was balling up the side of the building. But Rose's eyes were locked into the Doctor's own.

'Found you,' he grinned.

She shook her head. 'I found *you* more like. Typical. Bet you forgot all about me.'

'Forgot how much you weighed,' he complained, gently disentangling himself. 'That was gonna be a perfect catch, too…'

Rose turned to find Robsen and Dennel running towards her from one direction, and Flowers flapping her way from the other. Her face was covered in soot, except for panda eyes shielded by her glasses.

'Rose Tyler, I presume,' she said, holding out a hand to help her up. 'The genius.'

'Genius at finding trouble,' Rose agreed. As the others arrived, and the flames licked and swirled around the shattered frontage of the building, she made brief introductions. It wasn't easy with Dennel, since he was in a kind of trance, staring at the flames.

'What's up with him?' whispered Flowers.

'He's got a thing about fire,' said Rose. When she saw the disapproving look on Flowers's face, she went on defensively, 'He never hurt anyone!'

'Only old buildings,' he agreed faintly.

The Doctor looked between Rose and Dennel suspiciously. 'You're not making things domestic again, are you?'

'No!' she protested.

'Only I know how you humans love your domestic stuff.'

'Just quickly, Doctor,' said Flowers, 'what happened?' She gestured at the inferno raging behind them, choked on a stray gust of oily smoke. 'What brought those monitoring platforms crashing down on us? We barely got out alive!'

'Yeah.' Robsen gestured to the caved-in wreckage. 'That one we were in got dragged through a half-mile of forest before it smashed into that building. Think I preferred the ride through that invisible tunnel.'

'Oooh, a warp-hole,' said Flowers sympathetically. 'Yes, they're nasty.'

'And you can make them nastier.' The Doctor looked suddenly sheepish. 'Flowers… you know I rigged that warp-hole portal? Set up a repulsion field to shunt anyone who followed us out of the way?'

She nodded – then groaned. 'Let me guess. To balance out

the repulsion field, you created a local *attraction* field to try to hold it stable.'

The Doctor pulled a face. 'But the screwdriver excited too many energy wavelengths in the portal.'

Rose felt she could hazard a guess. 'And your local attraction became a big draw, right?'

The Doctor nodded. 'Gravity and anti-gravity fields colliding, *collapsing*. Anything using similar energies got drawn into the vortex.'

'Anything with anti-gravs, for instance,' Dennel realised. 'Say bye-bye to a few monitoring platforms!'

Rose dug her elbow in the Doctor's ribs. 'You are *so* jammy!'

'It was skill,' he said, affronted.

'It was a cock-up!'

'Making cock-ups at the right moment is a skill!'

'Er, excuse me?' Robsen was pointing past them. 'Would you call *this* a cock-up?'

Rose turned and her heart sank.

The Doctor and Flowers weren't the only ones to make it out of the building alive.

Through the smoke and the flames and the fumes, Blatchereen were spilling from the caved-in entrance. Six, eight, twelve… They emerged in an unending stream, sooty, battered and extremely fed up. Their terrible claws were clenching and unclenching, and their black eyes held a hunger for blood.

'Back into the forest,' snapped Rose as the monsters approached, 'it's our only chance.'

As one, they turned and ran, the Blatchereen lumbering in pursuit. Rose felt like a fox trying to outrun a pack of hounds. It was a strangely silent pursuit, no growls or threats or gloats – only the creatures' footsteps thump-thump-thumping on the ground behind. Somehow that made it more frightening.

Flowers started to tire first. 'I can't keep up,' she wheezed.

'You have to!' snapped the Doctor.

'If we can just make it to the forest,' said Robsen, 'perhaps we can lose them.'

'There it is!' cried Dennel. The sight of the treeline spurred him on; he broke into a sprint.

Then he skidded to a halt as four more battered Blathereen burst out from the forest, fanning out to head them off.

'Must be the ones we knocked down,' said Robsen gravely.

'We're trapped,' said Dennel, running back to join the group.

They huddled together as the Blathereen advanced, gurgling and salivating, clicking their monstrous claws.

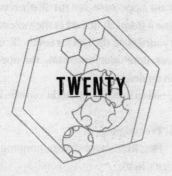

TWENTY

Rose shut her eyes, waiting for the inevitable. But then another sound carried from the forest. A cheering and clattering and crashing and shrieking…

She opened her eyes again in time to see hundreds of borstal kids come piling out of the forest, waving sticks and fists, yelling in fear and anger and liberation. A huge, terrifying lynch mob out for blood. Blathereen blood.

'Get them!' bellowed Maggi. 'Stop the monsters! It's the only way we'll get home!'

'Her again,' muttered Robsen.

'Never knew she had it in her,' said Rose, while Dennel just stared.

The mob wasted no time getting stuck in, and the Blathereen blocking the way to the forest were soon overwhelmed through sheer force of numbers. Rose could see the other Blathereen swapping glances, wondering whether to finish their hunt and stay and fight, or to stuff this for a game of soldiers and go get some new orders.

For now, they decided to stuff it, and retreated back towards the burning building.

There was no hope now for the Blathereen who'd been ambushed. Rose's stomach turned as the violence escalated.

'Friends of yours?' said the Doctor faintly. 'Running wild, no plan, no organisation, underestimating the opposition – they could all finish up dead.'

Flowers turned to Robsen. 'Shouldn't you be keeping an eye on this lot?'

He winced. 'I've resigned.'

'Hang on… Hey, Riz!' shouted Rose, jumping up and down. 'Look, Dennel, it's Riz!'

Riz, face scratched, hair wild, stared over in disbelief. 'Rose!' She rushed over and flung her arms around her, doing that slightly spaced laugh of hers. 'Are you OK? None of us knew what happened to you. It went all round the block… You're like everyone's hero! And Dennel – are you all right? And…' She grinned as she saw Robsen hanging back. 'Warder Robsen!'

'You can drop the warder bit,' he told her. 'I'm like you now. Just trying to stay alive.'

'Better stay out of sight then,' she suggested. 'That lot weren't good to the warders they met on the way.'

'Is… Is Jamini OK?'

'When I last saw her,' said Riz shiftily.

'How'd you get here?' asked Flowers. 'Through a warp-hole?'

'This little black platform in Blanc's bedroom. Maggi said it would lead us to safety, but it took us here…'

Rose couldn't believe it. 'They're really taking orders from *her*?'

'She showed them Blanc and the Governor were monsters – got them killed. After that, this lot seem to think she knows what she's talking about.'

'What about Kazta?' asked Rose. 'Thought she'd be well in there with a ruck going on –' Then she saw Kaz emerge, bruised and bloody but satisfied, from the heaving throng. She marched straight over to Rose. And offered her hand.

'Sorry for what I done.'

Rose took the sticky red hand gingerly. 'Just be careful what you're doing now.'

The Doctor swapped an impatient look with Flowers. 'Well, this is a nice get-together, but there's stuff to do. We've got to –'

'We've got to take the monsters' lair!' bawled Maggi at the top of her lungs. 'There'll be ships for you all there! Ships that can fly us –'

'Do you mind not interrupting when I'm trying to save the world?' shouted the Doctor indignantly. 'Quite a few worlds, actually!'

The rabble piped down a little for all of about two seconds.

'Who the hell are you?' Maggi demanded.

'Yeah, who's he think he is?' came an angry voice from the crowd.

'He's hanging with a screw,' said another. 'Probably a screw himself!'

Kazta set them straight. 'He's hanging with *Rose Tyler*!'

At this, an awestruck silence settled over the mob. The Doctor looked mildly miffed for a moment.

'Never mind her –' Maggi began.

'Oh, shut up a minute, Jalovitch!' Kaz bellowed.

Riz nudged Rose. 'You've become a bit of a hero since you've gone.'

'Speak to them,' the Doctor urged.

'All right, you lot,' Rose began uncertainly. Having any kind of control over a mob made her feel deeply uncomfortable.

'You've got to calm it down a bit, yeah? These monster things are dangerous – I know, believe me. And you won't have the element of surprise any more.'

'It's not the Blathereen themselves you need to destroy, anyway,' the Doctor added, and this time the crowd stayed quiet. 'It's their technology. You're on Justice Delta right now, the nerve centre of all Justicia. Once, the buildings here were filled with people. Now they're stuffed full of alien computers, working out how to end all life on –'

'Destroy the buildings!' someone yelled impatiently. 'Let's do it!'

'Wait a minute!' Rose shouted.

'Yeah, Rose is talking!' Kaz bellowed.

Rose turned to Dennel. 'You know how to do in buildings properly, don't you? Fire boy.'

He nodded, his eyes shining. 'I can do this, Rose. I can do this.'

'When Dennel was your block-walker, he listened to you when you had problems,' Rose told the mob. 'Well, now we've all got problems, and you've got to listen to him. He'll show you how to torch every building here, but you *have* to do as he says, yeah? No offence, Maggi...' She trailed off. 'Where *is* Maggi?'

The girl had gone.

'Who needs her, anyway?' yelled Riz. 'We got *Rose* now.'

'Sorry.' The Doctor put his arm round her. 'I need her more than you do.'

'You've got Kaz,' said Rose. 'And Dennel.'

Dennel pressed something into her hand. It was his lighter. 'Something to think of me by,' he said.

'Won't you need it?'

'Nah.' He shook his head and pulled a handful of tacky plastic lighters from his pocket. 'I don't smoke and chocolate gives me a rash. What else do I have to spend my block-walker's wages on?'

She grinned. 'I'll see you again.'

He kissed her awkwardly on the cheek and turned to the mob. 'All right, let's do it!' He and Kaz ran off to lead the mob onwards.

'And look after yourselves!' Rose added.

'I'll keep an eye on them,' Riz promised. She squeezed Rose's hand – and pressed a big kiss on Robsen's lips – before dashing off after the crowd.

'Madness,' said Robsen, wiping his lips. 'All madness.'

Flowers didn't watch them go. She was looking at the broken bodies of the Blathereen at the foot of the forest. 'I do hope Dram and Ecktosca avoid that mob,' she said.

'A couple of Slitheen con-merchants we know,' the Doctor explained to the others.

'I know they're wicked,' Flowers sighed, 'but I wouldn't wish that on anybody.'

'Me neither. But if we don't get on with the job in hand, there'll be more death and destruction than you can imagine. We have to get back to the SCAT-house.'

'You've got a gravity amplifier to dismantle,' Rose agreed.

The Doctor stared. 'How'd you know?'

Flowers was impressed. 'You really *are* a genius!'

'No, we just earwigged on your little meeting with the big Blathereen.' She shrugged. 'Well, if you *have* to be stuck inside a monitoring platform…'

Robsen looked worried. 'Did that thing in charge get out of the building, Doctor? Can it do all it says?'

'We have to make sure it can't. Can you show me the warp-hole you came through?'

'Yeah, we can follow the trail cut by the capsule,' said Rose. 'This way!'

Flowers thought her sides were going to physically split by the time they reached the clearing. Then her stomach started to churn as she took in the human remains lying about – those poor souls who'd been forced through the portals before the planets were fully in alignment.

The Doctor's friend didn't seem so bothered as she tramped over to the black platform. Flowers couldn't help but wonder how much the girl had seen in her short life.

'So, this warp-hole can take us to anywhere in Justicia?' Rose said. 'Back to where we left the TARDIS?'

'Hope so. Later.'

'How did those borstal kids get through?' Flowers asked. 'The warp-holes can only be primed by natives of Raxacoricofallapatorius, remember?'

Rose looked at her. 'And Riz said that the Blathereen inside Blanc and the Governor were killed. So how did Maggi lead them here?'

'That's easy to explain.'

They turned to find that Maggi had entered the clearing. And just behind her –

'Look out!' Robsen shouted. 'More of those things!'

Rose grabbed the Doctor's arm. 'Do we run for it?'

'It's all right,' said the Doctor. 'At least, I think it is.'

'Ecktosca! Dram!' Flowers beamed. 'So you *did* make it out!'

Ecktosca nodded his dry, blackened head. 'Thanks to our dear aunt here.'

With surprising dexterity, he dragged a silver zip across Maggi's forehead. Tiny birds clattered from the trees as a now familiar blue electric light crackled across the clearing from the girl's oddly immobile face.

Robsen stared in horror. 'Oh, my God...'

'Their aunt,' croaked Flowers. '*Another* Slitheen.'

'I was wondering how come Maggi had changed so much,' said Rose sadly.

'More than you realised,' the Doctor agreed.

The Slitheen finished stripping off its human skin and stood before them, panting and sweaty. 'That thing was a tight squeeze,' she said, turning to Ecktosca and Dram. 'Now have one yourself!' And she gathered them to her in a warm and sticky embrace. 'Come to your auntie Callis.'

"Scuse me?' the Doctor called. 'How'd *you* get here?'

Callis Fel Fotch opened her claw to reveal what looked to be an ornate gold brooch. 'A local teleport device. Very handy. I can use it to pop up here, there and everywhere.'

'Remember, we told you we had help coming!' said Dram triumphantly.

The Doctor shook his head. 'I meant how did you get past Justicia's defences, into the borstal and that poor girl's body and... well, *here*.'

'With stealth, ingenuity and cunning,' said Callis modestly. 'I hid on a passing space-wreck, teleported across to the Blathereen mothership, disguised myself as one of them, got myself sent to Justice Gamma – where I discovered they actually have the most fabulous shops! – and then I –'

'Never mind! Thanks anyway.' The Doctor turned back to scrutinise the warp-hole platform.

'Why d'you kill Maggi?' Rose demanded.

'She was the right size for my fuller figure,' said Callis, striking a sultry pose, 'and she had the right contacts. I knew it
would take a small army to help me liberate my nephews, and
that borstal rabble fitted the bill admirably. But if I showed off
my true self…'

'So you used that teleport thing to pop up wherever you
needed to,' Robsen deduced.

Callis sniggered. 'Yes, and I used her warp-hole to reach
Justice Prime. But I was too late. The warp-log showed that the
last several outgoing journeys had been to Justice Delta.'

Dram frowned. 'What warp-log?'

'It's hidden in the tree trunk!'

'S'pose it *is* a log,' the Doctor muttered.

Rose glared at Callis. 'You told all those kids in the borstal
you could make them free. But you were just using them for
yourself. You could have got them all killed!'

'They got me through enough Blathereen bodies to pick up
my nephews!' Callis shouted. 'That's all that matters to me!'

'So,' said Flowers brightly, 'perhaps we could all introduce
ourselves properly?'

'Indeed,' said Ecktosca. 'Callis Fel Fotch, this is the woman
who treated us like menial slaves and who sought to steal our
science to make her human masters rich.'

'Let me kill her,' she said. 'Let me kill all of them!'

'What, even me?' called the Doctor. 'The bloke who's going
to take care of your unbeatable rivals? Who's going to put an
end to the Blathereen's plans for this place?' The Doctor shook
his head. 'That's lousy business sense.'

'Big words, little human!' rasped Callis. 'What makes you
think you can stop Don Arco where we have failed?'

'He escaped the bombardment, Doctor,' said Ecktosca. 'We

saw him vanish. His chair was built upon its own warp-hole.'

'Paranoid scum,' spat Dram.

'Well, he was right to be, wasn't he?' Ecktosca placed a claw on his aunt's muscular arm. 'Callis, I've seen the Doctor at work. He's resourceful. Intelligent.'

'Haven't we had enough for one day?' Dram moaned.

'Oh, you can clear off if you want. Cut your losses, see ya.' The Doctor waggled his fingers in farewell. 'But if Don Arco wins today, the Blathereen will lord it over you for ever.'

The Slitheen looked at each other.

'Oh, all right then,' sighed Ecktosca.

'Good.' The Doctor nodded, and kicked the black disc. 'Then set that thing for the SCAT-house. I can't figure it out.'

Callis had a go, muttering under her breath.

'Can you trust them?' asked Rose.

'Don't have a choice,' the Doctor admitted. He turned to Flowers. 'You know we've got to destroy everything you've worked for?'

'Let's just get on with it,' she said.

'Warp-hole is primed and ready,' Callis announced sourly.

'Then let's finish this,' said the Doctor. 'One way or another, this is gonna be the final showdown.'

Flowers found that the trip through the warp-hole was easier second time around. Materialising back in the aquaculture compound, she realised that this wasn't good news. The planetary alignment must now be entirely perfect. The Blathereen would be poised for action.

'So what's our plan?' asked Rose.

'Good question.' The Doctor sighed. He was looking down at Nesshalop's eye, still where he'd left it beside the tomato plant. It sat closed now, a delicate frosted oval. 'But there's gonna be payback.'

'Doctor,' said Ecktosca. 'I propose we turn your earlier bluff into reality – wreck the gravity warp above this place. That will disrupt the space tunnel network.'

'Good idea.' Flowers pointed to the inspection ladder. 'Ermenshrew went up there unprotected, so the workings must be safely below the surface.'

'Right, Ecktosca, Callis – get busy,' said the Doctor. 'Robsen, you stay on guard here, all right?'

'I'd rather not,' he said, with a nervous look at the Slitheen.

'We're on the same side now,' said the Doctor. 'So I want to take Dram with me.'

Dram narrowed his enormous eyes. 'Why?'

'Muscle. In case of trouble.'

'Run along, Dram,' muttered Ecktosca, turning to the inspection ladder.

'Good luck,' said the Doctor. 'The rest of you, let's move it. The main event'll be happening in the gravity workshop – this way!'

At long last, it was ready.

In the workshop, Ermenshrew surveyed the completed gravity amplifier console with grim satisfaction. It was a gleaming dome of chrome, plumbed into a fearsome criss-cross of heavy-duty cables and junction boxes that filled half the cavernous workshop. There was a large space left in the latticework, but now that was ready to be filled.

She had lost her daughter and her cousin. Many of her more distant family had died in the sudden attack on the Blathereen HQ. But their deaths would not be in vain. The operation would be a success in spite of everything these tedious humans had tried to do.

Blista, Yahoomer, the Sucrosian creature she'd had to maul in order to show who was boss around here – they were all slumped against the far wall, exhausted by their labours. If she had any spare globs she'd have had the filthy aliens removed to their cells. But the ones the Doctor hadn't managed to destroy were busy elsewhere.

Don Arco sat slumped in his chair, sucking in the fuggy atmosphere from the many salve-candles arranged all around him, staring miserably at a wall-screen. It showed the humans systematically burning down the Executives' towers, cheering and dancing and gloating.

He clenched his claws. 'Our analysis engines, our forecast systems – all destroyed!'

'They'd already given us most of the data we need,' Ermenshrew reminded him. 'We'll build new ones. This place will be our base of operations now.' She smiled. 'At least they can't get their nasty little hands on the guidance controls.'

'We should have stayed to kill the little vermin.'

'And lose valuable human breeding stock?' She shook her head. 'Those children will keep. There's no way off that world. They'll soon start to starve. Then we can round them up with ease and use them to start building more storehouses.'

'I know, I know,' sighed Don Arco. 'But it sticks in my craw that these humans should get one over on us.'

'Maybe this will take your mind off things.' She gestured to the amplifier.

'It's ready?' Don Arco writhed in his chair with excitement. 'This is going to do it? This is going to shift the entire system through space?'

'Once the guidance system is connected, yes,' said
Ermenshrew.

'But without the gear on Delta to collate the data –'

'Oh, we can't go out on a business trip,' Ermenshrew
agreed. 'It won't be precise and measured and controlled. But
we can go for a little joyride, can't we? Burn up some planets.
Knock whole suns off their orbits and watch them whizz
away…'

'Then what are we waiting for?' Don Arco struggled up
from his chair, his blubber quivering majestically. 'Guards,
help me stand. Technicians – connect the guidance systems!'

Four guards helped hold him carefully upright while two
technicians took the chair. They broke off the sides, heaved off
the seat – and revealed the pristine panel of ultra-technology
beneath it.

Don Arco chuckled, setting his candle flames quivering.
'The two most priceless things in the universe, side by side all
this time. That guidance system – and my butt!'

Ermenshrew began to giggle with glee. The technicians tit-
tered too as they made the necessary connections. 'Still warm!'
said one. Then the guards joined in. Tahoomer, Blista and
Nesshalop huddled together as the laughter grew in volume.

'Now it begins,' hissed Ermenshrew. 'The warp-holes will
start collecting the potential energy of the planets' flight
through space. The energy will be amplified, it will be sent
from portal to portal, picking up speed and power… An enormous, four-dimensional centrifuge generating enough force to
rip open chasms in the fabric of space itself!'

Don Arco sniggered. 'Bring it on!'

TWENTY-ONE

Outside the workshop door, Rose, the Doctor, Flowers and Dram Fel Fotch were all listening in with gloomy faces.

'Sounds like they're almost ready to go,' said Flowers.

'I might have known they wouldn't stop to fix the damage on Delta first,' the Doctor complained. 'They're like kids at Christmas. Can't wait to play with the new toy, even if they break it cos they've not read the instructions first.'

'You'd be the same,' Rose retorted.

'True. But today *I'm* the one who sticks that toy back in its box.'

'But it sounds like there're loads of them in there,' whispered Flowers. 'You can't just walk in.'

'Can't I?'

'No.' Flowers gestured to a red light to the side of the doors. 'For a start, she's locked the vault from the inside.'

Rose frowned. 'Doors that lock from the inside – in a prison?'

'In an emergency, the Consul can use a special code to seal herself in any room. For her own protection.'

'Well, this is an emergency all right.' The Doctor pulled out the sonic screwdriver, but it barely produced a glow. 'And that's not going to help us. So what *can* we do? How do we get them out?'

'Got any bombs?' Dram wondered.

'No,' said Flowers flatly.

'We could wait for the other Slitheen to sabotage that gravity warp thingie,' said Rose.

'There's a chance Justicia could move, even if that's out of action,' said the Doctor. 'Only with even worse results.'

Flowers nodded. 'The gravity network would be left unstable. The second they move through the portal, every planet in Justicia could be sent spinning off into outer space – or into a rip in the fabric of space, never to be seen again.'

Rose looked at them in alarm. 'Then shouldn't we tell the Slitheen to stop until we've nobbled Don Arco?'

'Then they'll use Justicia to destroy some other solar system, and then another.' The Doctor shook his head. 'No way.'

'So we need a distraction.' Rose reached into her pocket and produced Dennel's lighter. 'We could set off the fire alarms! That might get the guards out of there at least.'

Flowers shook her head. 'Any fire is neutralised locally by the auto-sprinklers.'

'Fire,' whispered the Doctor. 'I wonder...' He turned to Flowers. 'Distraction time. Take Rose, and get off to the systems hub. I need zero gravity again. Just around this section.'

'What are you going to do – float up and crawl through the glob holes again?'

'Never mind that now.' He grinned. 'Everyone wearing watches? Give me fifteen minutes, then hit it.'

Rose looked at the Doctor. 'What are you up to?'

'Taking risks. Pushing my luck. The usual,' he told her,

taking Dram by the claw. 'But first, we're going to the solar workshops. See you soon!'

'You'd better,' said Rose, and she set off after Flowers.

Ecktosca and Callis were gasping for breath after the long climb up the inspection ladder. It was dark, the only light coming from streaks of luminescent gel scratched into the rocks by the Blathereen engineers.

A chrome cylinder extended down from the ceiling, glinting in the half-light. The gravity warp device was like a massive tooth – the mechanical roots of it were down here in the SCAT-house, while the structure itself must stretch up for hundreds of metres through the planet's crust.

'Will there be security overrides?' wondered Callis. 'Booby traps?'

'Even if they knew about the existence of this shaft, no prisoner would be permitted to enter,' Ecktosca reasoned, testing the housing of the warp with his claws. 'And if there are any globs still functioning, they wouldn't have access to a Blathereen hidey-hole.'

'Globs?'

'Bio-machines. Warders… Don't worry, I think we'll be –'

But as he ripped away a panel in the metal, bulbous shapes floated from out of the near-darkness at the fringes of the inspection shaft and fixed themselves to the Slitheen.

'*These* things are globs, right?' sighed Callis. They began to glow a greenish-yellow, and she swore with the pain. 'What are they doing?'

'Ermenshrew must have reassigned them,' Ecktosca gasped. 'To disable *anyone* tampering with the warp.'

'Never mind disabling.' The globs glowed brighter and

brighter as they sucked greedily at the Slitheen life essences. 'They're going to kill us!'

The Doctor rushed into the solar workshop, Dram thumping along behind him. 'You created a compression field that could contain some of a star's solar flares, right?'

Dram nodded. 'The compressor beams out from an orbiting satellite.'

He stared round at the weird technology in the room. 'What range does it have?'

'I'm not sure. Maybe 100 million miles?'

The Doctor pulled the gravometer from his pocket and consulted the screen. 'That may not be enough.'

'For what?'

'For what I'm thinking.' He gave Dram a wild smile. 'Power her up, Dram! We have to try!' He checked his watch. 'Only ten minutes left.'

Flowers and Rose ran through the corridors. Rose had to keep stopping to let Flowers catch her up. She was trying very hard not to let her agitation show.

'Sorry,' Flowers wheezed. 'But don't worry. The hub isn't much further.'

Rose dragged her along by the arm. Soon, Flowers swung her down a black-and-yellow side corridor.

'It's down here.' Now Flowers led the way. She pulled out her passcard and fed it into the slot by the grey bulkhead door.

Rose watched the door slide open to reveal a room full of what looked to her like posh fuse boxes. 'How long will it take to fiddle with the gravity?'

'Not long,' puffed Flowers. 'Oh.'

One of the fuse boxes was bound shut with a huge chain and padlock.

Flowers bit her lip. 'Seems Ermenshrew doesn't like to fall for the same trick twice.'

Ermenshrew clutched hold of Don Arco as the lattice glowed with pristine white light, as the amplifier started to tremble with subtle energies.

'The power-build's beginning,' she breathed, intoxicated not only by the moment but by the candle-fumes.

'Where shall we go?' wondered Don Arco. He giggled as a technician called up a star map on a nearby wall-screen. 'How about somewhere local for starters?'

'Say, within twenty light years?'

'Somewhere with loads of people…'

Ermenshrew gave a belly laugh. 'Imagine how the human investigators will scurry about trying to work out what happened!'

'Even if we told them they'd never believe it!'

And the two of them laughed and laughed till they felt sick.

Robsen was waiting helplessly in the sterile calm of the aquaculture compound. For all he knew, the Blathereen's first trip in Justicia could be to incinerate the world where his kids lived. They'd be wiped out in an instant. Them and billions of other lives.

And what was he doing about it? Waiting around as lookout for a couple of bug-eyed monsters.

He heard the cries and shrieks echoing down from the shaft. He peered up into the gloom.

'Use the teleporter!'

'I need both hands for that, I can't move!'

'What is it?' Robsen shouted. 'What's happening?'

Then he became aware of a frantic rustling sound close by. It was coming from a tomato plant.

To his baffled disgust, a big, egg-shaped eye was jostling the plant's roots and winking at him furiously. No, not at him – at something just *behind* him.

Robsen turned to find a Blathereen bearing down on him, reaching out with its killer claws. He dived aside, crashing into a bay of plants and flowers. As the Blathereen reached for him again, he rolled over backwards out of reach.

'Always humans…' rumbled the hideous creature. 'If there's one thing I *hate*, it's you ruddy humans!'

'Then don't look up that shaft,' Robsen warned him. 'There's eight of us having a real party with your gravity warp.'

Enraged, the Blathereen swatted Robsen aside and started climbing up the inspection shaft. 'Fun time's over, little humans,' it called. 'I'm coming to get you…'

Then, a few moments later, it screeched and fell with a resounding crash to the bottom of the ladder. It lay still. Robsen staggered up, and saw a cluster of weird, grey blob things nestled over the Blathereen's head and neck like giant warts. Slowly they detached themselves and drifted back up the shaft like balloons. But the guard didn't stir.

Robsen turned to the eye that had saved his life, lost for words. It stared back at him demurely.

And then it fluttered its eyelashes.

Seconds later, Ecktosca and Callis scrambled down from the gloom, brushing more globs away from their heads and shoulders. The two Slitheen trampled the guard's body in their haste to get clear.

'You saved us,' panted Ecktosca. 'Enough globs attacked the guard to free our limbs, let us scoot down the ladder.'

'For such pathetic animals, you humans do come in useful,' Callis added. 'On occasion.'

'What about you?' said Robsen. 'Did you fix the gravity warp?'

'No,' Ecktosca admitted. 'Barely even got started.'

'Then we have to fix those glob things so they can't stop you! That teleporter of yours! You... you could work in shifts, zip away every time it got too much.'

'Now hang on,' said Ecktosca. 'Those globs really hurt.'

Robsen imagined his children staring up at the sky, gasping in wonder as three more suns appeared – then burning to dust. 'I... I could run up the ladder and let some of the globs get me. Distract them from you like the guard did – buy you time!'

They stared at him, their alien faces unfathomable.

'*Please.*'

Rose was running full pelt, looking for the maintenance cupboard in which Flowers reckoned she'd find some cutting gear. She kept repeating Flowers's directions, over and over. Sure, she was the faster of the two of them – but if she got lost now, or couldn't find her way back...

Seven minutes left.

The Doctor sat poring over the controls for the solar flare compressor, referring to the gravometer now and then, barking out instructions at Dram.

'You're changing the direction of the compressor beam,' the Slitheen noted.

'But we don't have the range.' The Doctor thumped his fist down on the controls. 'We need to boost it somehow.'

'Any extra energy will have to come from –'

'The gravity amplifier! Yes!' The Doctor gave Dram a big kiss on the head. 'Can you feed the energy through from here?'

'Everything in the SCAT-house runs through the same power relays,' said Dram, calling up a screen full of complex equations. 'But we won't be able to get any of that energy until Don Arco hits the go button, tries to shift us all through space.'

'Suits me fine,' said the Doctor. He checked his watch. 'Six minutes left. Can I help?'

'Only by shutting up,' said Dram.

Robsen cried out with pain as the globs bobbed out of the dark and settled on his shoulders. He hung grimly to the ladder as they throbbed with a vivid yellow light. He felt weak and sick. Burning up.

He could hear the Slitheen somewhere up above him, clanking and cracking at the cylinder. 'Hurry!' he shouted, willing himself to hold on.

Then two of the globs slithered up against his face. They were fat, round and incandescent, little suns. Like the suns that would blink into existence in some distant sky before…

His feet slipped off the rung, and he slid two metres down to land on the prone body of the Blathereen. The impact brought him back round.

Callis appeared beside him from nowhere, her claws on her brooch. 'You'll have to do better than that,' she snapped, as Ecktosca's shout of pained surprise floated down from the darkness. 'Take it seriously!'

Robsen staggered to his feet, the world spinning. Hauled himself slowly back up the ladder.

* * *

'How long till the power's at optimum?' asked Don Arco in excitement.

'Four minutes,' a technician reported.

'Here we are,' said Ermenshrew, tapping at the star chart. 'The New Washington system, 18.9 light years distant. Twelve worlds, four of which are inhabited.' She chuckled. 'They're due to hold a peace conference on one of them next year.'

Don Arco grunted. 'They can hold a *pieces* conference.'

Ermenshrew cackled, and her tail wagged contentedly. 'Technician, set in the co-ordinates.'

Rose had come across a cupboard. But was it *the* cupboard? It was locked. She pulled out the passcard, the white plastic slippery in her hand, and slotted it into place.

The door slid open. There were tools of various kinds strewn about. Rose started rifling through them. Most of them were high-tech gadgets she didn't recognise, and panic started to build.

Then finally her hands closed on a jemmy that was almost as thick as her wrist.

'Yes!' she gasped. 'Yes, yes, yes,' and sprinted back off down the corridor.

It had taken her three minutes to get here. She had to push herself faster. *Faster.*

'I'll have to leave you to it, Dram,' the Doctor said. 'I've got to reach the gravity workshop in time.' He paused in the doorway. 'Can I trust you?'

'Can we trust *you*?' Dram countered, his claws tapping at the touch screen, making the connections.

* * *

Rose threw herself down the small side corridor. 'I've got the jemmy!' she shouted.

Flowers grabbed it off her and set to work on the chain that held the fuse box shut. 'I'm used to tools a touch more delicate,' she admitted.

'Then give it here!' Rose wrested the jemmy away, rammed it between the chain link and the fuse box, and heaved on it. The chain rattled but didn't break. 'All right, this needs both of us. Help me!' she gasped.

The Blathereen technician rose from the amplifier. 'Power build-up completed.'

'I think the honour of hitting the on-switch should be mine, Ermenshrew,' said Don Arco grandly. 'Don't you?'

He shuffled towards the console with his entourage, claws extended.

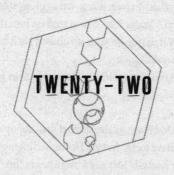

TWENTY-TWO

Flowers lent Rose her strength and the two of them pulled with all their might on the jemmy. Finally the chain cracked open, and dragged the jemmy with it as it fell to the floor.

Rose's hands were throbbing and red. Flowers opened up the panel. 'I have to cut the gravity in the workshop area.'

'You said it wouldn't take long, right?'

'How long do we have?'

Rose checked her watch. 'Oh, God, thirty seconds!'

Flowers peered at the controls. 'My glasses are all steamed up,' she complained.

'Quick!'

'Happens when I get flustered…'

'Fifteen seconds, Flowers!'

'Can't localise it! I'll have to zero-grav the entire SCAT-house. Hang on!'

Ermenshrew squawked in alarm. She was floating.

'What's happening!' shouted Don Arco as he too rose into the air. His entourage clung on to his great fat limbs in alarm as they slowly spiralled upwards together.

'Doctor!' yelled Ermenshrew, struggling uselessly against the air. 'It's you, I know it is!' She stared up into the darkness of the ceiling. 'Watch out for him up above! He'll be trying to get in through there!'

But Don Arco was pointing downwards in horror. 'Look!' he croaked.

'It worked!' cried Rose as she started drifting up into the air.

'He won't have long,' fretted Flowers, clinging on to the fuse box to steady herself. 'Just a few minutes before normal gravity is reset.'

'Let's hope it's enough.' Dennel's lighter floated out of Rose's pocket. She grabbed it, and started nervously thumbing the flints. 'Whoa!'

The lighter didn't produce the usual spike of yellow flame. Instead a weird blue blob, undulating like mercury, glowed from the metal. Tiny little specks of blue fire detached from it. The lighter grew suddenly hot and Rose had to let it go.

'That's it!' Flowers gasped. 'Fire in zero gravity behaves completely differently. *That's* what the Doctor's up to!'

Without gravity, flames can't rise upwards – and so Don Arco's candles had become spitting balls of intense blue flame. A technician drifted helplessly on to them, screeching as the fire scored holes in his flesh and the hot wax seared the wounds.

And there was nothing to make the healing smoke rise either. Don Arco's precious fumes were palling close to floor level, where they started to smother the crackling flame-balls.

'No!' he croaked, slowly somersaulting, struggling to reach them. 'My lungs! My lungs won't cope!'

'Where are you, Doctor?' shouted Ermenshrew, still scanning the ceiling for any sign of him. She didn't notice the injured technician smash the door controls, desperate to escape to safety. As he left, the Doctor, who'd been gripping hold of the doorframe outside, swung himself into the room.

'Come out and face me, Doctor!' shouted Ermenshrew.

'OK!' said the Doctor, drifting underneath her and waving.

'Guards, get him!' she shouted.

A guard floating nearby made a lunge for him. But the Doctor braved the smog to kick up a storm of spluttering candles. The blue blobs of flame multiplied, spat away from the wicks, blinding the guard with their incandescence. But now another guard had drifted close enough to grab for the Doctor's arm. In a gruesome ballet, the two skirted past each other, narrowly avoiding contact.

'My candles!' sobbed Don Arco. 'My lungs! Give up, Ermenshrew, he'll kill me!'

'I'll slaughter you for this, Doctor!' Ermenshrew promised. She grabbed big clawfuls of air, propelled herself towards him.

The Doctor couldn't get clear in time. The talons reached out for his throat.

But then, with a ferocious squeal, a sticky great blob of sweetness collided with the livid Blathereen, knocking her clear. As Nesshalop spiralled upwards to accompanying cheers from her fellow prisoners, she winked at the Doctor with one of her remaining eyes, little sugar crystals spattering from her smile.

Yahoomer, the furry mammoth, meanwhile, had dug one ivory tusk into a bank of controls to anchor himself. With one trunk he hauled Nesshalop down from mid-air, and he stiffened another for the Doctor to hang on to.

'Doctor, come on!' Don Arco pleaded. 'We can do a deal!'

Ermenshrew shouted, 'Don't be so pathetic, Don Arco!'

'All right, yeah – we *can* do a deal!' the Doctor agreed. 'You hand yourselves in. You help the humans remove all the Blathereen from this place.'

'I'll pay you anything you want!' Don Arco cried.

Ermenshrew frowned. 'You will not!'

'Stick your money. Those are my terms!' the Doctor insisted.

'Which we do *not* accept!' Once again, Ermenshrew had manoeuvred herself into an attack position, claws outstretched to rake his flesh.

'I hate zero gravity!' shouted Callis, clinging on to the spindly branches of the poppito tree in the aquaculture compound. 'It gives me the trots! Let's get out of here.'

'That idiot human has floated up the access shaft,' sighed Ecktosca, clinging to a rung on the ladder, staring upwards. 'The globs will kill him.'

'Never mind the human!'

But Ecktosca did mind. The thing had shown a bravery of sorts. They'd never have been able to rig the gravity warp without his distracting the globs.

Now the bio-creatures clustered about the drifting Robsen, milking him of his remaining life. They would drain him dry. Grumbling, Ecktosca propelled himself up the ladder, gripped hold of Robsen's ankle in his massive claw, and pulled down hard.

The human bounced at the bottom of the shaft and the globs scattered. Ecktosca felt a familiar agony as the nearest ones bit into his own flesh.

And then the gravity kicked back in. With a yelp, Ecktosca fell to the ground below.

'You silly, headstrong boy,' Callis cried. '*Now* can we get out of here?'

Gravity snatched Ermenshrew away from the Doctor seconds before she could get him. She fell with a squelch and a crunch on top of the remaining candles.

The Doctor landed lightly on his feet, still supported by Yahoomer's sturdy trunk. But smoke from the candles was suddenly free to squall up into the air, and it created a thick fug in the room. The bright white light of the wire lattice gave the smoke a sinister glow.

He turned to Yahoomer, gestured to the exit. 'Everyone out! Go on, shift!' Nesshalop and Blista took hold of a trunk each and bustled away with Yahoomer through the smoke.

'Don Arco, where are you!' shouted the Doctor. 'We can still do that deal.'

'You're wasting your breath,' hissed Ermenshrew from somewhere in the gloom. 'My leader can't speak to you.'

Suddenly she loomed up, holding Don Arco by his bloodied throat. Her talons had punctured the thick, blubbery flesh.

'He seems to have something wrong with his neck,' she said, black eyes agleam, standing between him and the door.

'You're bonkers, aren't you?' said the Doctor sadly.

'I'm head of the family now! And my first duty will be to dispose of you.'

She raised her free claw. But then, with a disbelieving yell, Ermenshrew staggered forwards as if someone had pushed her. She smashed into the wall, while the Doctor ducked between her legs and came face to face with his rescuer.

'Rose!' he beamed.

'You sure those things are made of living calcium and not

brick walls?' she asked him, coughing as she panted for breath, her eyes streaming in the smoke.

Suddenly the floor shook beneath them, and the sound of a colossal explosion carried. Rose clutched hold of the Doctor's arm.

'It's OK. Must be Ecktosca and Callis stuffing up the gravity warp on the surface.'

The smoke was starting to clear now. Both Rose and the Doctor reacted as a massive, powerful shape loomed over them.

But it was only Dram. 'All done,' he reported.

'Great.' The Doctor clapped him on the arm, looked about. 'Wait. Where's Ermenshrew gone?'

'Over heee-eeere...'

The Doctor stepped forward, peering through the haze. Flanked by three bewildered guards and a technician, Ermenshrew was standing beside the gravity accelerator console. Her claw was hovering over the start button.

'We're all charged up,' she said, her voice an icy whisper. 'Justicia's ready to move on out.'

'No,' the Doctor said. 'Please. Don't do this.'

'At last you respect me as you should.' She nodded smugly. 'Yes, it came to me in a flash. I shouldn't just kill you. I should morally outrage you first! Murder millions of innocent lives just to test my engine's working. *Then* I should kill you.'

'We've destroyed your gravity warp on the planet surface. If you try to move Justicia through space now –'

'Another pathetic bluff, Doctor?'

'I thought you might think that. All right then, let's try a threat.' He gestured to the Slitheen. 'Dram has rejigged the solar flare compressor. It's now aimed at your mothership – it'll crush it to the size of a postage stamp, and the second gravity warp with it!'

Ermenshrew shook her head, the smoke eddying around her. 'The compressor is in a probe in close orbit around Justicia's suns. It doesn't have the range.'

'We've boosted the range – it'll draw on the same energy you'll release by pressing that button!' The Doctor's voice was hoarse, and not just with the smoke. 'Please, Ermenshrew. When you hit that switch, the only lives you'll be taking are those of your own people on board the mothership.'

'Pathetic,' she said, her claw outstretched.

The Doctor raised his voice. 'And there'll be massive feed-back into that thing! You'll die too, Ermenshrew. I'm begging you –'

'I will stand no more of these pathetic attempts to deceive me!'

'In that case – everybody out!' the Doctor roared.

The Blathereen hit the switch.

Rose, the Doctor and Dram hit the deck the other side of the doorway.

Nothing happened.

Rose stared in him in horror. 'So it *was* a bluff?'

The Doctor wouldn't look at her, his forehead resting on his arm. 'Ask Ermenshrew.'

Rose looked back into the workshop. Ermenshrew was standing there, frozen in fury as a delicate white light started to play around her form. Her skin began to turn translucent, revealing all the mysterious alien organs that beat and pulsed beneath. A scream escaped her twitching lips. Smoke and sparks clouded all around her. Her claw was still gripping the control as both crumbled to ash.

'The feedback,' Dram realised. 'We're not safe here. We've got to get that door closed!'

'Wait!' Rose produced Flowers's white card from her pocket and slapped it in the slot.

The doors began to slide slowly shut.

Flowers arrived, panting like an elderly dog. 'What happened?'

White light had engulfed the workshop and was starting to spill out into the corridor, dissolving the floor. Rose shielded her eyes.

As Ermenshrew's screams reached a pitch surely high enough to break glass, the door slammed home, shutting off the light and sound.

Seconds later, the corridor rocked as an ear-splitting explosion went off in the workshop. The door bulged outwards as if some enormous bowling ball had smashed into it. The tremors seemed to last for a whole minute, and the ringing in Rose's ears went on for far longer.

'It's over,' whispered Dram. He clutched his chest, staggered as if he'd been struck. 'Ecktosca? Callis?'

'What is it?' said Flowers.

'I think… I think they're…'

He thundered off down the corridor.

The Doctor still lay face down on the floor. Rose sat beside him, placed her hand on his head, ruffled his close-cropped hair.

'You did it,' she told him.

He rolled over and looked at her, no triumph on his face.

'I know,' he said.

TWENTY-THREE

Robsen sat in Ermenshrew's old office, staring at the screen, willing someone to answer his signal.

Suddenly the image of Tiller was staring at him incredulously. 'Robsen? What the hell –'

Jamini's anxious face leaned into view. 'Are you OK, John? What happened?'

Robsen opened his mouth. Where to start?

Where to finish was a bit sketchy, too. He'd woken in a bed of roses, to find an explosion had torn out most of the inspection shaft. Ecktosca and Callis must have been caught in the blast; all that was left of them and the Blathereen guard was a pile of burned remains and a badly singed compressor field. That and the terrible pain that Dram felt at their passing.

'We can't get hold of anyone in authority,' said Tiller, jolting him back to the present.

'All in mourning,' Robsen muttered. 'Or scarpered. Look, I've got so much to tell you. I'm on Justice Prime right now –'

'You're *where?*'

'But I'm coming over. Soon. I'll explain everything then.'

'There'll be lots of mopping up to do,' the Doctor told him. 'There are

still Blathereen impostors across the system. The space tunnels won't work now, so you must hunt them down before they can find another way out. Make them tell you who they've hidden in EarthGov, get them rounded up.' He looked down at his feet. 'There won't be much fight in those left behind. They'll have lost so much. So many loved ones.'

'Think of how many loved ones they were going to take away on the planets they were ready to burn,' Rose told him gently. 'You can't feel bad about this. They did this to themselves.'

Robsen thought about his own loved ones. Justicia never let its staff vidlink to friends or loved ones outside the system. Security risk, they said. He'd gone months without talking to his children.

But the old Justicia was finished now. And things were going to change. He'd help see to that.

He set Consul Issabel's vidset to a priority channel and put through a call to his kids. To tell them he'd see them soon.

Flowers sat in her office, working out just what it was she'd let the Doctor talk her into.

'Justicia's finished, Flowers. When the news of this scandal gets out, when the rulers of Earth's empire realise how close they came to disaster... When they hear how so many people were held on trumped-up charges and what the real Executive was getting away with... They'll never let that happen again.'

He was right, of course. And he was right that someone in authority had to reveal the truth of the whole affair to the EarthGov officials, once they knew who they could trust. They would have to help assess who were the real criminals in Justicia, and who deserved freedom. For starters, the Doctor nominated Blista, Yahoomer, Dram Fel Fotch and Nesshalop to be freed at once for their part in saving billions of lives.

Nesshalop had looked at him fondly, her regenerated eye doing well, and blown a sugar-frosted kiss that melted on his cheek.

'All well and good,' Flowers sighed. 'But when will *I* be free?'

It could take years to sort out this mess. And the Doctor couldn't stay, of course, oh no. Not his style. He was already on a shuttle to Justice Alpha to pick up his ship. The overseers never had managed to get inside, or to shift it an inch.

'You've got to make your rulers see, Flowers. Crime and punishment raise tough issues, anyone knows that. But when people in power stop even asking the hard questions… When they pay someone else to make the whole thing go away… That's the biggest crime of all.'

'OK, getting a bit Jerry Springer now, Doctor,' said Rose.

He grinned at her. *'D'you think?'*

She punched the air, started chanting, *'Doc-tor, Doc-tor, Doc-tor…'*

Flowers shook her head fondly. Those two truly baffled her.

With sudden determination, she called up the central register of Justician inmates and started trawling through the 'male – petty crimes' section, sorting the best pictures into cute, fetching and drop-dead gorgeous.

She smiled. Yes, this would be a long and drawn-out business. And she would need at least twenty or thirty very dedicated personal assistants to help her through each day…

Rose stood beside the TARDIS, back on Justice Alpha after what felt like a lifetime away. The ground had been well churned up by the silver ship that had come for the Doctor. But somehow, though the area around it looked like something out of the Battle of the Somme, the spindly red flower still stood.

She smiled. 'Reckon we're two of a kind.' And she could see there would be others. The tips of green shoots were pushing through the rucked-up soil. New life was well on the way.

Dennel stood at the precipice, looking out over the unfinished pyramid below. A massive funeral pyre had been erected at its tip. He was watching the preparations, restless, edgy. 'This is going to be some fire.'

She joined him, the lighter gravity putting an extra spring in her step. 'Aren't you flamed out yet, after razing every Executive building down to the ground?'

'This is different.' He sniffed. 'Sort of spiritual.'

'Uh-huh. Right.'

'Reckon the Doctor thinks so too.'

'He just wants to be sure Don Arco gets off without a hitch.'

Rose remembered them finding the sole surviving Blathereen technician, weeping as he roamed the SCAT-house corridors, all the fight knocked from him. He'd fled the wrecked workshop, his hide blackened with burns and scalded by wax. He'd been lucky: it was a very different place in the aftermath, scorched almost bare. Of Ermenshrew there was no trace at all, nor of those who'd been standing beside her. But somehow, slumped in a far corner, the big, bloated corpse of Don Arco had been left more or less untouched by the incredible energies that flooded the chamber.

The technician had asked to cremate his dead Patriarch in a sacred place before submitting to imprisonment. He had suggested one of the pyramids here, and the Doctor agreed.

Aware there could be desperate Blathereen stranded on Justice Alpha, Rose had persuaded him to stop off at Delta to pick up the borstal mob for protection. Kazta, Riz and about a hundred others were now gathered on the pyramid, keeping an eye out for trouble – on the understanding that the shuttle was theirs for the taking afterwards. And the Doctor agreed they had earned their freedom.

'Then again,' he said, smiling, 'by the time they've worked out how to fly it, their sentences might be over in any case.'

As it happened, Rose needn't have worried about finding trouble. The valley was eerily deserted, the scattered pyramids standing like sentinels in silent majesty. The slave-labourers had taken their chance and scarpered when their overseers failed to show, but Flowers and the authorities would catch up with them all before too long.

She saw the Doctor and Dram Fel Fotch, standing a pace behind the creature as he set the pyre alight. The flames roared into fierce red life.

'Awesome,' breathed Dennel.

'I hate funerals,' Rose muttered.

'Nah. You're just sad cos you're saying goodbye to me.'

She looked at him with his dopey haircut. Smiled at the humour in his eyes. 'Come here,' she said, and gave him a hug.

'Ugh!' cried Dennel. 'God, no!'

Rose jumped away, confused. 'What is it, what did I –'

Then she realised he was looking past her at the pyramid, heard the gasps and shouts of the onlookers far below, and turned to see.

The Blathereen guard had thrown himself on the fire, to embrace his great father one final time. The flames blasted vengefully into the air.

Rose saw Riz and Kazta lead the others away. She saw the Doctor turn his back on the flames and walk away too. Only Dram kept staring into them, as if searching for something inside.

Dennel placed a hand on her arm. 'You'll be leaving soon, won't you?'

'Uh-huh. Wanna come?'

He shook his head. 'I wanna find my dad. I wanna set him free.'

'Flowers will help you,' said Rose, smiling.

He nodded, grinned back at her bashfully. 'I'd better get back to the shuttle. Don't want Kazta taking off without me.'

'Good luck, yeah?'

'You too,' he said. 'Wherever you end up next.'

And this time they hugged with no interruptions.

The funeral fire was all but spent by the time the Doctor appeared, hands jammed in his jacket pockets, barely out of breath from the long journey. He joined Rose, standing on her own at the edge of the rise.

'Dram stayed watching for ages,' she said. 'Gloating?'

'Perhaps,' said the Doctor. 'Or perhaps he just wanted to be sure nothing was left of the creatures who killed his family.' He nodded. 'I can understand that.'

The suns were starting to set, stretching the pyramids' crimson shadows.

'Will the TARDIS take off OK? If it was grounded here –'

'Shouldn't be a problem since we've knackered the space tunnels. The gravity warp the Blathereen hid here is useless now – except to Flowers as evidence of what was going on. She'll find it. And make sure the right people get to see it.'

'Then it's really over,' Rose murmured.

'Yeah,' said the Doctor. 'It is.'

They watched the funeral ashes carry on the warm breeze, fluttering over the valley.

Some hours later, Dram Fel Fotch stood beside a huge doorway set into the base of one of the great pyramids. All around was deserted. The human children were all busy trying to start their shuttle.

So he sneaked quickly inside.

Inside, Don Arco's corpse and the Blathereen guard were balancing at the top of the enormous chrome tower that housed the gravity warp.

'About time you showed up, you skiver,' called Don Arco.

In the blink of an eye he had appeared in front of Dram. With a leering grin, he unzipped his head...

To reveal Ecktosca, quite unharmed.

The two Slitheen giggled and gave each other a huge hug.

'Stroke of luck you found Don Arco's corpse intact,' Dram tittered. 'Perfect way to sneak off without arousing suspicion!'

'Can you believe I pinched the skin of the Blathereen Patriarch?' Tears of laughter were rolling down Ecktosca's face. 'And did you hear the crowd when your auntie jumped on me in the flames? I was almost sorry when she zapped us away with her teleport, we couldn't hear them down here.'

'They went on about it for ages,' roared Dram. 'Shock! Horror! Practically wet their pants over it!'

'Oi!' Callis was shrugging off the last of her burnt Blathereen flesh-suit. 'Get busy, you two! It'll take us a good day or two to strip this warp thing down and learn how it works...'

'What'll we do with it?' wondered Dram. 'Flog it on, or use it ourselves?'

'Plenty of time to figure that out.' Ecktosca grinned at him. 'All that matters right now is that the Blathereen are finished – and the Slitheen are back in business.'

Callis belched happily. 'Here's to a new golden age of crime!'

Acknowledgements

This adventure was shaped and shared by many. I am grateful to them all. But extra, planet-sized thank-yous are due to…

Russell T Davies – so generous with his time, enthusiasm and Slitheen, and who let me take Rose to her first alien planet.

TV series script editors Helen Raynor and Elwen Rowlands – who gave encouragement and brilliant notes when they were both so busy themselves.

Justin Richards, the indefatigable driving force of the *Doctor Who* books – for inviting me on board in the first place, for friendship and support, and for all that he does unsung behind the scenes.

And to Mike Tucker as always – provider of good nights out and Daleks.

About the author

Stephen Cole used to edit magazines and books, and in the late 1990s looked after the BBC's range of *Doctor Who* novels, videos and audio adventures. Now he spends most of his time writing, chiefly books for children of all ages.

Recent projects include *The Wereling*, a trilogy of horror thrillers for young adults, the ongoing fantasy series *Astrosaurs* for younger children, and the surreal school mystery series *One Weird Day at Freekham High*. His wife, Jill, and baby, Tobey, suspect *he* may be the real Monster Inside, especially when he has a book to finish and is running out of time…